SANA' WATTS

The Almost Perfect Match

A novel by Sana' Watts

This book is a work of fiction. Names, characters, Places, incidents, and dialogues are either products of the author's imagination or used fictitiously.

Any resemblance to actual persons, living or dead, or events is coincidental. Scripture quotations from The Authorized (King James) Version.

Fiction and Literature: Inspirational
Christian Romance

Disclaimer: Contains mild adult situations and the consequences

ISBN-13:978-1-968792-19-0

Chapter 1

Eleora didn't know she'd meet someone who would change her life forever that Monday morning.

Per her phone call with the school principal, she arrived half an hour early to meet the transfer student. As she entered the office, she stopped in her tracks, stunned by the most handsome guy she had ever seen.

Well, he wasn't the most handsome guy she'd seen in her life (hello, Michael B. Jordan, anyone?), but he was definitely the most handsome one at her school. He looked to be over six feet tall and had russet brown skin. His lineup was fresh, and his smile was the kind that could make knees buckle. She gave a quick glance at her reflection in the glass wall to check how she looked. Satisfied with the state of her natural curls, she headed toward Ms. Allen.

"Good morning, Ms. A."

"Now come on, Eleora. You know no morning is good until it reaches noon."

"But by then, isn't it the afternoon?"

"Exactly. By then, the morning's over and I can properly start my day."

Eleora laughed. "Funny how you despise mornings

but chose the profession of Head Secretary, which requires you to be here early."

"Sometimes the job chooses you. It may not make sense to anyone else—or even to you—but you know it's right."

"It's the morning wisdom for me! How's everything going with getting your master's done at U of T?"

Ms. Allen smiled. "Pretty good. By the time you graduate this year, I'll be done.

"And on that note, let's get to why you're here early this morning when this is your day to come for 9:30. Eleora, meet Chadwick—the new student you'll be showing around." She gestured toward the handsome guy.

Eleora tried to hide her shock. The student she had to show around was him? Maybe mornings weren't so bad after all.

"Chadwick, this is Eleora James—I mean, Gonzales. Eleora Gonzales. Eleora is the president of the twelfth grade and will show you around. If you have any trouble settling in, questions, or need any help— you go to her. And since it's now 7:55, Eleora only has twenty minutes to show you around this morning, so I suggest you get to it."

"Ms. Allen, I'm going to need his schedule and locker number."

Ms. Allen gave them to her, and they left the office.

"So, I'm Eleora, as Ms. Allen said, and for the next twenty minutes, I'll be showing you where your classes are, your locker, the gym, and the cafeteria." Eleora tried her best to sound normal, though she was freaking out inside. She had never felt such an instant attraction to a guy before.

"And as Ms. Allen told you, I'm Chadwick Knight." He stuck out his hand. They shook hands and both held on a second too long. "Sounds like we've got a lot to get to this morning. What's first?"

She didn't answer. She was staring in confusion at the papers in her hands.

"Is something wrong?"

"No, not wrong. Just weird. You and I have just about the same schedule, and your locker's next to mine. So first, we'll head to our lockers, and then I'll show you where your classes are." She looked around to make sure no one was nearby. "Then I'll give you the inside scoop on the teachers."

"Sounds like this'll be top-secret info. Should we say it aloud or write it down in invisible ink?"

Eleora smiled at him, playing along. "We can't. I forgot my lemon juice at home."

"But if we're overheard, we'll be doomed."

"That is true." They looked at each other and started laughing, slapping high fives.

"So, what brings you to our school? We rarely have transfer students."

"Well, I was performing in a school play, and afterward, a teacher from here approached me. She mentioned I should think about auditioning to come here—and I got in. I'm in drama and piano; composition."

"Well, I'm glad you're here," she told him with a big smile that he returned in kind. "And now we are at our lockers," Eleora said. "I'm 119 and you're 118. I'm assuming you got your combo from Ms. Allen?" she asked, and he nodded.

"Yup. Okay. I'll just dump my stuff while you figure out your combo and such, and then I'll show you the gym, the auditorium, the cafeteria, and bring you back—so that maybe you can make homeroom, which seems to be one of the few classes we don't share." She explained, then went through her locker routine. When she was done, she turned to see that Chadwick was just finishing up.

"Done? Know your combination and everything?" she asked.

"Yep. So what's first on the tour?"

"First off is the auditorium. Since you're a royal, I figured I'd show you that first. Plus, it's on this floor." She walked toward the office.

He followed her. "A royal?"

"It's our nickname for drama kids here. Some of us are kind of over the top, like drama 'queens,' but since we're gender inclusive, we use the term 'royals.'"

"Oh. Wait—did you say us? You're a royal?"

"Yup. I'm a royal, a stretch, and a scales."

"Let me guess. Stretch is for dance and scales is for singing?"

"Right and right."

"Wow, you're like a triple threat. The only thing you don't do is draw." He sounded impressed.

"Yeah, I can't draw to save my life." She shrugged, and he laughed. "And here is the Audi," she announced, opening the doors to the auditorium. They walked into a vast room with a majestic stage and balcony.

"You've performed on that? That must be incredible!" Chadwick's eyes shone with awe.

4

"Yup, and it is. And don't worry, you'll be performing here someday too." They exchanged a smile.

"Now come on. We have a few more stops on the tour and not much time left." Eleora playfully pushed his back to get him to exit the room.

He laughed and didn't move. "Look, since you're obviously so weak, I'll walk out on my own."

"Look, I am not weak. You are just freakishly heavy." She walked out behind him.

"Yeah, yeah. You just keep telling yourself that."

"Now, down this hallway on the left is a stairwell, which is where we're headed next."

Two gyms, one cafeteria, and five classrooms later, they were heading toward his homeroom.

"You are a pretty wonderful tour guide."

"Thanks. Comes with the job. I have to help create a 'healthy learning environment for all students—new ones and old ones,'" she quoted, and they laughed.

"So what are the clubs like here?"

She took a deep breath and started to explain. "You've got the obvious drama, arts, and dance here— but they're broken down. There's drama appreciation, where you go through plays and analyze them, and then an actual drama club that performs in the community. There are, like, a trillion art clubs. Some for anime, still life, painting, pottery, and so on. For dance, you've got teams broken down into styles—hip-hop, jazz, contemporary, tap. Then you've got the Piano Club, Guitar Club, Woodwind Family Club, and others. And then the non-Arts clubs, which are interest-based— from religions to political affiliations."

"About the religious clubs. Which ones do you

have?"

"We have Islam, Hinduism, Sikhism, Judaism, Baha'i, and Christianity clubs. Why?"

"I was just interested in the Christian club. Do you know when they meet?" he asked.

"Umm, you shouldn't ask me that. I know little about that club." Eleora's voice turned curt, and she picked up her pace.

"Hey, what's with the vibe switch?" he asked.

"Well, I'm not religious. I identify as an atheist."

"I'm curious. Why do you believe there isn't a God?"

"It's hard to believe in this powerful and loving Being when there's so much hell here on Earth. I feel like 'salvation' is something somebody made up to make others feel better. So they can think that if they live right and eat right and do everything right, they can make it to heaven. When in reality, all the heaven and hell we'll ever have is on Earth."

"The problem of evil is a real and genuine philosophical problem—but it sounds like there's a personal element here too."

"Let's just say that for people who are supposed to be 'following God,' I've met my fair share of horrible people who are Christians. And we are now at your homeroom classroom."

Then Eleora's face brightened, and she broke into a smile. "Jason!" She ran to hug a tall, green-eyed blond guy approaching their class.

"Elle!" He hugged her back.

"Jason, this is Chadwick Knight, a new student I've been showing around this morning. He's in your homeroom, and his next class is mine. Do you think you could bring him there for me? This is my 9:30 day, and I'm hoping I can take a break and go relax somewhere," she explained.

"Sure. No prob, Triple." Eleora rolled her eyes, laughed, and shoved his shoulder.

"Okay, so to make the introductions: Jason, this is Chadwick. Chadwick, this is Jason."

They nodded to each other.

"I guess that was your way of acknowledging each other. I'm going to see if I can take a nap. Later, Jason. Bye, Chadwick."

"Later, Triple!" Jason replied, then turned to Chadwick. "Let's head in," he said, and they entered the classroom just in time.

Eleora walked down the hall toward her favorite part of the school: the library. On her way, students said hi. She pretended her morning was going great. She pretended her heart wasn't in turmoil, breaking as she walked. When she reached the library, she headed to a little-known meeting room in the back where nobody went. It was reserved for student council members. Inside was a couch, a kettle, a mini fridge, a microwave, and a blanket. It was her home away from home. She flopped onto the couch and cried.

It figured that the one guy she was interested in would be a Christian. And she couldn't love another Christian again. Her heart wouldn't be able to take it.

Chapter 2

Chadwick headed to his locker and saw Eleora already walking away. He'd just missed her.

Crud.

He wanted to smooth things over with the beautiful girl who'd already become a steady presence in his classes and his mind. He had never felt so attracted to someone so quickly, so instantly connected, like they really could've finished each other's sentences.

His mind flashed back to the series his youth pastor had done on dating. He felt like he wanted to apply those lessons to someone.

And she just had to hate his faith.

What was he to do now?

Talk to someone.

Chadwick smiled at the impression placed in his mind. He knew that was God speaking, and he knew exactly who to talk to.

He opened his locker, took out his coat and other books, then left to catch the bus. As he waited, he pulled out his iPhone and called his mom.

"Hello?"

"Hey, Mom, I w—"

"Hello, honey! How was the new school? Do you

like it? Are the Lions as bad as everyone at your old school said they are?"

"The school's superb, and I made the basketball team."

"I thought the season had already started?"

"It did. But the captain of the team, Jason—he's becoming a new friend of mine—when I told him I was on the team back when I was an Eagle, he took me to see the coach during lunch. I had a quick tryout, and Coach made me a power forward. I start at the next game."

"That's fantastic, sweetheart! I'm so proud of you."

"Thanks, Mom, but I was calling to let you know I'm going to stop at the church before I come home."

"Thanks for that, Chad. You know, you're so thoughtful that way. I think you get that from me," she joked.

Chadwick laughed. "Yeah, yeah. See you later."

"Love you, honey."

"Love you too," he whispered as he boarded the bus.

He ended the call, showed the bus driver his student pass, then headed to the back. When the bus reached his stop, he got off, thanked the driver, and walked down the street toward the church. He entered and smiled at the familiarity. This place was his home away from home. He walked down the hallway with the offices and checked to see if his youth pastor was there. Shoot, it was empty. He turned around, disappointed— and saw Pastor Gabe behind him.

"Hey, Chadwick, did you want to talk? I have some work to do, but if you need to talk, I have time."

Chadwick nodded.

"Then step into my office," Pastor Gabe joked in a game show host's voice, and the two went in and sat down. "So, Chad, what's going on?"

"Well, there's this girl. Her name is Eleora. She's gorgeous—about 5'9", with long, curly dark brown hair and the most beautiful gray eyes you've ever seen. But it's more than her looks. She's funny and kind. But she's an atheist and has a very low view of Christians." His voice went from dreamy to glum.

"Well, thanks for being vulnerable with me like this. But I think you know that Christians and non-Christians aren't supposed to get married."

"Yeah, but I'm not trying to marry her. I just want to date her."

"But the purpose of dating is to figure out if that's someone you could marry, and with her beliefs, you know that takes her out of the running from the get-go," Pastor Gabe pointed out.

"I know you're right, but that doesn't mean I like what you're saying," Chadwick admitted.

"I won't pretend what I'm about to tell you is easy, but I suggest you just become her friend and put aside your romantic feelings. Ask God to help you with that. As friends, she can observe the faith in a non-threatening way. I believe Jesus is knocking at her heart's door. You have an opportunity to partner with Him in her joining the faith."

"I knew I should come to you right away. You always know what to say and have the best advice." Chadwick got up from his seat.

"Hey, before you leave—I wanted to check in on how you're doing regarding pornography. I know watching it was something you were struggling with when we last talked."

Inwardly, Chadwick sighed. He wasn't emotionally prepared to have this conversation, but he knew it was important. Truthfully, he would never be ready to talk about the addiction struggles he'd had with pornography. It caused him so much shame. What started out as occasional watching when he was thirteen had grown into a daily habit. It was only in the last six months that Chadwick had come clean to Pastor Gabe. While he'd had a few slip-ups in the last few months, they were becoming fewer and farther between.

Chadwick sat back down and leaned into his chair. "It's been okay. The software you recommended to block the content has helped a ton. Even when I've wanted to go on my usual website, I hit a firewall."

Pastor Gabe nodded. "Content restrictions are like cutting off the branches of the tree—it prevents the emergence of new fruit. Have you been able to notice any patterns in what you're thinking or feeling when you've felt the most tempted to re-engage with porn?"

"You mean what's at the root of our metaphorical tree?"

"Yes, exactly that. Normally, the roots are boredom, fatigue, loneliness, and stress. As I mention these common triggers, did any stand out to you?"

He thought for a moment. "I think it may be stress and loneliness."

"Okay. How does pornography medicate those things?"

"I think it's just an excellent distraction, and it has a physiological payoff? That sounds so dumb, doesn't it?"

"Not at all. When we feel something, we have thoughts or beliefs that accompany it. You've used pornography to avoid all of that instead of working through it. But maybe it's time to do that. What do you think?"

After turning it over in his mind, Chadwick answered honestly. "It sounds wise, but also uncomfortable and difficult."

Pastor Gabe smiled knowingly. "Oh, it is. But there's freedom on the other side of it."

Freedom.

The idea seemed foreign to Chadwick. To not feel like he had to battle with porn—to imagine he could even be without the impulse to watch it—was mind-blowing. Almost too good to be true. But he trusted Pastor Gabe and how God used him. If he thought it was possible, then it must be.

"Okay, I'm down."

"Sweet. I'm proud of you. I'll text you a list of common beliefs that people who struggle with watching porn hold. I want you to imagine being lonely or stressed and then consult the list to see what resonates. I'll also send you some reflection questions to help with your discerning. We can touch base in a couple of weeks to talk about it?"

Chadwick sighed in relief. They would go at a slow pace, one he could handle. "Sounds good to me. Would you mind praying for me before I leave?"

Pastor Gabe smiled. "You beat me to the punch. I was just about to offer! Let's pray." They both bowed their heads and closed their eyes. "Yahweh, our glorious Triune God, thank You for this time to meet together. Thank You for Chadwick—for his vulnerability and humility in disclosing his desires and inviting counsel. I ask that You would help him submit his desires to You—that he would consult his feelings as a gauge for where he's at, but not a guide for where he should go. May You guide him, Lord our God. Would You work through him to bring Eleora to faith? Would You continue to sustain the freedom he's been experiencing in his pursuit of sexual holiness? We ask these things in Jesus' name, amen."

"Amen. Thanks again. It's a blessing to have you as a spiritual mentor," Chadwick said with a smile.

"You're welcome, Chad. I'm glad to help. It's a privilege to have this role in your life," Pastor Gabe said. "Will I be seeing you at youth group this week?"

Chadwick nodded and stood. "Yep. Bye, Pastor Gabe—see you then!"

Chapter 3

Eleora had been avoiding Chadwick for the past two weeks, which hadn't been as easy as Maryliz had made it sound when they'd debriefed their attraction and differing beliefs.

Chadwick was intent on being friends. He tried to sit with her and waited for her at their lockers.

Eleora sighed. Every day she found more and more reasons to like him. He had an incredible work ethic, was intelligent, a talented actor, and so kind to people. He was unlike any of the guys she knew. And she had gleaned all this from a safe distance. She couldn't imagine how much deeper her feelings would grow if they were actually friends. She needed to remember that he was a Christian. And they were deceitful hypocrites. In the end, even though he seemed different, Chadwick would end up being the same.

Thank goodness it was choir with Ms. Stevens. She was amazing. Also, she didn't share this class with Chadwick, and it was a relief not to have to worry about avoiding him—or rather, failing to avoid him and liking him even more. She could just be herself without having to double-check her actions, and that felt liberating.

"Good afternoon, my singers! Today we are going to work on—" The class phone interrupted Ms. Stevens by ringing. "Sometimes I swear I hate that thing," she muttered, and the class laughed. "Eleora? Can you lead the warm-ups for me, please?"

"No problem, Ms. S." Eleora got up from her seat and led the class through warmups until Ms. Stevens returned. With a nod from Eleora, they all sat down and drank some water.

"You guys sounded excellent, and I'm sure you're all warmed up and ready to sing. But choir is cancelled today. Everyone now has a free period, so you can do whatever you want."

Eleora sighed and began to pick up her bag.

"All except for you, Eleora."

Surprised, she went to her teacher. "Is something wrong, Ms. S?"

"Quite the opposite. You know how Joseph moved away last week?"

"Yeah, he was our pianist."

"Exactly. Well, we may already have a replacement."

"Who?"

"Chadwick Knight. He's on his way over right now. That's why choir is cancelled—to see how well he plays. He's going to sight-read two of our songs and then play one of his own. That's also why I needed you here. We need to see how he plays with someone singing, and since you have a fantastic voice, I figured you'd be perfect."

Eleora put a smile on her face, though inside she was vexed. Her class—the one she'd looked forward to because it was one of the few without him—was being cancelled so she could spend an entire period with him?

She closed her eyes and breathed in and out to calm herself as he walked into the room and sat at the piano. She desperately hoped she looked like she was doing breathing warm-ups for singing and not that his very presence was unnerving her.

"Okay. Chadwick, the two songs you'll be playing today are Seasons of Love from Rent, and Dancing Queen from Mamma Mia. Take a glance at them for a few seconds and then I'll signal you when to start," Ms. Stevens instructed.

Inside, Eleora relaxed a little. Those were two of her three favorite choir songs.

"Okay, Eleora, just stand by the piano. When he starts to play, sing. You can improvise a little, but not too much. And if he makes a mistake, just continue, okay?"

Eleora nodded and walked over to the piano. She stood up straight and waited for Ms. Stevens's signal.

"Chadwick, the first song is Seasons of Love. Don't worry about the tempo, just play. Eleora can and will adapt."

He played the opening strains of the song.

Eleora took a deep breath and began. "Five hundred twenty-five thousand, six hundred minutes. Five hundred twenty-five thousand moments so dear. Five hundred twenty-five thousand, six hundred minutes... How do you measure, measure a year? In daylights, in sunsets, in midnights, in cups of coffee. In inches, in miles, in laughter, in strife."

And from there, Eleora got into the song. She sang with confidence and contentment. The only downside was that she couldn't forget who was playing the piano.

Chadwick didn't mess up once. His timing was perfect, and the notes were played just loud enough to support her vocals.

At the end of the song, Ms. Stevens clapped. "Okay, now Dancing Queen. Chadwick, please."

He started to play the chorus, and Eleora began.

When they finished, Ms. S clapped again. "One word: perfection." She sat down. "Okay, Chadwick, let's hear your original piece."

Chadwick nodded and suddenly looked very nervous.

Unused to seeing him like that—and compelled to fix it—Eleora said, "Don't worry. You'll do fine."

He looked up at her, surprised by the encouragement. "Thanks," he said, smiling.

Then he began.

The song started slow and had an R&B feel. When he struck the last note, Eleora and Ms. Stevens both clapped.

"Chadwick Knight, we would love to have you as our choir pianist," Ms. Stevens said enthusiastically. "I'll head to the office right now to change your schedule. Eleora, you can leave things as they are for the next class and go enjoy your free period. There's about twenty minutes left."

"She's an enthusiastic one, eh?" Chadwick joked, and Eleora laughed.

"I guess that's one way to describe her. But she's amazing. And she only accepts the very best, so her getting excited about you is a big deal."

Wait, she wasn't supposed to be friendly with him!

"Anyway, I've gotta go." She backed away from the piano.

"Seriously? I thought we were vibing." He sighed and played a trill on the keys. "I know I came on strong when we were last discussing our beliefs, and I'm sorry about that. I care about you, and I want us to be friends."

"Why?" Eleora didn't mask her frustration.

"Because we have a lot in common and we'll be around each other most of the day. It feels like it'll take less energy to be friends than to not."

He had a point. It was exhausting trying to avoid him. But would being friends really be easier? Would she be able to keep her heart in check? Something—call it intuition—told her that agreeing to be his friend would change her. Her life wouldn't be the same with him in it. Was that a risk she was willing to take?

She chanced a glance at him, and what she saw solidified her answer. His eyes conveyed a patience that made her breath hitch. He wouldn't rush her. And if she couldn't give him an answer now, she was confident he'd wait. He thought she was worth waiting for—even just for friendship. The maturity and kindness that required wasn't lost on her.

He would be a good friend to her.

"Fine," she muttered.

"Fine?"

"Fine."

"So… are we friends now?" His eyes lit up.

"What are we, in kindergarten?"

"Well, if we are, I call the box of non-broken crayons!"

"Just try to color inside the lines."

Chadwick and Eleora bantered back and forth, then started laughing.

"Does that answer your question, Chadwick?" Eleora asked teasingly.

"Yes. Yes, it does," he replied. "And yes, that was a Phineas and Ferb reference," he joked, and Eleora laughed.

"Well, I have to go. Might as well start the biology homework," Eleora said with a grimace.

"You don't like biology?"

"I despise it."

"Then why are you taking it?" Chadwick's confusion was clear.

"Short answer? Because my mom wants me to. What about you? Do you like biology?"

"Yeah, I do. I want to work in neurology—treat people who have multiple sclerosis when I grow up."

"See, if I were like you, my mom wouldn't always be on my case about my future. I bet your parents love that you want to work in medicine."

"Please. My parents don't want me to work in neurology. They say I'll work too many hours to be involved with my family."

Now it was Eleora's turn to be confused. "Then what do they want you to be?"

"Someone in ministry—like they used to be before I was born."

And there it was. Their proverbial elephant had made itself known.

"Well, on that note, I should probably head to my next class." She gathered her stuff and walked to the door.

"Bye, my new friend!" Chadwick called out.

Eleora looked back and smiled. "Bye, seventeen-year-old kindergartener!"

Eleora left the room to the soundtrack of his laughter—and it sounded better to her than the music they'd played in there earlier.

Chapter 4

Chadwick put his plates in the dishwasher as his father took up the placemats from the table. As usual, his mom was lying on the couch with the remote in her hand.

"Honey, do you want to, maybe, help us clean up?" his dad teased.

His mom glanced up and then looked back at the TV. "Nah, it's alright. I'm good here." You could almost hear the smirk in her voice.

"Chadwick, I hope you don't inherit your mother's laziness," Aaric said, making them laugh.

"Hey, I cooked that wonderful dinner you two just had. I deserve a break. This—" she motioned to herself lying on the couch "—isn't laziness, it's..."

"Relaxation?" Chadwick offered.

"Yes! Relaxation after some hard work."

"Fine, honey, you win. But after these leftovers are gone, I'm making dinner and will relax afterwards."

"You mean ordering pizza and taking out the plates?" Nina teased.

"It's still making dinner. And you know, dialing the number and then walking to the door to pick up the pizza is hard work."

"Mhhm, and I'm the lazy parent," Nina said sarcastically.

"It's not laziness! It's energy efficiency!" Aaric said as he finished with the table. He kissed Nina gently on the forehead and then grabbed the remote, lounging on the opposite couch.

"So let me get this straight. I'm going to be inheriting my mother's 'relaxation' and my father's 'energy efficiency'? My future wife is going to love me." His parents laughed. Glancing at the time, he said a quick goodnight and went upstairs to write for a bit, read his Bible, and then go to sleep.

He sat on his bed and opened the laptop lying beside him, his document open on the screen. Chadwick sighed, wracking his brain for something good to put down, but all that came to mind was Eleora. Trying once more to push her out of his mind—and failing—Chadwick set the laptop aside, lay down, and took some time to think.

Yesterday, he was trying to be friends with this incredible girl and she was bent on being cold to him. And now... now they were becoming friends—which was what he'd wanted. Okay, that wasn't true. He'd wanted to be more at first and... still did. But that wasn't an option right now. Not until she became a Christian. And she had a long way to go before that could happen. At least now they were at a middle ground, and she was in his life.

It was amazing—and a little scary—how well they got along. She was as good a friend as Chadwick had imagined she'd be when he'd first met her. Funny, accommodating, caring, with a lot of mutual interests and hobbies. Today was officially the first day of their friendship, and yet it felt like they'd known each other for years. He wished he had known her for that long— that he knew everything about her. But with the way their friendship was progressing, they'd be learning new things about each other soon. If he didn't lose his head like he had in Writer's Craft.

When they'd arrived at the lab, only half the class was there, and instead of avoiding him like she'd been doing for the past week, she'd sat beside him and they'd talked about their chosen topics for their poetry assignment.

Eleora opened up the Google Doc for her poems and smiled in glee.

"Okay, I see that smile. What have you written?" Chadwick asked.

"Just this:

I want.
Is an invitation
to intentionally indulge imagination
In an impactful and inspirational instance,
I want.
An authentic awareness that
acquaints itself with appeal
Audacious in its aspiring ambition
I want.
It seems dangerous to desire
Like a dalliance with deceit
And a dance with disappointment
I want.
I can wax eloquent about this tension
Obliterate my opportunity for introspection
Alliterate and rhyme my way out of reflection

But it doesn't change my plight:
I want.
I don't want to be found wanting.
I want to want well."

"That was great, Eleora." He noticed her nod her head and look at her hands.

"Thanks," she said softly, surprising him.

This Eleora wasn't the same one who laughed when guys flirted with her in the hallway, or who took compliments in stride and returned them with wit. This Eleora seemed unsure of her talent.

"Thank you," she repeated and gave him a bright smile.

"You're welcome. But why do you seem so unsure of your writing? It's fantastic—like your singing."

"But that's what everyone always says. 'Your singing is angelic, Eleora.' 'If you were on So You Think You Can Dance Canada, I would vote for you.' 'Omigosh, Elle! You should totally be on Disney Channel and, like, have your own show.'" Eleora adjusted her voice for each saying, making Chadwick laugh.

"No, but legit. Everyone is always complimenting me on my singing, dancing, acting, grades... when you're complimented all the time, you can't tell who's telling the truth and who's just saying it because everyone else is. I mean, I know I'm pretty good at all of those things, but... with my writing, it's different. I take it really seriously. That's why I hardly share it with anyone—I don't want to receive any fake compliments."

Without thinking, Chadwick took her hands in his

and looked straight into her eyes. "Eleora, I don't give out fake compliments. I'm horribly honest sometimes. So believe me when I say—your writing is fantastic."

"Really?" Her eyes still held a trace of disbelief.

"Yes." He answered firmly, his hazel eyes aiming to erase all doubt in her gray ones.

Chadwick noticed a loose curl and gently tucked it behind her ear. Their faces were so close they could have kissed—until Mr. Williams cleared his throat.

"Ahem. Could you two please save the romance for your poems?"

Eleora drew her hands away from his as some people in the class snickered.

"So, Mr. Knight, care to share what you have so far? If you haven't been too busy," Mr. Williams added with a wink.

Now Chadwick blushed, his russet-brown skin turning even more red. He turned to the computer and shared what he'd written.

"My idea for my series is personifying inanimate objects. This poem is from the perspective of a pen:

I make thoughts tangible
And ideas accessible
I require authenticity
Sometimes, it can get messy
Since I do not hide mistakes
I put your true self on the page
This is actually a blessing
Because real life has no erasing
There's no Control-Z to undo your actions
No rewinding your infractions
I'm not just a tool, but a reminder

Every time you put me on paper."

When he was done, Mr. Williams gave him an encouraging smile. "Nice job, Chadwick."

Chadwick cringed at the memory. They hadn't even been friends for a full day, and he'd already almost crossed the boundary and kissed her? How could he have almost done that? And more importantly, why did he hate what happened so much? Was it because he'd nearly crossed a line—or because he hadn't?

He couldn't deny it: he'd wanted to kiss her. Especially after she showed him that vulnerable side today. How could this beautiful, talented girl also be insecure and unaware of how incredible she was?

Well, he was determined to help her see that—and to be with her. Not to be seen with her. And he would do anything to prove that. For now, that meant spending as much time with her as possible.

He sat up, turned off his laptop, and placed it on his nightstand. Then he went to the side of his bed. On his knees, he prayed:

"Lord, my God, thank You so much for answering my previous prayers and for the opportunity to have a friendship with Eleora. Please help me not to overstep the boundaries of this friendship. Help me rein in my emotions and my hormones whenever I'm around her, so that we can continue to learn more about each other the right way. And that she'll become a Christian."

Chadwick got up and felt energized from that time of prayer. So much so that he felt motivated to do the work Pastor Gabe had given him.

He checked his texts to find the list of beliefs and

copied them into a note on his phone:

I'm a bad person
I'm worthless
I'm unimportant
I'm irrelevant
I'm unlovable
I'm shallow
I'm unwanted
I'm stupid
I'm foolish
I'm weak
I'm useless
I'm a freak
I'm faulty
I'm a mistake
I'm needy
I'm greedy

Then, he thought back to the last time he'd felt the urge to watch porn. It had been a few weeks ago. He was feeling stressed about starting at a new school and having to make new friends. That brought on the familiar, lonely feeling.

He glanced at the first reflection question: "And why does that bother you?"

That wasn't too hard.

Well, without friends, I would be alone.

Next question: "What does that say about you?"

Uncomfortable. He wanted to stop. But he felt God giving him strength to sit in the discomfort long enough to answer. Then it came to him:

It means no one wants to be with me.

He blinked, surprised by the words he'd written. Tears welled in his eyes. The next question: "And so what, what if that were true? What are you worried that might mean?"

Nope. This is too hard. I can't do this anymore.

He wanted to escape—but instead, he felt nudged to check the list of beliefs again. One popped out:

I'm worthless.

Chadwick got up and paced. Did he really believe that about himself? That his worth came from others' approval? Was he really that motivated by how others saw him?

Yes. He was.

From school to sports to church, he wanted everyone—his parents, friends, teachers, pastors. He wanted their approval so much.

It felt like trying to breathe underwater, and he was running out of air. The realization overwhelmed him. This had been beneath the surface all along.

God, help me. Free me from being motivated by others' approval. He prayed.

Then Hebrews 11 came to mind. He grabbed his phone, opened his Bible app, and pulled up the chapter. As he read, he understood why God sent him there.

It was all about faith. Faith—saving, persevering, active faith—is what makes us approved by God. He treasured the first part of verse 39:

"And all these, having gained approval through their faith..."

He had God's approval. That truth could free him from striving for everyone else's.

He wasn't approved because of what he did—but because he believed.

As these truths settled in him, Chadwick felt like he'd broken the surface. He wasn't drowning anymore.

He still had a way to go to shore—but now he could breathe enough to swim.

Chapter 5

As Eleora and Chadwick walked down the hall together, she suddenly remembered something.

"Hay nako," she gasped, stopping in her tracks.

Chadwick stopped as well and looked at her with concern. "Is something wrong? Also, what did you just say?"

"It's Tagalog for 'oh my gosh,'" she explained.

"Tagalog?" He looked confused.

"It's the language most used by Filipinos."

His eyebrow quirked in surprise. "You're Filipino?"

"Filipina. And yes, half. My other half is Black Jamaican. But I don't really have contact with that side of my family." Her voice went flat.

"I'm sorry to hear that." He patted her shoulder.

"Thanks! Anyway, I just realized that I have a free period today. My classes don't start until 9:30."

"So, I'll see you in Drama then?" he asked.

"Definitely." Eleora gave him a smile and walked toward the library.

When she reached it, she went to her special spot and settled into her favorite couch, picking up the book she was reading: Ophelia by Lisa Klein. As she found her page—Eleora rarely used bookmarks—thoughts raced through her head.

It had been one week since the almost-kiss in the computer lab. Eleora still didn't know whether to be relieved or disappointed that it hadn't happened—and that nothing similar had happened since. There been no lingering gazes, no leaning into each other, nothing.

Why did that upset her?

He was treating her platonically, as he should. They were supposed to be friends.

Except... she had never been this attracted to a friend before. And not just physically. It was his character that drew her most. He was thoughtful, kind, gifted, and patient. She could only imagine what he'd be like as a boyfriend.

Well, she imagined that. Often.

Before Eleora could be drawn into another Chadwick daydream, she pushed the thoughts aside to focus on the book in her hands.

She may have been too successful, because the next time she looked up from her book, it was already time for her next class!

She dashed to the auditorium and grabbed a seat right beside Chadwick.

"So why were you late?" he asked after attendance was taken and they were instructed to break into pairs.

"I was so caught up in the book I was reading, I lost track of time."

"Really?"

"Yeah... I love reading. And the book I was reading, Ophelia, is so good!"

"What's it about?"

"Okay, so you know how Shakespeare wrote Hamlet, right? Well, Ophelia is like Hamlet but from his lover's—Ophelia's—point of view. It's everything! There's this part where Hamlet is writing a letter to Ophelia to convince her father that he's in love with her—you need more background info, but that's, like, the gist—and he writes:

Doubt that the stars are fire,

Doubt that the sun doth move,

Doubt truth be a liar,

But never doubt I love.

I think I must've read that part for, like, five minutes straight," Eleora said in one long breath.

"Whoa, breathe, Eleora."

She took a deep breath and smiled. "I'm good—just enthused by a wonderful book."

"It sounds great, even though it's not the genre I usually read. What was the part you liked again? 'Doubt that the stars are fire. Doubt that the sun doth move. Doubt truth be a liar. But never doubt I love'?"

"That's it! I shouldn't be surprised by your excellent memory though, you being a royal and all. So anyway, how was class? Did I miss much?"

"Not really. I figured you might want to hear it though, so I asked Mr. Williams for permission to record the lesson on my iPhone to give to you later, and he gave me the okay. So I'll send it to your email after class."

Her eyes brightened, and she impulsively gave him a hug, catching him off guard and nearly knocking him over. His arms instinctively slid around her waist as her head rested beside his neck. Eleora turned her head so that her mouth was right beside his ear, her hair slightly tickling him.

"Thank you," she whispered.

"You're welcome."

She drew away and glanced around the stage, but everyone was still talking exactly as they had been a few minutes ago.

How could no one notice the moment between her and Chadwick? How could everything seem so normal when something monumental had just happened?

And something had happened.

That hug felt intimate. Like it had shifted something in her. The tectonic plates of her heart had moved, unearthing a chasm of longing.

She yearned to be held, and seen, and loved.

And for all these things to be true… with someone like Chadwick.

Or Chadwick himself.

Chapter 6

Chadwick watched the countdown to the start of the church service with anticipation. After a rollercoaster of a week, he needed to be in the house of God with the people of God. He was thankful he wasn't serving in the worship band this Sunday—it meant he could engage in the service without distractions.

When the countdown finished, an older Black woman came onto the stage holding a mic.

"Welcome, everyone, to Agape Community Church. I'm Marielle, and we're so glad you joined us today to worship and learn from God. I'm going to pray for us, and then the band will lead us in song. If we could all bow our heads and close our eyes to avoid distractions, that would be great."

Chadwick obeyed. Even before she prayed, he felt peace settle in. He knew God was already present.

"Yahweh, You are good and worthy of praise— worthy of our very lives! I ask that we would experience Your tangible presence this morning. Be with Pastor Tavish as he unpacks Your Word so that we may hear it and do it. In Jesus' name, amen."

"Amen," Chadwick said in unison with the hundreds gathered in the sanctuary.

When he opened his eyes, the worship pastor, Pastor Ben, stood at the center of the stage, the band behind him. Even from where Chadwick sat, he could see the excitement in Pastor Ben's blue eyes, his brown hair pulled up in a man bun.

"Alright, if you're ready to worship our God in song, stand up and join us!"

Chadwick stood and clapped along as the band began to play. Then Pastor Ben sang:

> Beauty for ashes
> Joy for mourning
> Praise for heaviness
> I am for Your glory.

Chadwick let the words wash over him. God had done so much for him—of course he'd want to live his life for God's glory.

"Alright, I want y'all to join in," Pastor Ben said, and the church sang the refrain with him. The song celebrated God's power to transform lives and give new beginnings.

Next, they sang Fountains:

> I will never forget
> The moment I met You
> The moment You called my name,
> Pulled me out of the darkness
> Gave me a promise
> To never thirst again.

As he sang, Chadwick was reminded of when he first placed his faith in Jesus—how alive he'd felt for the first time. He sang about finding his satisfaction in

Jesus.

Then came As the Deer. The lyrics about ongoing longing for God struck deep:

> You're my friend and You are my
> Father
> Even though You are my King,
> I love You more than any other
> So much more than anything.

Did he really love God more than anything?

They closed worship with King of My Heart. As he sang, Chadwick recommitted his heart to the kingship of Christ:

> Let the King of my heart
> Be the fire inside my veins
> The echo of my days
> Oh, He is my song.
> 'Cause You are good.

God's goodness and faithfulness made Him worthy to be King. As the band wound down, Pastor Ben prayed:

"Yahweh, our life is in You. Our desire is You. Our King is You. We love You, Lord, but only because You loved us first and showed Your love for us in this: You came to earth, lived a perfect life, died a sinner's death, and rose from the grave. Hallelujah. Lord, be with Your servant, Pastor Tav, as he unpacks the Word this morning. In Jesus' name, amen."

The lights dimmed, and the congregation sat, awaiting their Sri Lankan pastor. When the lights came back up, Chadwick was surprised to see Eden, a

Ghanaian girl from the youth group, onstage. And then he got excited. Every so often, artistic elements were incorporated into the service. Eden's presence meant that was happening today.

She began to speak:

> "I still want you
> But I cut and bleed
> with every grasp
> A sting of self-sabotage so familiar
> When recovery became
> Relapse
>
> The truth is,
> Poison doesn't leave the system
> quickly
> This curing process excruciating
> Crucial
>
> Killing all that's unhealthy in me
> So that a new creation
> Can rise in its stead
> Resurrection
> Requires something to be dead
>
> We want the Phoenix
> Without realizing that the fire
> Burns
> And it's more comfortable
> But not better
> To avoid it altogether
>
> Easy

But not free
True freedom is
Saying goodbye
But why is this goodbye
So hard to say?

Can hope be hope if it's cautious?
Does this conflicted stance cancel out
the courage?
My resolve to change is unsteady
But still greater than our fatal
fellowship

Alas,
At last,
Goodbye."

Chadwick snapped along with the congregation's applause. What a powerful poem. It built his anticipation for the sermon.

"Well, hello church!" Pastor Tavish greeted them, smiling warmly from his dark brown face. "Praise God for the worship we've engaged in through music and poetry. Now, we will worship through the Word of God. We're continuing our series in the book of James. Turn your Bibles or scroll to James 1—we'll focus on verses 13 through 17."

He cleared his throat and read the passage aloud. Chadwick followed along. These were challenging verses.

"I've got to tell you, church," Pastor Tav said. "This won't be a light sermon. Today we're talking about temptation. Here's where we're going: the progression of temptation and how we respond to temptation and sin in our lives. And I mean our—this is a word for me too! Are y'all ready?" Pastor Tav loved the congregation's participation.

"Yes, Pastor!" a Trinidadian-sounding voice called out. The congregation chuckled with Pastor Tav.

"This text outlines the progression of temptation. It starts with desire. Now, we need to remember. Desire is not sinful in and of itself. There are normal desires—hunger, longing for intimacy—but desire can become evil. It lures us and entices us until we commit an act of sin, like gluttony or sexual immorality. Sin that continues on without repentance leads to death."

Chadwick nodded as he followed along with Pastor Tav.

"So, what happened here? How did we go from desire to death? It starts with us being lured and enticed to sin by our desire. This is us bring led by desire instead of being led by the Spirit. When we surrender our desire and follow the Lord's leading in the fulfilment of our desire, whether he says yes or no, we cut off the process from the get-go. But let's say we let our desire lead us, and then an act of sin is committed. We have decided to get our desire fulfilled on our own terms. We have chosen to be the god of our lives."

Chadwick shivered. God was speaking to him. He had a desire for a romantic relationship with Eleora, but he couldn't let it lead him. He needed to find his satisfaction in Christ. No matter how beautiful and good a relationship with her may seem, it would lead to death.

"This is what happened in Eden. Let's go to Genesis 3, Reading from verse 6: 'The woman saw that the tree was good for food and delightful to look at, and that it was desirable for obtaining wisdom. So she took some of its fruit and ate it; she also gave some to her husband, who was with her, and he ate it.' See what happened there? She desired it and she chose to listen to the serpent instead of to God. And where did that leave humanity? Dead in our sins. Church, when we don't kill our sin with repentance, it will grow up and kill us."

"That's good!" someone called out from the congregation. Chadwick smiled. It was a word, no doubt about it. He needed that reminder.

"A sister in the faith, Rosaria Butterfield, said this about repentance: 'The Bible teaches that what separates a believer from an unbeliever is repentance. (...) Repentance refreshes the believer, gives glory to God, and bears Christian fruit. Repentance is a gift from God, for only believers can repent.' Can I get an amen?"

The church responded with an enthusiastic amen, which made Pastor Tavish smile.

"So, we've seen two stops where we can get off the temptation train. Stop number one is right at the beginning by giving our desire to God. This is what we sang about, finding true satisfaction in our Lord. The other stop is after we've sinned. We get off by repenting, by turning away from our sin. We heard about this in the poetry that was spoken over us. It is difficult. And typically, the longer we've gone without repentance, the harder repentance will be. But, in the power of the Holy Spirit, we can say no. We have authority. It doesn't have to end in death, saints."

Chadwick felt peace and hope. He had everything in God to get off the train every time it came by.

"Our brother warns us not to be deceived. Deceit is when true things are used to lead us to a lie. Let's take sex. It is true that sex is good. It is true that, for most of us, sex is something we desire. But, in deceit, these true things can lead us to sexual gratification outside of the covenant of marriage. Instead, we ought to surrender our desire to God and trust Him. Why do we do that? It says it in verse 17: God is the giver of good and perfect gifts. Not us. Not our flesh. Not the world. Not Satan. God. He will either say yes and give you what you desire right away. He may say no, and we can trust that denial is the good gift. Or, He may say not yet to that desire. Remember, church, the right thing at the wrong time is still the wrong thing."

That line hit Chadwick to the core. Maybe a relationship with Eleora was the right thing. But if she didn't follow Jesus, it would always be the wrong time. He wanted to honor God. He wanted the right thing at the right time.

"But take heart! Even though Adam and Eve failed—and even though we fail—Jesus didn't. He had desires but never let them lead Him into sin. Yet He took on our consequence—death—through His sacrifice on the cross. That's why we can say no. And even when we don't, we're still loved and still have life!"

Chadwick felt a fresh wave of awe and gratitude. Jesus had defeated sin and death. He had given Chadwick the authority to resist temptation. No matter how many times he heard the gospel, it still stunned him with its beauty and power.

"Together, let's sing praise to Jesus! Let's declare that He is enough. That He is what we want. And that we will leave temptation behind."

Pastor Tav nodded to Pastor Ben and the band, and they led the church in singing Christ Is Enough.

While others stood, Chadwick remained seated. God had spoken clearly. He needed to respond.

"Lord, I hear You. What You're asking of me isn't easy. But it's doable through the power of the Spirit. Help me, Lord. In Jesus' name, amen."

He finished his prayer, then rose to join his brothers and sisters in worship.

Chapter 7

Eleora wiped her sweaty palms on her jeans as she waited for Chadwick to arrive. They were trying something new—spending time together outside of school; meeting at the library to get work done.

Why was she so nervous? This was Chadwick, her friend. He was one of the people she felt safest with. Second only to Maryliz, he was the person she trusted the most. Over the past week, their friendship had only grown. They had fallen back into their natural rhythm of banter and support. These nerves made little sense—except maybe they did. Maybe hanging out together like this, alone and not at school, felt like they were legitimizing their friendship. That it wasn't restricted to a certain part of life, but open to all parts of life. All parts of her.

She sighed and shook her head to dislodge the thoughts as she leaned against the glass wall by the library entrance. She could take comfort in being at one of her favourite places—the largest library in her city. Across from the mall and in the same building as a recreation centre to boot, she always enjoyed coming here.

Just as she was about to pull out her phone to see if

he'd texted about running late or not showing up, she saw Chadwick walk through the door. She spotted him looking around for her and lifted her arm to wave. When his gaze landed on her, he smiled.

She felt her heart rate speed up as she took him in. Somehow, he could make plain jeans and a cream sweater look amazing. And the leather jacket he was wearing? She was a sucker for two things on a guy: a suit and a leather jacket.

He walked up to her and lifted an arm to give her a side hug. She cherished it way too much, considering they were just friends.

"Ready to go in?" he asked, and she nodded, following him inside the library. It was fairly empty, but that made sense. This wasn't where people wanted to be on a Saturday morning. They found a table big enough for both to have their laptops out and set up.

"What are you planning to work on?" she asked, turning on her MacBook.

"A lab report for chemistry. You?" His actions mirrored hers as he opened his PC laptop.

"The bane of every twelfth grader's existence: university applications. Dun, dun, dun."

He laughed. "Yo, it's only October, fam. Don't we have until January to send these in?"

Eleora shrugged. "The early bird gets the worm."

"Says the night owl."

Now she laughed. "But legit, I don't want the future to be this looming unknown thing to get anxious about. I figure the earlier I apply, the sooner I'll hear back and figure out what my next steps are."

"That makes sense. So, where are you applying to and for which programs?"

"The nursing programs at Mac, Queens, and U of T."

His eyebrows raised in surprise. "What? You want to be a nurse?"

She mustered up a perky smile. "Yeppers."

"You don't have to do that with me, you know." The serious tone of his voice caught her off guard.

"Do what?"

"Pretend. You can be real with me."

"What makes you think I was pretending?"

"Your smile didn't reach your eyes."

Her eyes widened in surprise. "I didn't realize I was so easy to read."

"I don't know if I'd say that necessarily. I'm not sure how many people have noticed it." Well, that was reassuring.

"But you did. How?"

He took his time to answer, looking thoughtful. "I guess I first noticed it when you shared your poetry with me in class. There's a light that comes to your eyes." He shrugged, looking sheepish. "That's not the only time I've seen it, but it's not as frequent as it could be."

Eleora nodded, taking in his words and hearing the question underneath what he'd shared: why does she pretend most of the time?

"Thanks for bringing this to my attention, Chadwick. Often, it feels easier to be what others want me to be instead of who I am."

He looked incredulous. "Easier? If anything, I would expect that to be exhausting."

Eleora laughed dryly. "You mean it's not normal to feel emotionally tired most of the time?"

"If it's so draining, why do it?"

She thought for a moment. "Because that's easier to deal with than people's disappointment in me, or worse, their rejection. Who am I if I'm not making people happy? If I'm not doing everything perfectly?"

"Someone that would still be loved, Ellie."

"Ellie?" She chose to ignore the other part of what he'd said.

"Well, your name is kind of a mouthful..." Chadwick said teasingly, his voice trailing off.

She playfully punched him in the shoulder. "I guess there are worse nicknames."

She liked it. No one else had called her that before. Even though they were just friends, she liked that there would be something in their dynamic that was distinct from others. "On the real though, thanks. For everything."

"You're welcome. For everything. But you didn't answer my question before... nursing?"

She snapped her fingers and said in a playful tone, "Darn. I hoped you wouldn't remember that."

Eleora paused before answering. How honest should she be? She was going to give him her practiced answer, but when she saw the genuine surprise and concern in his eyes, the truth came out. "No, I don't. Not even a little."

"Then why apply for that program?"

She sighed. "My mom wants me to do it. And it's not like I can't handle blood or needles. I know it's a job I can do."

"But it's not a job that you want to do." It wasn't a question, but she nodded in answer anyway. "Have you thought about telling your mom how you feel?"

"It's a non-starter. I have to do one of the big three: healthcare, law, or engineering. Out of that, nursing appeals to me the most. She wouldn't understand me not doing it because I don't want to. That's not a sufficient reason."

"I will say that our North American culture has conditioned us to see our jobs or careers as the locus of purpose and fulfillment. And that's not supposed to be the case. Still, I wrestle with you not being passionate about what you're going to be spending hours of time and thousands of dollars on."

"It's the philosophical wisdom for me," Eleora joked, and they laughed together, breaking the tension that had been building.

"But, humour me—if you could go with your passion, what would you want to do? Where would you want to go?"

"Well…" she had told no one this, not even Maryliz. But she knew she could trust him. "There's this program at the University of Victoria in BC that is the dream." She couldn't stop a smile from spreading across her face.

"Go on. Tell me more." He leaned forward on the table toward her.

"Okay, so it's a Fine Arts degree in Writing with a minor in Theatre."

"Now that program sounds like the Eleora I've been getting to know. Why BC?"

"Well, it's where my mom and I lived when I was in middle school. I love it. The temperature is pretty moderate, it's often rainy, which I love, and you can go to the ocean or the mountains. It's gorgeous."

"Okay, Ellie, ditch the program you just told me

about and become a tourist agent. You've sold me on visiting or living there." He teased, and she laughed.

"On the real though, I wish you could see what you looked like when you were talking about that program. Your eyes even lit up."

She felt herself beginning to blush. "Ah well, it'll probably stay a dream."

"Why don't you just apply and see what happens?"

She shook her head.

"Seriously, what's the worst-case scenario if you do?"

The words came out before she could stop them. "I could lose another parent."

Chadwick's face was a mix of surprise, concern, and caution. "Do you want to elaborate on that a bit more?"

Eleora sighed. "Let's just say that my bio dad isn't a part of my life anymore. Things went south with him during my parents' divorce in grade five. That's part of the reason we moved to BC."

He reached over and took one of her hands in his. It was shaking. "I'm so sorry, Ellie."

His words wrapped around her like a warm hug, and she felt her eyes sting with tears. "Thanks." She turned away from him so he wouldn't see the tears beginning to fall.

She felt his hand on her shoulder. "Hey, Ellie, you really don't need to do that."

She sighed and turned back, but looked down. "Do what?"

Gently, he lifted her chin until they were making eye contact. "Hide the fact that you're crying. It's okay." His sincere eyes broke through her, and she sobbed.

"Come here." He stood and opened his arms. Without thinking twice, she stepped into his embrace. There, she felt safe—even safe enough to fall apart.

After several minutes of crying, she pulled away and wiped her face with the sleeve of her sweater. "Thanks. I feel like that's the word I seem to use the most. I didn't mean to burden you."

He looked at her, shocked. "Eleora, you could never be a burden to me."

She believed he meant it, but she didn't believe it was true. She definitely felt like a burden.

"This is part of being your friend," he continued. "Being there for you when you need support. No thanks necessary."

"Tha—" she caught herself and grinned sheepishly.

"Okay." She chose that instead and then gave him a warm smile.

"There it is! A genuine smile from Eleora Gonzales, everybody!" he said in an announcer's voice.

She giggled and realized they were still holding hands, so she gently pulled hers away. He let go without any indication it affected him. He leaned back in his chair, away from her.

"You're right though," she said after a few moments. "I can just apply and see what happens. At least I won't have to live with uncertainty and regret at not trying."

"So you'll do it?" He looked so boyish in his excitement that she laughed.

"Yes. What about you? Have you given any thought to where you'll be applying? You want to work in neurology, right?"

He smiled at the fact she remembered. "Yeah. I'll probably do a Bachelor of Science. I'm not sure where yet, though. The Ontario universities you mentioned have come to mind since they're like the Canadian Ivy Leagues."

"That's why I chose them. It's the bougie and nerdy part of me, I guess?"

He chuckled. "I love that. Bougie Nerds. That should be an official club! Of course, you will be our president."

"And you may be my vice or chief of staff, unless you feel weird about being under a woman." Eleora realized what she'd just said. "I mean... not literally under..." she stammered, and he laughed.

"I gotchu. And no, I'm not intimidated by women in leadership positions. If you're the most qualified for the role and have upright character, nothing else should matter."

"Is it sacrilegious if I say amen to that?" she asked tentatively. He laughed.

"You're good, fam."

"Well then, am—" Eleora was cut off by a ringtone.

Chapter 8

"Oh gosh, I thought I'd put this on silent. Give me a sec." Chadwick pulled out his phone and turned down the volume.

"Was it a call? Should you have answered?"

"Nah. It was a reminder about a movie that's now in theatres that I've been waiting for."

"Let me guess, another Marvel movie?"

"Whoa, am I sensing hate for the MCU?"

"Hate is too strong a word. I guess fatigued?"

"Fair enough. But no, it's not a Marvel movie." He twirled his phone in his hand.

"Colour me intrigued. What's the movie?"

He sighed. "Don't make fun of me, but The Magician's Nephew."

To his surprise, Eleora squealed. "Are you messing with me? They're making a movie of that book?" In her excitement, her words rushed out. It took Chadwick a moment to catch what she said.

"Wait, you know the book?"

She gave him a "duh" look. "The Chronicles of Narnia is a freaking classic, Chadwick. Of course, I know the books." She rolled her eyes. "I was so cheesed when they skipped the first book and never went back to it. It puts The Lion, the Witch and the Wardrobe in context. You're telling me it's been made?"

He nodded, still surprised. Did she know a Christian who integrated spiritual themes into the books wrote it? "Yeah, it's been released to a smaller number of theatres. Seems like we're in the minority wanting to see it."

"That's wild to me!" she exclaimed and then remembered they were in a library.

He breathed deeply and took a chance to see if she would go with him. It wouldn't be a date. Just two friends hanging out. "Do you want to go see it together after we're done here?" He kept his voice casual.

"For sure."

He released a breath he hadn't realized he'd been holding.

"I'd probably just be seeing it on my own anyway. Better to do so with a friend."

He smiled. "Cool, I'll buy our tickets right now." He started tapping on his phone.

"Oh, let me know how much it is and I'll e-transfer you."

He shook his head. "Nah, let me cover it."

"I can afford a movie ticket, Chadwick." Her sharp tone made him look up. She was peeved.

"Whoa, Ellie. Chill, it's not that deep. I'm using scene points for the tickets, so there's no reason to pay me back. I'd be making money off you, which would be weird."

At his explanation, she calmed down. "Oh. Sorry."

"No problem. Was your objection purely feminism, or was there something else going on here?"

"I didn't want to be a burden on you." She refused to meet his eyes.

"Hey, look at me, Eleora." She turned toward him as soon as he said her full name. "You could never be a burden. Not to me or anyone."

By the tears beginning to form in her eyes, he could tell his words had hit her hard.

"Thank you, Knight."

He smiled at the use of his last name. "Knight, eh? I like it. Let's do Trinity for the theatre. What time do you think is best?"

Eleora thought for a moment. "I'm free all day. I just want a time when the theatre would be emptiest."

"Are you trying to get me all alone, Ellie? Do you have something nefarious planned?"

She laughed. "You're not that special, fam."

"Wow." He stretched out the word, faking hurt, then started laughing too.

"I agree with you, though." He said when their laughter died down. "Actually, I have a confession that may make you rethink seeing it with me." He started to feel apprehensive. He really wanted to go on this not-a-date with her.

"I already know you're a Christian."

He snorted, which made her giggle.

"Nah, for real. I talk during movies. I like to give a running commentary as I'm watching. When I watch with others, I try to do it under my breath, but it can still annoy people."

Eleora looked at him dubiously. "That's crazy! I do the same thing! It's why I often watch movies alone."

He relaxed. "Bruh. Are we the same person? Okay, let's do the later showing at 7:30. That way, most families will probably be at home." He reasoned aloud, and she nodded.

"Works for me. We should get something to eat, eh? I'm high-key craving some Jollibee. I'd be happy to have that for dinner tonight. You good with that?"

"Sure, I'm down. But, what's Jollibee?"

She gasped. "Are you serious? It's a Filipino fast-food restaurant that has the best fried chicken ever!"

He smirked in amusement at her response. "Whoa, seems like I struck a nerve. What about Popeyes or Church's?"

Eleora shook her head. "Nah. Trust me when I say that Jollibee is better. That settles it. You need a fried chicken education. We're going there for dinner. It's just at the mall across from this rec centre."

"Alright, let's say we wrap up working by 5:30 then? That should give us enough time, right?"

"Yeah, that sounds good." She agreed. "Now, we should do what we came here to do and get some work done."

"Facts. Let's check in with each other in an hour?" he suggested.

She nodded and turned toward her MacBook screen. He shifted his attention to his Chromebook and saw a message from Pastor Gabe confirming their meeting that evening.

He had forgotten.

Chadwick pushed aside his guilt as he typed out a message asking Pastor Gabe for a raincheck on their meet-up. It was a struggle to decide between the two. The last time they'd met and discussed the core beliefs that had surfaced had been powerful. He was looking forward to more time with Pastor Gabe, but in the end, he chose Eleora—a fact he was trying his best not to read too much into. It's not like he was choosing her over God, right?

To distract himself from these thoughts, he got to work on his chemistry lab report, then his calculus homework, then rewriting notes for his biology test. They worked in silence, and time flew by. He was surprised when Eleora tapped him on the shoulder.

"It's Jollibee time! Ready to have your mind blown?"

"Promises, promises, Ellie," he teased.

"And like Amazon Prime, I deliver."

They packed up their stuff. During the quick walk to the restaurant, they debriefed everything they'd done at the library. Upon arriving, they grabbed a booth and dropped their stuff.

"I'll go order for us, that is, if you trust me to do so?" Eleora offered.

He held up his hands in surrender. "This is your domain. It's all as you wish."

"Alright, I'll be back in a few." She walked toward the counter.

Chadwick had to hold himself in check as she walked away. He had never noticed her butt before, but he couldn't help looking now with her in those leggings. And the sliver of skin he'd seen between their waistband and her sweater was more enticing than it had any right to be.

He shook himself. He could do this. He could just be her friend. "Lord, you're really not making this easy for me to do. Holy Spirit, help. I need You." He whispered the prayer and felt a peace come over him. He felt heard and seen by God.

In almost no time, Eleora returned with a bright red tray full of food. He took stock of the bounty she spread before them on the table: a bucket of fried chicken, two small containers of white rice, two small containers of what looked like gravy, and a large box filled with—he didn't even know what.

"Sorry, I didn't realize you were buying out the entire store." His teasing earned her a smile.

"Teenage boys have a reputation for eating a lot and I love their food, so I needed to be sure we had enough."

"Gotcha. How much do I owe you?"

Eleora shook her head. "Nothing. It's a treat on me." He wanted to argue, but it wasn't like this was a date. If it were, he would have fought to pay more, but they were just friends. He could enjoy a friend's generosity.

"Well, thanks." He bowed his head, closed his eyes, and sent off a silent, quick thanksgiving prayer. When he opened his eyes, Eleora was staring at him, but he couldn't read the emotions on her face.

"Nickel, for your thoughts?" he asked.

"They're still in draft mode. Can we eat first, and then I'll share later?"

"For sure. Let's get into this. It smells amazing."

She smiled and gave him a paper plate.

"So, I got us some mild and spicy chicken. I figured with your Jamaican background, you'd want the spicy?" He nodded. "Great. I wanted the mild anyway. While I can handle some heat, I just prefer this chicken without it," she explained. "There's rice and gravy and..." She opened the mystery box. "Spaghetti. It's not Italian, though, so it may not be what you expect.

Shoot. I forgot to get us drinks since I have a water bottle in my purse already." She looked worried.

"No worries, I have my own water too."

Eleora immediately relaxed. "Okay, well, let's dig in!"

They shared the food enthusiastically. He took a bit of a chicken leg and was transported to a magical land of perfect fried chicken. He took another bite to see if it was a fluke, but it wasn't. He noticed Eleora was waiting for his verdict.

"You have won this battle, Eleora. This chicken is... perfect. The only word I have for it is perfect. If Jesus was a piece of fried chicken, He would be this." The Christian-themed joke slipped out naturally before he considered its impact.

Thankfully, she just laughed. "I'm so glad you like it! Now try the spaghetti."

He complied and took a forkful of noodles. He tried to school his face to hide his reaction, but Eleora missed nothing.

She giggled. "You don't like it, eh?"

He hesitated. He didn't want to hurt her feelings, but she didn't seem to take it personally. "Not really. I think this is more sweet than savoury, and I prefer savoury."

"That's okay." She shrugged. "It's not for everyone. It just means more for me."

They spent the next little while in companionable silence as they both enjoyed the food. As was true to their friendship, they didn't feel the need to fill the silence needlessly. It was easy.

"Okay, I think I'm ready to share my thoughts now that I have a full belly."

Chadwick gave her his full attention.

"When you were praying before the meal, it reminded me that you're a Christian. I guess I'd forgotten somehow? Anyway, it made me sad and confused. Like, you're an intelligent and kind person, so I have no idea why you choose to subscribe to this faith."

He could tell she'd chosen her words carefully, and he smiled at her thoughtfulness. "Well, one, thanks for sharing all of that with me. And two, I genuinely believe that it's true. Not because it was what I was raised with, but because of how it has impacted me. And three, there are so many people who think like you and embrace the Christian faith." Just then, Chadwick remembered something. "Like the person who's responsible for us hanging out tonight."

Eleora looked at him quizzically.

"I'm talking about C. S. Lewis. He was an atheist who became a Christian. I think he even wrote a book about his journey."

The surprise was plain on her face. "I was today years old when I learned that."

He could tell she was ready for the conversation to end. "I know we didn't meet today to have spiritual conversations, so let's table this discussion."

This earned him a smile that made it hard to remember they were just friends. "I appreciate that."

"How about we clean up and head to the theatre?"

She nodded in agreement. They left the restaurant soon after and headed to the vehicle Chadwick had driven. As they walked, they talked about parts of the movie they were looking forward to, both resisting the urge to hold the other's hand.

Chapter 9

They left the movie with awed smiles on their faces.

"That was…" Chadwick's voice trailed off.

"Yeah, I don't have words for it either. Other than to say I loved it." Chadwick nodded in agreement. "I've just gotta go pee, and then we can head out."

"Sounds good. I'll wait for you by the water fountain."

With a thumbs up, she went to take care of business and appreciated these few minutes to herself to think. Not just about the movie, but watching it with Chadwick. She'd had so much fun with him. There were only a few other people in the theater, so they could whisper to each other while watching. His commentary often made her laugh. Often, they were thinking the same thing and just on the same wavelength.

During their time discussing religion at Jollibee, she had been worried. Maybe they wouldn't have a good time and would see their friendship should be restricted to school. Relief and disappointment warred within her at the thought. But she needn't have worried. Things were as easy as they'd ever been. If anything, she felt closer to him than before.

After washing her hands, she walked toward him, where he was waiting. In silence, they went to the car. Once he was done backing out of his spot and started to navigate through the parking lot, he broke the silence. "So, can we start by just saying that the visuals were incredible?!"

"Yes, they were. The VFX, or whatever it's called, was on fleek. Like that scene where Aslan sings Narnia into existence... gosh, it was gorgeous."

"Agreed. I'm so glad we saw it in IMAX so we could get the full effect. Okay, favorite part?"

She thought for a moment. There were so many! "I think when Aslan creates the world and gives the animals the power of speech for justice and joy. In this way, he almost makes them human, which shows us as the humans watching what Lewis thinks we should be like. You?"

His response was immediate. "When Digory resists Jadis tempting him to take an apple for himself. It was so powerful to see him confronted with what he wants most but doing the honorable thing. It shows his growth from just giving into his desires and ringing the bell earlier in the movie."

Eleora nodded. "That was pretty inspiring to see. I also loved seeing Frank and Helen become the first King and Queen of Narnia. I appreciated how they gave us more insight into why they were chosen by showing that montage of their kind actions and humble character."

"You seem to be drawn toward the characters stepping into their purpose," Chadwick pointed out.

"I hadn't even realized that, but you're right. I

believe we have purposes in this world. I just wish I knew what mine was, you know? I want to know that I'm doing the right things."

"Makes sense to me. Is there anything you didn't like about the movie?" Her emphatic nodding made him laugh. "Please, share."

"Okay, I wish they had put in a love story for Polly and Digory."

"Nah, fam. They honored the source material and the author's intent."

She shook her head. "Well, they were fine doing their own thing when they wrote in a romance between Susan and Caspian. And that served no purpose. It was unnecessary!"

"And it's necessary for there to be one between Digory and Polly?"

"Yes!"

Eleora noticed they had just driven up to her house. Disappointment hit her. She didn't want their time together to end.

"I need to hear your argument for this. You okay if we chill here and keep talking?"

This was just what her heart wanted. She nodded.

"Cool, okay Ellie. Convince me." He took the key out of the ignition and turned on the lights in the car so they could see each other.

She turned in her seat to face him. "My argument is this: think of their respective spouses. They're always going to have shared this life-changing thing with someone they're not married to, something they could never even explain to their spouses. No one would believe their story."

"Hmmm. I think I see what you're getting at.

There's an intimacy they would share that their spouses wouldn't have access to."

"Exactly." She nodded. "I'm not saying they would cheat, although that could be a real danger in situations like what we're describing. But it would be so hard for me to be married to someone who I couldn't enjoy…" She paused to land on the right words, "…reciprocal full disclosure with. Does that make sense?"

"It does. You're saying that marriage is a place where you should be fully known and fully know your spouse. Complete intimacy. I agree with you."

"Thank you. So, that was my main reason. My second is like it—I just always root for friends to get together. In my head, it's like you already care for each other so much, it's often just the physical stuff that's missing. And, I don't know, I think that can grow." The words came out without her realizing the implications of what she'd said. This is how she's always felt about romances and how she would want to end up in a relationship, starting as close friends.

This is what she wanted to happen with Chadwick and her.

"I root for the best friend to be the love interest when I'm watching a rom-com or something. Like, this might be controversial, but I think Katniss should have chosen Gale, not Peeta," he shared.

"Oh my gosh, yes! I've always thought that, too!" Her voice rose in excitement. "So, you see where I'm coming from? Like the movie Brown Sugar. Have you seen it?"

"My mom loves that movie. The one with Sanaa Lathan and Taye Diggs, right?"

Eleora nodded. "Yep, that's the one. Like, they

wasted so much time and energy and hurt other people's hearts by not just getting together from the get-go."

"You're not wrong. Okay, you've convinced me. This is an area where C. S. Lewis made a mistake." He pretended to bow in defeat and she laughed.

"Thank you, thank you!" With a pang of her heart, she realized she should probably leave now. She really didn't want to, though. She wanted to stay with him… and maybe never leave.

The thought surprised her and was just what she needed to end their time. Eleora put her hand on the door handle. "Hey, it's approaching 11, and I had some work to get done, so I should head inside."

She saw something flicker in his eyes while he nodded. Was that disappointment she detected?

"True. Well, thanks for introducing me to perfect fried chicken, watching the movie with me, and processing it afterward."

Eleora gave him a warm smile. "You're welcome. It was a great time. See you at school?" She opened the door and gave him a wave before closing it and walking up to her front door.

She went upstairs to her room and flopped onto her bed. She really liked him. What was she going to do?

Chapter 10

Chadwick sat down at his desk and read over the worksheet Pastor Gabe had given him to work on for their next meeting. Thankfully, rescheduling the one he'd missed could work out, and their last session had been powerful.

They were working on crafting a vision for his life—something to motivate him to remove porn from his life. His homework was to assess how he was doing in eight aspects of being human by reading them, rating himself, and reflecting on each.

The first was fun and recreation. "Fun and recreation are the desires to be creative and enjoy life. These are stimulating activities," he read aloud.

Hmm. How much fun did he really have? What did he do for fun these days? School, work, church, repeat. Chadwick grimaced and rated it a 5.5 out of 10.

Next was rest and relaxation—activities that are enjoyable but slow you down. Well, watching movies and playing piano fit here. Chadwick thought about it and gave himself an eight out of ten.

Then there was work. "Work is what you do to contribute productively to society in a way that is rewarding," he read to himself. He scored that a nine.

He enjoyed tutoring and being a student in high school—his vocations, which he did well.

Chadwick sighed as he read the next one: contribution—giving back to society by serving others in an altruistic, sacrificial way. Besides youth group compassion projects, this area was lacking. He gave himself a six.

He brightened at the next category: spiritual growth. Chadwick scored this a nine, confident that he was consistently praying, reading the Bible, and going to church.

Family was next—a higher rating at eight. His biological family was his parents, whom he felt close to and loved by.

The last two were much harder: friends and romantic relationship.

For friendships, this was where much of his loneliness came from. He didn't feel like he had close guy friends who really knew him, loved him, and would be there no matter what. This was a four. Chadwick cringed. Maybe really a three, he thought.

For romantic relationship, he was single but wanted to be with Eleora. She was funny, kind, gifted. Eleora saw him and got him. Even though they didn't share the same faith, she was his closest friend. A friend he wanted to hold, kiss, and... other things—things meant for marriage.

It had been two weeks since their first study time that turned into a dinner and movie non-date. He was struggling to hold back his feelings for her. With her, the aching loneliness he'd always felt eased up. When he struggled and needed a compassionate perspective or a laugh, he could go to her.

He needed her.

You need Me alone.

God was right. He may want Eleora—desperately—but he didn't need her. All he needed was God.

But she's here. I can see her and touch her. God, You feel less accessible.

Chadwick felt the tug-of-war inside himself. Choosing Eleora as the solution to his addiction felt easier. But was that better? Was that what he should do? Shouldn't he go to God?

Blessed are those who did not see, and yet believed.

Chadwick smiled. If he remembered right, that was what Jesus said to Thomas after His resurrection.

Going to Eleora didn't require faith. Believing in God did—but there came the blessing.

He would trust God to heal him. He would trust God's timing.

Or, at least, he would try.

As he evaluated the eight categories, he noted his lowest scores: fun, friends, and romance. He could see how porn was a counterfeit substitute for these things. He used porn for stimulation, for distraction from the lack of friends, and as a mimic for the intimacy he was longing for. Chadwick realized that if he invested in these areas of his life healthily, he could kick porn to the curb.

Satisfied with his work, he put down his phone and bowed his head to pray.

"Lord, thank You for this time of reflection and revelation. Thank You for showing me how porn is a poor replacement for what I'm longing for. And Lord, grow my faith in You. Help me trust Your timing with Eleora. Amen."

Chapter 11

November came with a chill, but there was still no snow, much to Eleora's relief. She didn't have to worry about stepping in slush or wearing her clunky winter boots outside. She found solace in these small blessings—especially since the last few weeks had been a sweet torment.

Ever since that weekend when they'd hung out at the library and the movies, her friendship with Chadwick was in a different place. Truly uncharted waters for her. She had many acquaintances and admirers, but few real friends. There were girls she got along with and spent time with for school-related things, and then there was Maryliz. Fate had put them together in grade nine, and she was thankful for her. She could always count on Maryliz for a funny meme, advice, or deep chats. It was like having the sister she never had.

Chadwick was different. He had become her closest friend—second only to Maryliz. But unlike her sister-friend, he didn't feel like family; she definitely didn't see him as a brother.

She knew she didn't want to go a day without interacting with him. Like today, she'd been looking forward to their regular Saturday study time when he told her he couldn't come because of a dentist appointment. She wanted to tell him it was unnecessary—his smile didn't need any help—but she bit back her words and feigned nonchalance.

It was hard to describe what he was beginning to mean to her. He felt like a whole new world she had the privilege of exploring. She wanted to hear his perspective on everything—from books and movies to what they were learning in class to politics. And she wanted to share more and more of herself with him. It wasn't just easy to be with him; he felt safe.

With each day that passed, his religious beliefs mattered less and less. It rarely came up. His character remained consistent—kind, humble, wise. And gosh, he made her laugh so much.

She sighed as she walked back home from the nearby Tim Hortons. Eleora had to admit, at least to herself, that she was falling in love with Chadwick.

It wasn't just attraction—she'd sailed past a crush ages ago. He made her feel at home. She hadn't even realized how unsettled she'd felt in her own life until she met him. Now, she couldn't imagine her life without him in it.

The question wasn't about her feelings, but about her actions. What would she do? Risk telling him how she felt? Or convince herself to be satisfied with their friendship as it was?

Eleora pondered what she should do as she walked through the front door. Kicking off her shoes, she heard Michael Bolton's voice coming from the kitchen. Her mom must be home. She smiled and hummed along with the familiar song, walking toward the kitchen.

There she found her mom dancing around, singing along to When a Man Loves a Woman.

"Kumusta, Nanay. Is that Turon I'm smelling?"

"Oo. Come and help me. Do you want to fry or wrap?"

"I'll fry."

Eleora washed her hands and helped. She put some oil in a pot with sugar and waited until it was hot. Then she grabbed the wrapped food and placed them in the oil. She and her mom worked in a peaceful rhythm, a dance honed over years.

When the frying was done, they each grabbed a turon and toasted before eating. Eleora almost moaned in delight. Somehow, the brown sugar–coated plantain and jackfruit always hit the spot. She grabbed a plate and filled it with a handful—okay, maybe more than a handful.

"I'll be taking these to go. Heading upstairs to work on my uni applications."

Upstairs, she sat at her desk, MacBook open and ready. Too bad she wasn't. She didn't know where to begin the essays asking her to describe herself. Should she start with ethnicity? Hobbies? Achievements? They weren't asking for a resume—they wanted a window into her identity.

The problem was she didn't know who she was any more than the application committees. No wonder it was taking so long. At least with Daylight Saving Time, she'd have an extra hour to work.

Then it hit her—maybe she could crowdsource some help. Satisfied, she picked up her phone and opened Instagram. She posted a story asking people to describe her in one word. Now maybe she'd get somewhere.

It wasn't long before responses came in:

Beautiful.

Talented.

Popular.

Flattering, but superficial. Did she not have any depth? Did no one know her?

Her vibrating phone took her from these thoughts. Her heart fluttered when she saw the caller: Chadwick.

She took a deep breath to calm her nerves and answered. "Hello?"

"Hey."

His voice sounded different—deeper, richer. It made her toes curl. "My answer would be 'wondrous.'"

She blinked, still adjusting. "What?"

"The answer to your Insta question? My word is wondrous."

Oh. She'd forgotten the post once she saw his name. Wondrous. Such a beautiful word, poetic even. But what did he mean?

"Care to elaborate a bit on this word?"

"To do so, I'll have to reference my faith. You okay with that?"

She appreciated his asking permission, the respect in it. She nodded, realizing he couldn't see her. "Sure. I'm curious."

"Well, there's a verse in the Bible that says every human is wondrously made. Woven into the DNA of every person is dignity, beauty, and wonder—because each human shows us a new way to see God."

Gosh, that was beautiful—even if religious. "Wow. That sounds lovely, whether it's true or not. But you said it's true for every human. How does this apply to me?"

"That's a good question. Well, you point me to God just by being yourself. Your thoughtful nature reminds me that God's actions are carefully considered and planned. I've seen how you treat people—making everyone feel valued and important. That shows God's kindness and care. You're creative with your writing, which reflects God as Creator."She was speechless. Had she ever felt so known? So seen? Tears formed, and she sniffled, wiping them away.

"Ellie, are you crying? Are you okay?"

She searched for words. "Everything you said was..." She shook her head. "I appreciate it..." Gah, why was this so hard? Talking to him was usually easy! "I didn't expect your response. I'm surprised by its depth and specificity. Thank you. Your words mean so much. I wish I could record this to listen to when I'm down."

Ack! Why did she say that? She'd been doing so well but just revealed something she hadn't meant to.

"Well, you're welcome. I meant every word." His warmth calmed her racing thoughts. Time to change the subject.

"So, what were you up to today?"

"Well, you know, that dentist appointment." His voice sounded pained.

She giggled. "It's giving disdain."

He chuckled. "That obvious, huh? I hate going to the dentist."

"Sounds like you need to get this first-world problem off your chest. Tell me more."

"I appreciate your compassion."

She laughed at his sarcasm.

"Even though I've gone to the same dentist since I was a kid, I still hate having hands in my mouth. Then there's the fluoride treatment—the worst. Especially when the flavor is something you don't even like. Today, it was strawberry. I'm not a fan of berries, so having it stay in my mouth felt like an eternity. Ugh. I'm disgusted just thinking about it."

"Sounds like deep trauma. What's your earliest memory of berries?"

He laughed. "I see how it is. I choose to be vulnerable with you, and then I'm mocked!"

His dramatic tone made her laugh even harder. "Okay, okay. Sorry, fam."

"All good. I knew you were kidding. Tell me about your day. Why the Insta post?"

"I've been trying to write my uni application essays but got stuck. I didn't know how to describe myself, so I asked others for help."

"Interesting. Why is describing yourself so hard?"

Eleora thought. How honest should she be? "I guess when I think about myself, all I see are failures. I can't seem to find good things to say."

She held her breath, waiting.

"I think there are tons of good things about you. I'm sorry you can't see that yourself." His gentle voice brought fresh tears.

"I know everyone else sees someone successful and perfect, but all I see are ways I'm not. There's a voice in my head telling me I'm not good enough—that I don't deserve the admiration people give me. If they knew how hard I worked, how it doesn't come naturally, they'd see I'm a fraud. And they'd despise me."

She sobbed.

"Ellie, I wish I could be there now, but I'm here. You can let it all out, okay?"

After a few minutes, her tears slowed.

"Welp, that was embarrassing. Can you erase the last five minutes from your memory?"

"Not a chance. And I wouldn't want to. You don't have to be ashamed of your feelings or expressing them. I'm honored you let me be there for you. It's not a burden—it's a privilege. Okay?" His voice was gentle yet firm.

"Okay." She sniffled.

"Fam, sounds like you need a distraction. Am I right?"

"You're not wrong."

"Aight. What movie? My family has all the streaming services."

She didn't even hesitate. "Beauty and the Beast."

He laughed. "Wow, that took you forever to decide! Favorite Disney classic?"

"Bet. It's all about love being what's inside. And he gives her an entire library. I'll wait for someone to top that."

"Okay, Beauty and the Beast it is. Animated or live action?"

"This might be the most serious question you've ever asked me."

His chuckle was way too sexy for her comfort.

"Live action. It does their love story more justice. Watch party on Disney Plus?"

"Yep. I'll set it up and send you the link."

Soon they were watching together, chatting on the phone the whole time. It was restful—just what she needed after such an emotional night. Once the credits rolled, she sighed.

But they just kept talking.

Eleora was surprised to see it was already 2 a.m.

"Yikes, it's getting late."

"You're right. Didn't even realize. Time flies, eh? At least we have fall back tonight. That extra hour's gonna come clutch—I have to get up early for church."

"True. Guess we should say goodnight then?"

"Yeah. This was a good time. See you Monday?"

"Yep. Lockers at 8:10."

"Okay. Good night... erm, morning." She laughed.

"Good morning to you, too."

She hadn't expected that call, but was grateful. It gave her the clarity she needed. Now she knew she couldn't be satisfied with their friendship as it was.

Something needed to change.

Chapter 12

Once the call ended, Chadwick went to the washroom to brush his teeth for bed. He couldn't believe it was already so late, but that's what spending time with Eleora was like. He was so glad he'd called her.

With the dentist appointment and missing their regular Saturday study time, he'd been out of sorts all day. He was so close to distracting himself with porn when, instead, he checked out Eleora's Instagram. When he saw the question in her story, he wanted to know what made her post it. And he wanted to hear her voice, so he called her.

It was the best decision he'd made all day.

Her voice was softer on the phone, more vulnerable sounding. Her trust in him to share all that she did was astounding. There was so much he wanted to say and do—but that didn't fit into them just being friends.

He didn't want to be her friend anymore. He wanted to date her. He wanted to spend hours with her. He wanted to show his feelings. He wanted to flirt with her and compliment her. He wanted to hold her. He wanted a unique role and position in her life.

Why wasn't he taking this step again?

What, because they didn't share the same beliefs? Was it that big of a deal? Besides, any time he brought up something faith-related, she was less and less hostile. Sometimes, she even seemed quite open. She might become a believer soon, anyway! Why did he have to wait for that?

She made him a better person. His struggles with porn were non-existent now. When stressed, he had her ready to make him laugh or think. And he was rarely lonely because she was such a steadfast friend. Eleora's presence in his life made him feel worthy. He had no need for the distraction and outlet of porn—not when he had her.

She made his life brighter. Fuller. Like he was now living in IMAX. With more clarity and beauty than ever before.

He was going to do it. He was going to ask her to be his girlfriend.

With this decision made, he went to sleep in an Eleora-themed dream.

Chadwick got to school earlier than the time he was supposed to meet Eleora at their lockers. He had been wracking his brain about how to ask her to be his girlfriend. He wanted it to be special and meaningful to her. He walked into the office and was greeted by a big smile from Ms. Allen.

"What can I do for you, Chadwick?"

"I was wondering if you had any records or information on Eleora before high school? Perhaps middle school or even as far back as elementary?"

Her eyebrows furrowed. "I'm not allowed to give out that type of information, Chadwick. Those are for the school board and Eleora herself—or her parents." Her voice was sad, yet firm.

"Are you sure? I wanted to see if I could find some places she used to hang out at when she was a kid—as a surprise for her..." Chadwick tried to sound as sad as possible. "But it's alright, I guess. I'll just have to think of something else." He waved goodbye and walked away. On his third step, he heard Ms. Allen sigh and knew he had her.

"All right, I can give you the information. Just don't tell anyone about this or we'll both be in trouble."

"What information?"

"Okay, it says she went to middle school in British Columbia, so that won't be of use to us, but hmm, let me see... aha! She went to Florset Drive Public School from grades 1 to 5, and it says here that she loved going to the park and had mentioned a park close to her house."

"Do you have her old address or the name of the park, by any chance?"

She raised her index finger, motioning for him to wait, then continued to hit the keyboard at a rapid pace. She paused for a second, hit a few more keys, then leaned back in her chair, satisfied.

"Here it is: 3819 Victory Crescent, Malton, Ontario. The closest park is just down the street. Apparently, you can't miss it—it has two sets of monkey bars, three slides, six swings, two poles, monkey bars, and a clubhouse to the side, all on top of a big hill."

"Wow. That's amazing. Thank you very much for doing this for me. You didn't have to, and you could get in trouble for it. I appreciate your help."

"It was no problem, Chadwick. Besides, I had fun doing it. It was like I was a private investigator for a few minutes. Now, I'll just print all this information for you." Her tone switched to one of efficiency.

Surprised by the change, he glanced around the office and saw that Principal Edwards had entered.

"Here you go—the schedule for basketball practices that you misplaced." Her eyes told him to play along.

"Thanks, Ms. Allen. I'll try my best not to lose them again." He took the papers and walked out, giving a little wave to Principal Edwards.

Each step toward his locker was infused with pep. He could take her to a park that was meaningful for her! Now all he had to do was ask her.

He waited at their lockers after dropping off his bag and grabbing the books he needed. Chadwick smiled as he saw her coming and waved.

She smiled back. "Hey!"

"Hey. So, I was wondering how you'd feel about swapping out our study time on Saturday for an adventure?"

Her head was behind her locker door, so he couldn't see her face. The wait for her response seemed like ages. Maybe this was a mistake. He was about to backtrack when she closed her locker, revealing a smile.

"Sure! What sort of adventure are we talking about?"

He inwardly sighed in relief. "That's a surprise."

She groaned. "Come on, can I get a hint?"

"Not a chance. Now let's go. We have class to get to."

Chapter 13

Tomorrow was to be her adventure day with Chadwick. She couldn't put her finger on it, but it felt different from their study times or even when they went out to dinner and saw a movie.

It felt like a date.

At least, she hoped it was one.

She could ask him, but how embarrassing would it be if he said it wasn't?

All this time, she had been struggling with her feelings about his beliefs. Eleora hadn't considered that hers might be a barrier for him as well.

Or a deal-breaker.

He may not even like her that way.

Realizing that possibility brought tears to her eyes as she grieved what she hadn't even had—only what she'd imagined.

In moments like these, when her emotions were just too intense, she pivoted to poetry. The words flowed out of her thumb as it tapped the screen, moving so fast it was a blur.

I want you to find me
But I'm hiding behind this veneer of confidence

Inside conversations with other people
Underneath the intricate quilt of
insecurities and desire,

Are you even aware of this game of hide
and seek? That occurs every time we
speak
You gain ground in finding me
And I want you to
And that scares me

Not that I want to be found
Because that's a longing
That I've always carried around

No, what makes me shiver from fear
Wait excitement
Wait nervousness

Wait,
it's an earthquake at my very foundation
My emotions are uprooted and shaken
awakened

For so long, I laid myself out for the world
to see
I altered myself for the present audience
And I divided who I am into what I
perceived people wanted from me.

But now, I'm tired
Of never being seen
So I've locked up heart like a gated garden

And I've thrown away the key

And then you happened
I saw you approaching
And I admired the view
But I didn't think it was going to be you

Wait, how did you get that key?
The one I had thrown away,
I'll admit a bit recklessly
In shock, I watch you enter my garden

You carefully and systematically explored
it
Always respectful but reluctant to leave
I continued to be blown away
By a gift I hadn't known I needed to
receive
Consistency

You changed the narrative for me
You wooed my heart into trust
And taught my eyes to not fear lighting up
Because they wouldn't necessarily be
destined to fade

If my heart was a guarded garden
Here and there you've been planting seeds
And pulling out weeds
that I had never even noticed

But I've been taught
The risk of trust

So I wait
And as I do, You come closer and closer
To the center of my garden
The location of my soul

There is nowhere to hide
And I now want you to find me
See me
Know me

But I will stay where I am
Lest this is all a game
And all that I think is happening is imaginary
My biggest fear is not that you would find me,
But that I made up you trying to in the first place

With that last line typed out, Eleora felt a bittersweetness. She loved the artistry of her words even as they brought her sorrow.

She hated this uncertainty and wished she could just know where Chadwick stood, if her feelings were all one-sided. Eleora was so desperate that she almost did something she hadn't done in years.

She almost prayed.

Chapter 14

Chadwick rang the doorbell, and it opened to reveal Eleora. In bronze flats, dark skinny jeans, a green very detailed top, a thick cream cardigan, a gold necklace and matching studs with half her hair up, half down in curls, she looked beautiful.

He had to hold himself back from saying so, though he hoped to have that privilege soon if everything went well today.

"So, where are we going?" she asked.

"Aht. Aht. Nice try."

"Will you at least give me a hint?"

"Alright, we have to take a few buses to get there and that's part of the adventure."

She smiled, just as he'd hoped. "Sounds good."

"Are you sure you're alright with taking the bus?" he asked.

"Yes, I am. This is going to sound weird, but I find it fun. It makes me feel independent and gives me alone time and opportunities for people watching."

"Same!" Chadwick looked at the girl beside him and felt himself like her a little more. "In fact, I—oh! We're here," he interrupted himself as they reached a bus stop post. "And here comes the bus, right on time."

They got on and found two seats together near the back.

"So, what were you going to say before we reached the bus stop?"

"I was just going to say that I enjoy making up stories about random strangers whenever I'm bored on the bus," he answered.

"I do that too!" Eleora exclaimed, and a few people on the bus glanced at her. "I also tend to speak too loudly and draw unwanted attention."

Chadwick laughed. "Okay, well, pick someone and we'll see what we can make up."

"Okay, the lady over there in the floral hat is staring out the window, wistfully thinking of her lover from last spring."

Chadwick nodded. "He was betrothed to another, but that didn't stop her feelings for him. In fact, that hat was a gift from him as a memento to the times they spent together in a beautiful garden."

"Yes, that garden was how they met. She's a landscape designer and his fiancé hired her to make the gardens spectacular because that's where the wedding was being held."

Chadwick thought for a second and then carried on the tale. "She was standing there in the middle of the field that was their backyard at the beginning of April, imagining a trellis and stone cobble paths and a rainbow of flowers when he showed up. Her beauty spellbound him."

"And she was nervous about meeting her clients because this was her first big job. They were millionaires, and she'd expected the groom to be attired in an expensive suit. So when she saw a handsome man in regular jeans, a t-shirt and messy hair, she didn't know it was her client and started a flirtation."

"That ended as soon as the bride arrived in a fancy pantsuit and a kiss for the man. She was so embarrassed about the previous flirtation that she ignored the groom and worked on the design of the garden. But that evening when she returned..." Chadwick continued.

"...he was in the garden waiting for her, and before she could say a thing, he kissed her, and that's when she became his mistress. They got together whenever they had a spare moment and made love in that garden." Eleora shook her head. "Three months passed, and it was July, only a few weeks until the ceremony."

"They had discussed many times running away together, but they couldn't bear the thought of hurting his fiancée because—throughout planning the wedding—she had also become a friend of his bride-to-be. So they'd decided to leave each other, though it hurt them both to be giving up the best love they had ever known; they knew it was the right thing to do."

"Then the day before the wedding at the wedding rehearsal, she came to him in tears. She was pregnant with his baby. She was reaching 10 weeks and would soon show." Eleora continued.

"He didn't know how to react. They both had no clue what to do. Eventually, they decided to run away together the very next morning a few hours before the wedding, leaving a very detailed note behind. They were to meet at the train station."

"But he never showed." Eleora carried on. "She waited there for two hours, crying at the end of it when she realized he wasn't going to show up. All those plans and sweet promises whispered in her ears were false. She left that day and never tried to contact him again."

Chadwick gestured to her as she stepped off the bus onto the sidewalk. "And this is where we end the story of the woman in the floral hat."

They laughed and gave each other high-fives.

"Our stop is next." Chadwick pulled down the yellow cord. With a "Thank you," to the bus driver, they got off and crossed the street to get to the next bus stop.

They sat down in the bus shelter together and chatted about the times that they'd missed their stops on the bus. Laughing, they got on their second bus and Chadwick had them sit close by the front.

"Why not the back, Knight? It's the best place for people watching."

"I chose the front because we're getting off in a few stops."

"Ohhh." Eleora glanced out the window and recognized where they were. "Are we in Malton?"

"Darn." Chadwick joked in a southern tone. "You found it out."

Chapter 15

Eleora giggled even as apprehension grew within her.

"Well, now we have to get off, and you can see what the rest of the surprise is." He offered her his arm and pretended to tip his hat like a cowboy.

She took it as they got off the bus. Eleora remembered the hill in front of her and the older houses surrounding it. Certain she wasn't right and yet hoping in her heart that she was, she ran up the hill as fast as she could, almost taking off her flats, and then she saw it. Her park.

The classic 6-piece swing set, the monkey bars, the jungle gym with the two slides and two poles, and the old clubhouse. Eleora slipped off her flats and let her feet sink into the sand. She closed her eyes as memory after memory came to her. Sliding down the poles, swaying on the swings, making shapes in the sand... her eyes opened and tears formed.

Eleora arrived at the clubhouse seconds later, not even realizing that she'd been running there. She climbed up the familiar steps and sat down, trying to stop the onslaught of tears. This was where she and her father had spent the most time together.

She heard creaks and glanced up, almost expecting to see her dad, so she was relieved to see Chadwick.

"How..." she paused and tried again. "How did you find out about this place?"

He sat down beside her. "I have my ways. I just wanted to choose someplace special that would be meaningful to you."

"It's meaningful alright, just probably not the meaning you want."

His face looked concerned. "Want to share?"

Eleora was about to shake her head no and shake it all off when she looked into his eyes. They were so filled with concern, and caring, and a need to protect her that she just broke down and decided that she'd tell him all. She'd tell him what she'd told no one else before.

"My parents, my bio parents, were atheists. They'd met at a debate between an atheist and Christian. They both came from religious homes and cultures and had chosen the rational way. This bonded them. Eventually, they fell in love, got married and had me. My grandmother was the only Christian I knew and I remember overhearing her say to my dad that one day, she would not be here—alive—anymore and she didn't want to worry about whether her son would go to hell or heaven. The next week, she was diagnosed with cancer.

"My dad freaked out and went through a mid-life crisis. He was pacing all the time and visiting her and then; he went to church one Sunday. He came back calm and refreshed and just at peace with himself. My mom thought it was just a coping mechanism and let it slide, but I—" Eleora's voice cracked, and she took a deep breath before continuing. "—I was curious. I wanted to know what had changed him.

"So, the next Sunday I went with him to church and I was changed. I just knew that all the years my mom and dad spent telling me there was no god was a total lie. And I could tell that my dad felt this way, too. I knew it wasn't just a phase for him. I knew it would stick. We joined a prayer group at the church, and five months later, the doctors declared Nana cancer-free. They were shocked and claimed that they'd never seen that happen before. My dad and I, we knew it was God. And it just made us have faith in Him even more.

"Over the next four years, we attended church faithfully. I was a part of the Children's ministry and my dad felt the call on him to be a youth pastor and went to seminary at Tyndale. We grew closer; my grandma, dad, and I. And it was at this park that my dad and I spent the most time together. It was always so awkward talking about God in front of my mom, so we walked down the street to this park and sat down in this clubhouse, looking more into the Bible.

"I can't say that everything was perfect though; I wasn't stupid. I knew that my mom and dad were drawing more and more apart. She refused to attend our church even once and was going out more, hanging out with girlfriends, talking on the phone a lot. I didn't know what it meant until one day when I came home from school and saw suitcases at the front door.

"My mom had been offered a new job across the country; Vancouver, British Columbia, and already had an apartment there too. She'd also drawn up a divorce petition. She'd done all the paperwork. All she needed was my dad's signature and an agreement on custody, and it would be all done. There was a flight scheduled that afternoon for us. The school already knew and my dad did too. It struck me as strange that he hadn't left a note saying goodbye, but I figured he would talk to me later." Eleora closed her eyes and breathed in and out for a few seconds, as if trying to stop tears from falling. After another deep breath, she continued.

"So, we hopped on a plane to Vancouver and got to our new apartment. Nanay told me that Daddy knew where we were, our numbers, address and that we'd figure out custody soon. I expected a phone call that night but... didn't get one. The next day, same thing. She assured me that he would call, that maybe he was just working the custody out so he could tell me when he'd see me next. And then I got an email from him. I read it repeatedly until I had it memorized. And then I showed it to my mom. That email broke my heart." Until that moment, she hadn't cried, but it was as if she couldn't hold them in anymore and they fell.

"It said: Eleora. Don't bother trying to arrange a time to stay with me. Just stay with your mother, I don't need you—" she shook, and Chadwick put an arm around her. "—nor want you here with me. I'll be happy with the two of you gone." It was hard for her to breathe now, but she pushed the words out. She'd held them in for too long. She had to let them go. "Don't contact me or try to find me. I have no desire to see or hear from you again. Gabe James." She finished and wasn't able to speak anymore, just opting to lean into him.

Chadwick held her and just let her cry. When she shook, he held her tighter. When she sobbed, he rubbed her back. She buried her head into his shoulder.

"I trusted him, Chadwick! He understood me, he helped me grow, he was my spiritual mentor, and he left me. First, I was kind of in denial. I checked the email address. I tried to make up a bunch of excuses for him. And then a week later, a week filled with so many tears, my dad called. I picked up the phone, heard my dad's voice, and for one second, I believed everything was as it used to be. And then the email came to mind, and I gave the phone to my mom.

"She then asked me two questions: Do I have an interest in staying with my father again? My answer was no. Do you want to talk to him again, in email, letters, or on the phone? My answer was again no. I said it on speaker so that he would hear. And that's the last I heard from him. It was my mom and me after that. I attended middle school in Vancouver and then my mom met Larry Jacobson, which is why we moved back to Ontario. I started high school here, and I even came back to this park, but..." she breathed in and out, and Chadwick noticed the tears were slowing.

"But I couldn't bear it. All the memories here just made the betrayal seem even worse. I'd been planning on visiting our old house to see if my—" her voice broke again "—if my dad was there. I mean, I know what I said that day and I also know how angry I was and how I wasn't thinking clearly, and how much I've been missing him for those years. He was the only one who got me. And the same with my grandma, who lived just across the street. But as I stood there, the email just came back, and I knew it was all a mistake for me to even come back to my old neighbourhood. So I left and haven't been back since.

"And my relationship with God? That just went

away. It was so linked to my dad that praying and reading my Bible all reminded me of him. If someone could act the way my dad had and claim to have faith in God, then what kind of God was that? What kind of religion says that's okay? I doubted whether this religion was good or real. And besides that, all my mother had ever done for me was stand by me and comfort me when my dad left. How could I disrespect her by continuing to engage in Christianity? I couldn't. So I stopped everything and became an atheist."

"Wow. That's a lot, Ellie. I don't even know where to begin."

Now a bit calmer, she moved away from him. While she'd enjoyed his embrace, she didn't want to presume that it was anything more than him just being a good friend. She wiped the remaining tears from her face. "Thank you for listening to my story. You're the only one I've ever told."

Chapter 16

Chadwick stared at Eleora with a combination of shock and compassion. All along, the real reason she didn't believe in God, the reason she couldn't stand Christians, was because someone who was closest to her betrayed her. It made so much sense now.

"No, Eleora, thank you. For telling me all of this when you didn't have to. After all you've been through, I—" he shook his head in wonderment, "—I can't believe you're even friends with me."

"Well, you showed yourself to be trustworthy." She gave him a big smile, and they enjoyed a moment of silence.

"This was not what I was expecting would happen today."

She gave him a quizzical look. "What were you hoping would happen?"

Chadwick thought for a moment. Did he want to share his feelings for her now? After everything? He was about to sidestep the question, but she looked so expectant. He adjusted himself to face her and took a deep breath. "Eleora, I planned this adventure today to create the right setting for telling you how much I care about you. I'm falling in love with you, Ellie, and I can't continue with just being friends with you. I want to be more. Would you consider becoming my girlfriend?"

There, it was all out now. He tried to gauge her feelings based on her facial expression, but it was no use. She was unreadable. As the seconds went by, he resisted the urge to fidget or backtrack. He'd said a lot, and she deserved the time to process.

"I feel the same way about you." Her voice brokered no room for doubt, which gave him confidence to touch her.

Slowly, so that she would have time to pull back, he put one hand at the small of her back and the other behind her head. His fingers ran through her curls and she leaned into his touch. Then he pulled her head closer to his until their foreheads and noses were touching. They breathed in tandem, and then he leaned forward and kissed her. Her arms went to his shoulders and her hands clasped behind his neck as she moved herself closer to him and deeper into the kiss.

He was lost in how amazing it was to kiss her and be so connected to her. It wasn't until he felt a familiar sensation in his pants that warning bells went off in his head and, reluctantly, he broke the kiss.

The raw desire on Eleora's face coupled with the question in her eyes almost tipped over the edge into another kiss.

Almost.

"I need us to take it slow."

She nodded, her eyes compassionate, and gave him a swift kiss on the cheek.

"Okay. Now I have a replacement memory for this clubhouse."

THE ALMOST PERFECT MATCH

"Want to make some more memories all over this park?"

"I'd love to."

They shared a sly smile as they exited the clubhouse, and then both yelled at the same time.

"I CALL MONKEY BARS!"

They raced for the monkey bars and got there at the same time. Eleora jumped, grabbed onto the bars, and pulled herself through them.

"What are you doing?" Chadwick asked.

A few seconds later, she was sitting on top of the monkey bars. "That's what I was doing."

"You know that the purpose of the monkey bars is that you move your arms across the bars until you get to the other side, right?"

"It's giving lack of imagination." She giggled. "What I used to do when I was younger was sit on top of these and then do flips off of them." She stood up on the monkey bars and jumped off, doing a somersault in the air, and landed perfectly in the sand. "That is much more fun."

"You're crazy."

"And you're just realizing this?" She ran to the jungle gym next and climbed up the rock-climbing wall in seconds.

"Are you going to flip off of that too?"

"No, I'm waiting for your slow poke self to get over here!"

He laughed and made his way over toward her.

"Let's see who can get down these poles the fastest." He suggested.

"You're on."

From then on, there was only laughter, races, and

just plain fun. They went down the slide together, swung on the swings for a while, and then finally were tired out and just layon the grass side by side.

"Did we make enough memories?" Chadwick asked, turning to face her propped up on one elbow. She followed suit.

"We just need one more." she winked.

They leaned closer to each other for a kiss and then Chadwick's stomach rumbled.

Eleora laughed and fell back on the grass. He stood up and offered Eleora his hand. "Let's go get something to eat."

She took his hand and got up with his help. Then he continued to hold her hand as they walked to the bus stop. A bus ride and a meal of Manchu Wok later, Chadwick and Eleora were sitting down in the Woodbine Mall food court, people watching.

"Is there anything you'd like to do here before we begin the trek back home?" He asked.

Eleora glanced around and then spotted a photo booth. She smiled and gestured towards it. "I've always wanted to do one of these things. I'd just never gotten the chance."

"Let's do it!" Chadwick held the curtain for her as she went in. Then he put in the required change and stepped in with her. "Okay, we only have a few seconds to decide. What type of pictures do you want to take?"

"One smiling, one hopefully laughing, one stupid, and then one..." she winked.

He laughed. "Okay, Ms. Photographer, let's go in that order."

He slipped his arm around her waist, and she leaned into him. They faced the camera and smiled.

They saw the flash and then Chadwick tickled Eleora's waist. She immediately started laughing and retaliated by tickling the side of his neck. He squirmed, laughed, and they saw the flash. Then Eleora grabbed her ears and held her breath, puffing out her cheeks, nudging Chadwick to do the same, and he obliged. Then Chadwick leaned down and kissed Eleora.

They pulled back at the same time and then exited the photo booth together, holding hands, to see the pictures. They'd come out perfectly. Eleora smiled gleefully, and Chadwick basked in her happiness.

They walked outside to the bus terminal, and Eleora sniffed the air. "It smells like it's going to rain."

"It's completely sunny out! It won't rain."

Two minutes later, torrents of rain fell down and instead of freaking out, like Chadwick expected, Eleora laughed.

"At least we know you have no career in meteorology."

There was no point in going into the bus shelter when they were already soaked by the downpour. From the darkening sky, they could see it wasn't going to end anytime soon.

"Okay, we need to get dried off. Whose house is closer?" Eleora asked.

"Yours is 3 buses away because you live on the far side of Brampton. Mine is two because I live kind of on the border between the two. We can go to my house, dry off, and I'll see if I can take the car to drive you home."

"Perfect. And the bus just came. Come on, let's go." She took his hand, almost pulling him towards the bus, having to hold on tight because his hand was wet and slippery because of the rain.

He pretended he didn't want to go. "No! You can't make me leave!"

"You would rather be at the bus stop than with me?"

"Actually, let's get on the bus." He gave her a quick kiss on the cheek.

She giggled and took his hand again, and they walked hand in hand on the bus, getting out of the rain.

Chapter 17

Eleora and Chadwick were thoroughly soaked. After getting off their first bus, they had to wait 10 minutes for their second one—and that bus stop had no shelter. Being on the second bus prevented them from becoming more drenched but did nothing to dry them off.

With the bus so full, Eleora and Chadwick were standing together. She leaned backwards against him, with his chin resting on her head and her hands holding his over her stomach.

Eleora felt Chadwick stiffen for the seventh time since they arrived on the bus and giggled. Some guy must be ogling her again. "What guy are you giving a dirty look now?"

"Some random guy at the back."

"You know that staring them down helps nothing, right?"

"I just hate when guys look at you like that. You're not an object."

"That's sweet, but I think you should stop focusing on them and pay attention to the bus stops."

"Oh, right." He listened to the lady over the intercom and then bent his head down so that he was whispering in Eleora's ear. "We're getting off now." He pulled the yellow cord behind him and soon they were off the bus. "My house is seven away."

Usually, that wouldn't be a long distance, but because these houses were large and detached, it was actually nearer to the end of the street.

"I'm so excited that I'll be able to see it!"

"It's not really anything special." He replied with a shrug.

Eleora nodded and then grinned. "Want to race there?"

"Are you crazy? It's pouring right now, and you could slip and hurt yourself!"

"That's a lot of words just to say that you're afraid to lose."

He looked at her hard for a moment and then nodded. "I'm house 57. Go!"

"Cheater!" she called as she ran as well. She was used to running in the rain; when she was on the track team, they had to run rain or shine. 51, 52, 53, she counted to herself as she passed them. She had her head turned to the houses, so she didn't see that she'd passed Chadwick on house 56 and then ran to the garage of house 57. As soon as she touched it, she turned to see Chadwick right behind her.

"What's that saying? Cheaters never prosper?"

He laughed at her teasing. "Something like that."

As he walked toward her, she took him in, and a thrill of awe went through her body. This gorgeous and gentle guy was her boyfriend.

He took his keys out of his pocket and opened one of the double doors. Chadwick let Eleora enter first. She took in the kitchen that was to the left, the spiral staircase on the right, and a dining/living room area that was in front of her. She noticed the walls were a golden yellow and that the many pieces of furniture were in shades of brown. Pastel pictures were hung on the walls and attractive vases were on the side tables. It was cozy, yet sophisticated. And neat. She liked Chadwick's house instantly.

"Honey? Is that you?" Eleora heard a woman's voice.

"Yes, mom!" Chadwick answered.

They heard footsteps and saw a shadow coming towards them on the wall.

"Oh, good, because I need your help with dinner."

Even without Chadwick saying so, she would've known that she was his mom. Eleora could see that Chadwick had her ears and smile. They also shared the same russet brown complexion. She had light brown eyes and dark brown hair that was straight and fell to her chin. She was around Eleora's height and was in good shape. Eleora blushed when she realized that she'd been scoping her out and then realized that his mom was doing the same thing. And remembering her wet appearance, she grew even more self-conscious and blushed more.

Chadwick cleared his throat. "Mom, this is Eleora. Eleora, this is my mom."

Eleora took a deep breath, smiled, and then extended her hand. "I'm happy to meet you, Mrs. Knight." She was relieved to receive a warm smile back.

"Likewise, Eleora. And you may call me Nina."

"Okay, Mrs. Nina."

She turned to Chadwick. "I like her. So, I'm

guessing you two were caught in the rain?" she asked.

"Yep, we came here to pick up a few towels and then I was going to bring Eleora to her house." Chadwick answered.

"No, no, no! That will not do!" Mrs. Nina said with dramatic flair, and Eleora laughed, earning another smile. "I just did some laundry. Eleora can borrow some fresh track pants and maybe one of your sweaters... if that's okay with you, dear?"

"C'est parfait!"

"Oh! Tu parles le français aussi!"

"Only a little. I was in French immersion when I was younger but was pulled out in grade five, so I've lost my roots."

"To be honest, I don't really know much French either; I just like to add in a couple words here and there to make it look like I do." They laughed together and then turned to Chadwick. "Hello? Are you going to show Eleora upstairs?"

"Oh, sorry! Sure thing, I just zoned out for a second there."

"Alright, dear, I'll see you when you come back down."

The walls around the staircase were white; but anything but plain because they held up a few baby pictures of Chadwick, the wedding picture of his parents, and the Lord's prayer. Upstairs, the walls were now a light forest green and there was dark brown furniture in a sitting room to the left of the staircase. The walls held a few pictures of golden sunrises and sunsets, and Eleora counted three doors.

"Wait right here," Chadwick told her and motioned towards the sitting room. But Eleora leaned on the railing, knowing that she was wet and did not want to ruin their leather. She saw him go into the room to the far right of the staircase and come out with a blue hoodie and then passed her to go into the room past the sitting room and emerged with dark gray track pants.

"Okay, so here's a pair of my mom's track pants and one of my light hoodies. The room that I just came out of is my parents' master bedroom and the room right there," he pointed to the room on the left, "is my bedroom. The one right in front of you is the guestroom and has its own adjoining bathroom so you can use those towels and change there."

She nodded and giggled.

"What's up?"

"Now, you're the tour guide."

He laughed, visibly relaxing.

"Look, why were you stressed?" she asked.

"What are you talking about?"

"Chadwick."

"I'm just nervous about you meeting my parents because you're, well, they'd want you to be a ..."

"... Christian." She finished for him, and he nodded. "I'm curious. Is there some kind of rule that you're not allowed to date people who believe differently than you?"

He shook his head. "No, but I know that would be their preference."

She released the tension that had been building in her after asking the question. She'd hate to not be with him, but she wouldn't want him to go against his faith, either. It was such a big part of who he was.

"Cool. Well, if I have to act like you're only my friend, then that's what I will do."

He gave her a warm smile and kissed her on the nose. Eleora sighed and gave him a small wave as she walked into the guest room. It reminded her of her room at home because the walls were a beautiful light blue.

She opened a door inside to find the bathroom, grabbed a towel, and dried herself off. She was pleased to see that the black camisole she'd been wearing underneath her green shirt was still dry and just threw Chadwick's hoodie on over it, zipping it up halfway. It smelled like him. She slipped out of her jeans, dried her legs, and pulled on the track pants that warmed her instantly. She glanced at her reflection in the mirror and pulled her hair into a high ponytail with a scrunchie that she'd kept on her wrist.

Eleora took another look at the mirror and was content with the way she looked. She folded the towel and placed it on a dresser in the room and then laid her clothes along the bathtub so that they could dry out. She turned off all the lights, left the guest room, and headed downstairs.

"So, what's for dinner?" she heard Chadwick ask as she got off the stairs.

"Well, your dad is loafing around the kitchen while I'm making some curry goat," his mom answered.

"Did I just hear curry goat?" Eleora asked, entering the kitchen.

The man beside Mrs. Nina laughed. It was obvious that he was Chadwick's father. He was past six feet and shared a lighter complexion, like her own. He had light green eyes and short, curly hair.

She gave him a warm smile and extended her hand. "Hi, Mr. Knight, it's nice to meet you. I'm Eleora."

He met her hand with a firm handshake. "Nice to meet you, too. You were interested in the curry goat?"

"Don't listen to this loser; I'm the one making the food," Mrs. Nina teased.

Eleora laughed and turned to Chadwick. "I hope you know how lucky you are! I haven't had curry goat since I was around 11," she joked, but he grasped the hidden meaning.

"Well, no one should go that long without this soul food. You should stay for dinner!" Mr. Knight said.

Eleora smiled. "I would hate to impose on your family dinner, Mr. Knight, but thanks for the of—"

"Nonsense!" he interrupted her. "It gets lonely with just the three of us sometimes. Join us!"

"Okay, okay, I'll stay. But at least let me help with making it."

"Now, see. No one else around here ever offers to help me with dinner! But, Eleora, you're a guest; you should relax."

"I want to help because, well, my grandma was teaching me how to make curry goat and I haven't seen her for a few years, so my lessons just... ended. I only got up to seasoning the meat and learned nothing about cooking it!"

"Well, allow me to take over where she left off."

Eleora smiled and pushed up the sleeves of Chadwick's sweatshirt. "What's the first thing that you want me to do?"

And so, under the direction of Mrs. Nina, Eleora chopped up some garlic and three different peppers while Mrs. Nina cleaned the meat. Then they added all the seasonings to the meat, talking and laughing the whole time.

"Now, there are two main ways that goat is cooked. There's on the stove boiling out or cooking in the oven. Now I prefer on the stove, so here's what we're going to do." She explained every step in the process as they went along, and Eleora tried to commit everything to memory.

"Now that the meat is on, we have about an hour and a half before it's going to be ready; and that's the bare minimum. So right now, we have time to kill."

Chadwick—who'd been watching football with his dad the whole time—suggested a movie.

"That is a brilliant idea, Chad. And we get to choose the movie because we've done all the cooking! So, what shall it be? A wonderful romantic comedy?" she asked, and the guys groaned. "How about a Disney Classic?"

"That's a good idea. What movies do you have?" Eleora asked her, walking over to the cupboard that she was standing in front of.

"I think the question is: what movies do we not have?" Mrs. Nina opened the cupboard to reveal at least five shelves full of Disney movies. "These DVDs don't really work anymore and we have Disney Plus to stream all of them, but I enjoy seeing the full collection."

"This is incredible!"

"I'm a Disney fanatic, one could say, so what shall we choose?"

"Well, there's so much! You have Mulan; total girl power in a musical!" Eleora scanned the shelves. "You have Little Mermaid 1 and 2 and oh my gosh! You have Cinderella 3! I've never seen that one before!"

"Well, I haven't watched that one since last year,

so we'll put it in."

"Okay, Chadwick, can you queue it up for us? And honey?" Mrs. Nina turned to Mr. Knight. "Please grab us a few blankets and pillows."

Eleora held back her laughter, and they exchanged mischievous grins as Mr. Knight went upstairs to get the requested items.

"And that is why you always cook, Eleora," Mrs. Nina told her with a wink, and then Eleora couldn't hold it back any longer and laughed.

Mr. Knight came down a minute later with the requested items and they pressed play on the movie. Eleora and Mrs. Nina lay on the ground together while watching the movie—almost like a sleepover. But they didn't just watch the movie; they paused it at different parts to discuss what was going on and if those discussions lasted for over five minutes, Chadwick or Mr. Knight would threaten to switch to sports and they would press play again. They also checked on the curry goat and the rice that was put on earlier. Eleora was having so much fun.

By the time the movie finished, the food was ready. Mrs. Nina had Chadwick set the table and then all four of them sat down.

Chadwick, Mrs. Nina, and Mr. Knight joined hands and then the realization dawned on her. They were about to pray. Seeing the worried look in Chadwick's eyes, Eleora smiled and grabbed his hand and his mother's. She gave his hand an extra squeeze to let him know she was fine with it all.

"Please, continue. I don't want to interfere with what you guys do." Eleora realized that she was being honest. She wanted to see how they did this. She received warm smiles from Chadwick's parents and her hand being squeezed by Chadwick himself.

They all closed their eyes, so Eleora followed suit and then Mr. Knight started, "Lord, we thank you for the food you have had prepared for us by my beautiful wife and by our beautiful guest, Eleora. Please let it do what it needs to in our bodies so that we may glorify you. Amen."

Eleora opened her eyes to see Chadwick and his mother mouthing amen as well and felt a little tug at her heart. The closeness that they had wasn't just because of them; a God held them together. Eleora remembered what that used to feel like with her dad.

The food was delicious, and the table was silent as they enjoyed the meal.

When they were done, Mrs. Nina broke the silence. "Alright, now, Chadwick and Aaric, please clean up the kitchen while Eleora and I relax and watch TV."

"No, it's okay. I'll help." Eleora rarely minded doing the dishes and she wanted a chance to talk to Mr. Knight more, since she'd spent most of her time with Mrs. Nina.

"Aww, you can't do that now, Eleora! You'll make me look lazy!"

"According to something I saw on the internet, it's not laziness. It's resting up before you get tired."

Mrs. Nina laughed. "Well, then. Now I won't feel bad."

Eleora giggled and offered to dry all the dishes that Mr. Knight rinsed while Chadwick cleared the table and swept the kitchen.

It was quiet for a while and then, as he was washing a dish, Mr. Knight sang in a beautiful deep voice: "Hey diddle, diddle, the cat and the fiddle, the cow jumped over the moon. The little dog laughed to see such a sport, and the dish ran away with the spoon; ran away with the spoon." Eleora laughed at the song and was impressed by his voice.

"Did you just make that up?" Eleora asked him, laughter still in her voice.

"Nope, it's a song that was taught to us in Jamaica, in what you would call Kindergarten." He replied, smiling.

"Can you repeat it?"

He nodded and sang it once more.

She took in every word and noted the notes he was singing. Then she opened her mouth to sing the ditty. Her voice rang out as she dried the dish handed to her and when she finished, Mr. Knight was staring at her, surprised.

"You sing?"

"Well, I'm in choir at school and my mom had me take lessons when I was younger."

Mr. Knight dried his hands and then gave Eleora a hug. Awkwardly, she hugged him back.

"Sorry, it's just that my wonderful wife here is utterly tone deaf. We have her sing to Chadwick when he's being punished."

"Hey!"

Mr. Knight laughed. "Honey, you know it's true." He replied.

"And you know that you're sleeping on the couch, right?"

"I love you too!"

Mrs. Nina stuck out her tongue at him and he laughed.

"So anyway, Chadwick inherited his singing voice from his mom. He can carry a tune but not much else." Mr. Knight continued.

"And I thought he was joking when he said that he couldn't sing."

"No, he was being quite honest. But now, there's someone who can sing with me! Chadwick, invite Eleora over another time!"

"I will, Dad, if not for you, then for Mom." Chadwick joked.

"Good, give me some notice so that I can plan to make oxtail with her."

Eleora glanced at the clock on the stove to see that it was almost 6:00! As if reading her mind, Chadwick said, "I should get Eleora back home."

"Eleora, I'm sorry, but your clothes are still quite damp. I'll run them in with our laundry and then Chadwick can give them back to you at school." Mrs. Nina told her, walking with them to the front door.

"Alrighty, that's fine."

"Okay, sweetheart, it was great meeting you. Come back anytime, alright?" Mrs. Nina hugged Eleora, who smiled at the term of endearment she was just called.

"I will, trust me. We have more Disney to watch, oui?"

Mrs. Nina nodded and waved as Chadwick and Eleora walked through the front door into the outside.

Chapter 18

They walked down the pathway side by side, and Chadwick opened the car door for Eleora, making her smile. Once inside, he turned on the car and blasted the heat. Then he drove down the street, turned the corner, and parked.

"I absolutely can't believe how amazing you were today with my parents," he started. "Usually, with my friends, they put on their fake perky selves. But with you, they were completely real, and you gelled with them so perfectly. They even let you stay for dinner—which is unheard of since dinner is considered this special thing for family. I knew they would take a liking to you, but I didn't know they'd love you this much!" He finally looked at her.

"I was just being myself, Knight, honestly. I didn't even know we'd get along so well. They feel like family. You're so lucky." Her eyes shone with earnestness, making her even more beautiful than she already was.

He kissed her forehead and nose, then came to her lips and whispered, "I am lucky because I have you," before brushing his lips softly against hers.

He wanted to linger. Delve deeper. Explore. But

something in him—rather Someone—bid him to have restraint.

He pulled away, put the car in drive, and they didn't speak the whole way to Eleora's house. The air was thick with intimacy-fueled tension, broken only by Chadwick's occasional kiss on her hand.

He pulled into her driveway, exited the car, and opened her door. Taking her hand, he helped her out and closed the door behind him. They walked up to her front door, holding hands. Eleora only dropped his to reach into her back pocket for her keys.

"Oh, crap."

"What's wrong?" he asked.

"My house keys are in the back pocket of my jeans," she told him. She saw the realization dawn on his face.

"Oh, crap."

"That's what I said," she joked, and he laughed, making her laugh too.

"Well, let's just hope the car is in the garage and my mom's home. If she is, there's something you should do when you greet her."

"Alright, what is it?"

"In Filipino culture, when we see an elder, we do something called mano po. You hold the elder's right hand and touch your forehead to the back of that hand. To initiate it, you say mano po, and then they'll give you their hand. It's a way to show respect. I know you probably think it's weird..." As she explained, she looked everywhere but at him, her hands fidgeting.

"Hey, Ellie." His voice was gentle as he used his right hand to lightly turn her head toward him.

Finally, he could see her eyes—they showed how

nervous she was. "I'm happy to learn about your culture and engage in its practices, okay? Your culture isn't weird; it's unique. That's something to be proud of."

At his words, she began to tear up. Seeing that, he opened his arms to her. She immediately stepped into them, resting her head on his chest just above his heartbeat. His arms wrapped around her, and they stayed like that for a few moments.

Once she felt better, she slowly pulled away. "Thanks for that."

"You're welcome. Although it isn't really selfless—holding you is becoming one of my favorite things." She giggled at the twinkle in his eyes.

"All right, here goes nothing."

Eleora rang the doorbell.

"Oh, honey, it's you!" Adalina said with a smile, then looked confused. "Where's your key?" she asked.

"It's a long story. I'll explain inside," Eleora answered. "Is Larry home?" she asked.

"No, he's working late today," she replied.

Eleora thought for a moment and shook her head—then remembered Chadwick was still there.

"Oh, who's this young man?" Eleora heard her mom say and couldn't stop the cringe.

"He's—"

"—Chadwick Knight. Pleased to meet you, Mrs. Edwards. Mano po?" Her mom gave him a big smile and held out her right hand. He bowed slightly, touching it to his forehead.

"Well, come on in, Chadwick." Her invitation was full of warmth.

He and Eleora went inside and took off their shoes. Mrs. Edwards led him to the living room, sitting down on the loveseat and patting the spot beside her. Chadwick obliged.

"So, Chadwick, how do you and Eleora know each other?"

"From school. I was the new kid, and as president, she showed me around and we became friends," he answered easily, noticing Eleora had her mother's smile and eyes—or at least their shape.

"Oh, what's your specialization?" she asked.

"I'm there for Drama and Piano—composition." She nodded approvingly.

Just then, Eleora entered with a bowl of plantain chips and a glass of Pepsi, her hair out of its ponytail. She settled into the armchair beside the couch.

"So, how much have you interrogated him yet?" she teased, making her mom laugh.

"I've barely asked him anything!" her mom insisted.

"Right, nanay. Sure. I totally believe you," Eleora said sarcastically, making her mom laugh even more. Eleora smiled happily and ate a chip.

"Well, I was just done anyway. I was only going to ask what happened today and why you don't have your key," her mom said pointedly.

Chadwick looked at Eleora, Eleora looked at Chadwick. After a few seconds, Eleora started.

"Chadwick invited me out today to go to a park and relax for a while," she started.

"And then to Woodbine Mall to get some lunch," Chadwick continued.

"But we were bussing it, and when it started to rain…"

"…we were caught in the downpour," he finished.

"So we went over to Chadwick's house because his was closest, and were only going to get towels," Eleora continued.

"But Eleora ended up staying for the making, eating, and cleaning up of dinner."

"And since I was soaked, I changed into Chadwick's mom's sweatpants and his hoodie."

"When we were ready to leave, her clothes were still damp, so it was decided I would bring her clothes to school once they were washed and dried," Chadwick added.

"And when I was on the porch, I realized my keys were in the pocket of my jeans at Chadwick's house."

"And here we are now," Chadwick finished.

Mrs. Edwards nodded a few times. "Alright, that makes sense. No harm done, then. Did you guys at least have fun today?" she asked.

Chadwick couldn't stop smiling. When he stole a glance at Eleora, he saw she was fighting a grin too.

"Yes, Mom, we had fun," she replied casually.

"Actually, more than that, Mrs. Edwards. I care about your daughter a lot and asked her to be my girlfriend today. She did me the honor of saying yes."

Eleora started to choke on the chip she'd just been eating while her mom's eyes widened in surprise. He went over to Eleora, gave her her glass of Pepsi to help wash it down, then patted her back lightly as she coughed. Once satisfied she was okay, he returned to his seat beside her mom.

She had watched the whole thing silently.

Eventually, she spoke. "I appreciate you being so forthcoming, Chadwick, even though you caught me off guard. With what you just shared, I'd love to get to know you more and ask some questions before you leave, if you have the time."

He nodded. "Of course, ask me anything."

"Well, iha [daughter], maybe you should get our guest something to drink. Maybe calamansi?" Her mom checked with Chadwick, who nodded, and Eleora obeyed.

"So…"

She started, and he sat up straighter. "I must confess I've never done this before. I guess, what do you like about my daughter?"

This question was easy to answer. "She's kind and funny and so bright. Her creativity humbles me. And, well, she's also stunning. It's been great being her friend, but my feelings have gone beyond friendship."

Eleora came in on the tail end of his answer and smiled at his words. She handed him and her mother each a glass of Filipino lemon-limeade. Her mom smiled, and he relaxed slightly.

"What are your hopes and ambitions for your life?"

"My goal is to work in neurology as a doctor. I want to help those with neurodegenerative diseases like Multiple Sclerosis or Alzheimer's." She looked impressed. "I'm applying for degrees in life sciences or biology for university next year. Although Eleora is definitely ahead of me on that. I haven't started mine yet." He gestured to Eleora, who promptly blushed at the praise.

"She does like to do things in advance, eh?" They laughed together. "What do you like to do for fun?"

"Besides spending time with your daughter?" he joked, earning a chuckle. "I enjoy composing songs on the piano, playing basketball, and watching movies."

"Those sound like healthy pastimes. What movie could you watch over and over again without getting tired of it?"

"I love that question. It would have to be Black Panther for me. Although, since Chadwick's passing, it carries a grief when I do."

She nodded. "He was very talented. May he rest in peace." She let a moment pass before speaking again. "Would you rather clean or cook?"

"Clean. I can follow a recipe, but I'd rather bring order to messiness."

"Well, you'll be happy to know Eleora can cook, so you won't starve," she said jokingly. He laughed, but Eleora looked mortified at the implications.

"Nanay!"

"Relax, iha. Chadwick knows it was just a joke."

"I've noticed you've used the word iha a few times. Is this a special nickname?" he asked.

"It simply means daughter," her mom explained. "Do you speak any languages besides English?"

"Not really. I can perfectly understand Jamaican Patois, but I don't have the right accent for speaking it."

"That makes sense. There's no shame in that. Accents are harder to acquire when you aren't born in the appropriate country," she said understandingly.

"Thank you for encouraging me to be more compassionate with myself."

"You're welcome. Self-compassion is a lifelong skill. Well, I don't want to keep you too long, so this will be my last question for now: what are your intentions for my daughter?"

"Hay nako!" Eleora exclaimed, covering her face with her hands.

Chadwick chuckled at her reaction. "Would you mind if I just whispered it to you?" he asked her mom. She nodded, looking slightly confused.

He leaned forward and cupped his hand to block his words from escaping. "Mrs. Edwards, my parents raised me with the perspective that you don't date for the sake of dating, but that dating is the process of determining whether someone is who you should marry. That's my intention—to see if Eleora and I are meant to be married someday. My parents are high school sweethearts who married young and have had a flourishing marriage. I'm hopeful to have a similar story."

He leaned back and tried to gauge her reaction. She was undoubtedly surprised but not angry or upset. That was a relief. He hadn't planned to say it all—that truthfully, he didn't even know he was feeling that way until asked.

She turned to Eleora. "I have no objections with him, iha. You've chosen well."

Chadwick could see the relief and joy on Eleora's face.

"You are definitely not like the rest of your peers, Chadwick. Your parents are probably expecting you, so we'll end our time here, but I know we'll be seeing a lot of each other," she told him and began to get up. He followed suit.

"Thank you for your hospitality, Mrs. Edwards," Chadwick replied easily.

"You may call me Tita Adalina." She gave him a quick hug.

"I'll walk him to the door," Eleora volunteered, jumping up from her chair.

They walked the short distance to the front door, and Eleora opened it, allowing Chadwick to go outside first, then followed and closed the door silently.

"I am so sorry about my mother!" she said immediately.

"What's there to apologize for? She's nice, and she clearly cares about you," Chadwick commented.

"Please, she's not as cool as your parents," Eleora said, shrugging.

"That depends on who you ask," Chadwick responded gently.

Eleora sighed dramatically. "You're not going to let me feel bad, are you?" she asked, and Chadwick nodded.

"Despite what you may think, your mom was great. I actually like her," he told her.

Eleora laughed. "You know, you're a terrible liar," she joked.

"But a wonderful actor," Chadwick said back with a wink.

"So, you admit you were just acting when you said you liked my mom!" Eleora replied with an eyebrow raised.

"No! I was just stating a fact that I can act. I was being completely honest when I said I like your mother," he insisted.

"I know that. I was just teasing."

"But you were giving me such a hard time!"

"That's called acting."

"And that was called acting," Chadwick teased back.

She laughed and playfully hit him on the shoulder. The movement made her hair fall in front of her eyes.

"So how are we supposed to decipher what's real or what's not?" Eleora said, laughter still in her voice.

"We're real, and that's what's important," Chadwick told her softly.

She'd just brushed back her hair when he said that and was immediately met with his gaze. What she saw made her blush and duck her head. But feeling his eyes on her, she raised her head again.

Chadwick pulled her into a hug and kissed her forehead. Bringing his head down to her ear, he whispered, "Your mom's watching by the window, so I'm not going to kiss you." Eleora nodded, and they pulled away, Chadwick still holding her hand.

"I have to go in," she said sadly.

"I know, and I have to go home," he said, echoing her disappointment. "I'll talk to you later." She nodded and went back inside.

Chapter 19

Eleora heard her phone buzzing and groaned with irritation. Could her alarm have gone off already? Was it really time to get ready for school? She rolled over to check her phone's screen and saw with surprise that it wasn't an alarm but a phone call.

"Someone better have a good reason for waking me up before my alarm," she muttered.

"Good morning to you too, Belle," Chadwick's deep voice came through, making her blush.

"Sorry about that, I'm not really a morning person," she said sheepishly, and he laughed warmly.

"I learned that about you the day we met," he replied, and she smiled, remembering that day. She settled back into the covers with the phone against her ear.

"So, what's up? What's with the early AM phone call?" she asked, curiosity softening her tone.

"I just woke up thinking about you, so I called." His voice was tender, and her heart fluttered.

"I think that you just made me a morning person— or at least a happy person in the morning," she told him, smiling.

"Oh no, Liz is going to kill me. I get the feeling

she's been trying to do that for years," he joked, and Eleora laughed.

"I can't wait to see you today," she said, blushing at her own forwardness.

"I feel the same way, Ellie. I miss you a lot. I guess that's why I called—I just wanted to hear your voice." Eleora giggled softly.

"And then you got my crabby, annoyed voice in response." She giggled some more, and Chadwick chuckled. "Sorry about that, Knight."

"It was really no problem; you're actually cute when you're annoyed," he teased gently, making her laugh.

"I'll try that one on Liz. Whenever I'm upset, I'll just be like, 'But Liz, I'm just being cute.' How do you think she'll take that?" Eleora proposed through her giggles, earning a chuckle from Chadwick.

"Yeah, you may need to rethink that, Belle. I don't think that's going to fly," he told her teasingly.

"You see, this is why I refrain from making plans too early—clearly they make no sense," she joked.

"And yet you still manage to use words like 'refrain,' so your vocabulary is always intact, eh?" he complimented her. "And don't worry about it—you have me, and unlike yourself, I am a morning person. I can take over the decision-making in the mornings and you can have the afternoons." He continued smoothly.

"Alright, that plan in itself is proof enough that we should go with that. Also, you've called me Belle a few times?" She didn't know what she was asking necessarily; she really wasn't all that coherent in the morning.

"Well, it means beautiful—which you are—and it

references Beauty and the Beast. I figured it was a perfect fit for a nickname," he explained thoughtfully.

Eleora smiled at his thoughtfulness. "I like it." Then, she heard her alarm go off. She sighed and turned it off. "Alas, tis now time for me to get ready," she told Chadwick.

"I shan't keep you any longer then. See you later, Belle," he said warmly.

She smiled. "See you." Eleora got off the phone with a happy sigh and slid out of bed serenely. She got ready for school in a daze of delight. It was almost surreal that this amazing guy wanted her, too. When Eleora arrived at school and saw Chadwick waiting for her, the daze broke. He was real, tangible, and hers.

They walked to class together, hand in hand, and separated when Eleora headed straight to her seat beside Maryliz while Chadwick waited at the teacher's desk to ask him something. Eleora had a large smile on her face that Maryliz immediately noticed.

"Someone's awfully happy before noon," she teased.

"Well, sometimes, people can affect your regular thoughts and routines," Eleora replied with a wink and sat down.

"I'm so happy for you!" Maryliz squealed. Eleora had filled her in on Saturday—well, the part about their new relationship, anyway. "We have to go on a double date sometime! I'm so happy that I get to do these kinds of things with my best friend now."

"Aww, Liz." She reached over to hold one of Maryliz's hands.

Maryliz squeezed it appreciatively. "It's just … you don't talk about your childhood often, so I know you must've gone through some hard things. And that hurts my heart. But now, you and Chadwick? I just love this for you. You deserve all the love in the world, Elle."

"Not you making me cry in first period," Eleora joked, subtly wiping away a few tears. Maryliz laughed.

"Whoa, what did I miss?" Chadwick asked, taking the seat on Eleora's other side.

Maryliz let go of her hand and, in a bubbly voice, said, "Just best friend stuff."

Before he could reply, their teacher started to take attendance and their day was underway.

What used to bother Eleora was now cause for celebration—namely, the way that she and Chadwick shared almost every class together. It was such a privilege to be with him in some way for almost the whole day. Is this what falling in love felt like? This unending craving for the object of your affection?

The desire she felt for him scared her. If things went sideways, how would she make it? Suddenly, she understood why Romeo and Juliet died the way they had. Living without Chadwick was truly unthinkable.

Eleora shook her head to dislodge her morbid thoughts. She didn't need to imagine the worst-case scenario. Instead, she needed to enjoy the present. Be in the moment.

Like, right now she was supposed to be working on a short story. She glanced at Chadwick to her right and saw him intently tapping away. He looked so focused, she ought to follow suit.

Eleora sighed. She was stuck. No ideas were coming to her. Desperate, she decided to employ Google to find some writing prompts. Maybe this would help stimulate her imagination.

As she searched through different links, she came across an interesting prompt: The protagonist buys an antique trunk from a junk shop and discovers a mummified body inside—a body that was murdered. Hmmm. What if the body was killed a long time ago and was related to the person who found it? And maybe they're an orphan, so this is even more meaningful! One of her quirks could be being into antiques, which is how she comes across the trunk. Maybe they could even take this to a fantasy genre and let the girl's origins be another world?

Eleora smiled—she had a story after all. The words came to her like a torrent; she was barely able to keep up with them. When she finished writing, she read it over and smiled in satisfaction. She had something she was proud of.

Eleora checked the time on the computer and was pleasantly surprised to see there were still about fifteen minutes left in class.

She took out a piece of paper and quickly wrote a note for Chadwick.

Just finished my story and would love to share it with you. Are you almost done yourself? — EG

She slid it to him beside her. He heard the movement and glanced down at the note, then up at her. He gave her a smile and opened it.

After reading it, he leaned closer to her and whispered in her ear. His closeness made her shiver. "I'm just about done. Want to trade seats and read each other's?"

Unable to speak, she nodded. Swiftly, before anyone could notice, he kissed her on the cheek and then got up from his chair. They quickly swapped seats. She was nervous to have him read her story but excited to read his.

It was so interesting! His story was about an alien prince running away from his planet to avoid an arranged marriage. He lands on Earth and begins to fall for a human girl. She found herself wanting more of the story when she was done reading it. Before she could say anything to Chadwick, the bell rang, indicating the end of the period.

"Alright class, you are dismissed," Mr. Williams announced.

She heard people begin to pack up and turned to see Chadwick still intently reading her story. Gently, she tapped him on the shoulder.

"Babe, we have to go to our next class." The term of endearment slipped out without her planning it.

"Babe, eh?" She started to blush. Gosh, what if he didn't like it? He laughed. "I'll take whatever nickname you want to give me. You can call me anything and I'll like it because it came from you."

She relaxed. "Good to know. But for real, we have to get going."

"Facts. Feel free to log out of my computer. I've saved my work. Is there anything you need to save here or am I good to log out for you?"

"You can go ahead."

Quickly, they went through the motions of logging out and packing up their stuff. When they were ready, Chadwick reached for her hand, and they speed-walked to drama.

"Your story is fantastic, Ellie. Here I thought you were just a great poet, but it turns out you're actually a great writer in general."

"Thanks for the encouragement. I felt like it was good, but I feel like I can't trust my own judgment when it comes to my writing," she admitted. "Also, yours was super interesting! I love the premise. It's the type of story I could see Netflix adapting as a TV show or movie."

"Coming from you, writer extraordinaire, that's high praise. Thank you."

They walked into the auditorium just as attendance was being taken. Instead of splitting off to sit with other people, they sat together. This did not go unnoticed by their classmates, many of whom gave them knowing looks.

Eleora started to feel apprehensive when she felt Chadwick hold her hand and squeeze it lightly. That little action restored calm to her. She squeezed back a thank-you.

Within a few minutes, she felt a note land on her lap. She glanced down at the paper and opened it quietly.

Sit together at lunch? — CK

She was about to nod and then had an idea.

Actually, do you mind if we head to lunch a little later? There's something I want to show you. — EG

At the corner of her eye, she watched the confused and curious look on his face. Then, he turned to her and nodded. Eleora nearly clapped her hands in glee—she couldn't wait for class to be over.

Chapter 20

"Okay, you've had me in suspense for a whole class! What are you showing me?" Chadwick asked once they were dismissed and people were packing up their stuff.

"You'll just have to see," Eleora responded in a singsong voice. They left the auditorium together, but instead of going right toward the cafeteria, she led them to the left.

Once they got to the library, she threw her arms out in a dramatic flourish. "Ta-da!"

He gave her a bewildered look. "I'm pretty sure you showed me the library on the first day," he deadpanned.

She laughed. "It's inside the library. Come on." Easily, she weaved in and out of the bookshelves and tables until they reached her secret meeting room. She opened the door for him and ushered him inside. His jaw dropped.

"What is this place?"

"A Student Council hideaway room, but I don't think anyone really uses it besides me." While he gathered himself, she dropped her bag on the floor and went to the mini fridge. "Would you like anything? We have a pretty good selection of microwave meals."

He walked over to her and scanned the options. "I'll take a spaghetti Bolognese meal."

"Cool. Mine has about five more minutes to go, and then I'll put yours in." She took out the meal he'd selected and set it beside the microwave, then went to sit on the couch and patted the spot beside her.

He joined her on the couch. "Hmm. I guess we never talked about this—are you a cuddler?" he asked.

"I haven't been in a relationship before, so I guess my answer is I don't know? But I would like to cuddle with you now if that's what you're asking."

"Come here then." He didn't need to tell her twice. Soon she was positioning herself against his side, moving one of his arms to wrap around her shoulders. Eleora leaned her head against his shoulder and sighed contentedly. She felt his body shift as he chuckled. "Yep, you're definitely a cuddler."

She giggled at his proclamation. He pulled her in closer and kissed her forehead. She tilted her head up to face him and then boldly kissed him on the lips. At first, he was still, surprised—but then he kissed her back. She leaned forward, deepened the kiss, and then climbed into his lap. She straddled him and wrapped her arms around his neck. He couldn't hold back a moan at the proximity of their intimate bodies.

And then the microwave beeped.

He jolted out of his lustful haze at the sound. Within seconds, Chadwick moved her off his lap and stood, backing away from the couch.

She looked at him, confused. "What's wrong?"

He went to the microwave and took out her food. He placed it on top of the microwave and put in his own meal. Then he handed Eleora the hot container along with a plastic fork he found.

"Chadwick?"

"Sorry for not answering right away. I'm just thinking and trying to figure out how to put my thoughts into words."

"Okay." She blew on her food and started eating, waiting for him to share what was on his mind. When his meal was ready, he grabbed it from the microwave and sat beside her on the couch.

"I'm really into you, Eleora. It's crazy how much. I didn't anticipate how strong attraction could be. You're the only girl I've dated. You're my first experience of everything—and it's been wildly amazing."

She smiled shakily. "I feel like there's a but coming."

"But we need some boundaries. I made a promise to myself and God that I would save sex and sexual touching until marriage. I want to honor that commitment. How do you feel about that?" He sounded nervous and hastily shoved some hot food into his mouth.

"Well, it's certainly honorable. I know I've never wanted casual sex. For me, it would have to occur within the context of a committed and serious relationship. But I'm good to respect whatever boundaries you want. When we're together physically, the chief desire of my heart is to show you how much I care about you and make you as happy as you make me. I wouldn't want to do anything you're uncomfortable with."

He visibly relaxed at her words.

"Thanks. So maybe no straddling. It was hard to

keep my head on straight when that happened. And I think we might need to have shorter kisses. How do those things land on you?"

"I can work with those boundaries," she concurred. Eleora finished her food and checked to see if he was done too. He was, so she took his container and went to throw out their garbage.

When she got back, she approached the couch cautiously. "Just confirming—cuddling is still okay, right?"

"Right." He affirmed, and she quickly snuggled up against him. They stayed like that and discussed ideas for their stories until the bell rang and lunch was over.

Chapter 21

Eleora almost pinched herself as she waited for Chadwick to arrive. She still couldn't believe they were together. It had been an incredible week. Yet, it all seemed so fictional—like maybe she'd wake up right now and realize she'd dreamed the whole thing.

But when the doorbell rang and she opened it to see Chadwick, she was reminded that this was her real life. She was going on a date with her boyfriend, who happened to be one of the kindest, most intelligent, and handsome people she'd ever met.

She greeted him with a smile, and he reached down to give her a tight hug before spinning her around. Eleora giggled as he did so. "Well, hello to you, too."

"I guess you could say I'm excited to see you," he said earnestly, causing her heart to flutter.

"Same! I look forward to seeing where we're going today." It was yet another surprise date he'd planned for them. Normally, she hated surprises. She loved well-laid plans and being aware of all the details. But she trusted Chadwick. The unknown wasn't scary with him.

Once he put her down, she locked the door behind her and turned toward the street to see a black Honda Pilot parked nearby.

"Is that the car you drove?" Eleora asked.

"Yeah. Technically, it's my dad's, but he was going to give it to me if I had all 90s on my report card at the end of the semester. I kind of persuaded him to let me have it early," Chadwick explained. Eleora practically ran to it, sliding her hands carefully over the doors.

"You like it?" Chadwick asked, amused.

"Like it? Bruh, this is my favourite car! When I was around nine years old, my family went on a road trip, and the rental place gave us this car. I fell in love with it and swore I'd drive it when I was older—either this or a Toyota Highlander. I love an SUV crossover," Eleora explained excitedly.

Memories began flooding back—her mom and dad joking in the front seat, old disco songs playing on the radio through the van, eating Doritos while reading Judy Blume, singing We Are Family with her dad whenever it came on. Such good times. She quickly wiped away the tears forming in her eyes.

"Hey, are you crying?" Chadwick asked gently, holding her face in his hands and wiping away a few tears she'd missed. Then he put his arm around her. She leaned into his shoulder.

"Yeah, it just brought back a lot of memories."

"I'm guessing those memories are related to your dad?" He asked softly. She nodded. "Well, if you want to talk it out, I'll happily do that for you. You're not alone."

"Thanks." She went up on her tiptoes and kissed him on the cheek. "I'm good for now. Let's head out?"

He allowed the subject change, knowing he didn't want to push her on such a sensitive topic. He opened the passenger door for her, and she slid inside.

Once she was settled, Chadwick closed Eleora's door and walked around to his side. When the car started, Only Hope by Mandy Moore began playing through the speakers.

Chadwick blushed. "My mom was listening to the A Walk to Remember soundtrack and must've left this CD in there," he explained.

"It's alright—I love this song. And that's one of my favourite movies! It always puts me in tears."

This led them to discussing their favourite movies. Soon enough, they arrived.

"And voilà! We're here!" Chadwick announced with an attempted French accent as he turned into the parking lot of Scooters.

Chadwick reversed neatly into a parking spot, then turned off the car. He began taking off his seatbelt, got out, and went to her side, opening her door like a true gentleman. Eleora grabbed her purse and stepped out, giving Chadwick a smile of thanks for his chivalry.

"So, have you been rollerblading before?" Chadwick asked as they walked across the parking lot.

Only all the time with my dad. "A little when I was younger. Hopefully, it's like riding a bike—you never truly forget how to," she joked, and he laughed.

"What about you? Do you rollerblade often?" she asked as they reached the entrance, and once again, he held the door for her.

"Yeah, I go at least once a month with my youth group. The youth pastor really likes rollerblading, and now he's got us hooked. Which is why I usually end up here pretty often." Eleora nodded and didn't even flinch at the mention of his church; she was too busy looking around.

The place looked almost exactly the same as when she was younger. They still had that snack bar that served pizza, hot dogs, hamburgers, chips, and Pepsi, and the layout was still the same too. The only thing that had really changed was the paint on the walls, which had been touched up.

"Chad!" she heard an older gentleman call out.

"Arthur!" Chadwick answered and gave him a side-hug. "And Arthur, this is Eleora."

Chadwick introduced her. Eleora gave Arthur a big smile and shook his hand.

"Nice to meet you."

"Likewise. So Chadwick, this is the girl you've been talking about!" Arthur exclaimed in a mild British accent.

Eleora turned to look at him, surprised. "Arthur, there's something called confidentiality," Chadwick joked.

"Oh! My bad, that's what you kids say these days, right? Well, if I haven't totally mucked things up, Chadwick, she's a beauty—and Eleora, I hope you enjoy rollerblading this afternoon. See ya kids around!" Arthur said, then walked away.

"So, who exactly is Arthur?" Eleora asked.

"He and his wife Judy run the place. And since I'm here so often, I know them well. Arthur's like my honorary grandfather," Chadwick explained. Eleora's smile widened. She knew she should probably let the moment slide, but she couldn't resist.

"So, you talk about me, eh?" Eleora teased, laughing when she saw Chadwick's brown skin take on a reddish tone.

"No comment," Chadwick deadpanned, and they both laughed as they reached the counter where you rented rollerblades.

"Hey Chad and Chad's pretty friend," an older lady greeted them—Eleora assumed she was Judy.

"Good afternoon, Judy," Chadwick responded.

"What will it be for today? Blades or skates?"

"Blades," they answered simultaneously.

"Chad, I already know you're a size 10 and sweetie, you're a...?"

"I'm a nine," Eleora told her.

"All right, I'll be right back."

They waited for what seemed like an unusually long time before Judy returned with two... boxes?

"Sorry about the wait. I was looking for the new shipment of blades that just came in so I could give them to you two. This is a special occasion," Judy said meaningfully.

Eleora fought back a laugh as Chadwick groaned. "Arthur got to you, didn't he?" he asked. That's when Eleora finally laughed.

"We appreciate this, Judy, despite Chadwick's rude tone," she said kindly.

"Well, at least someone's appreciative," Judy said sarcastically, and Chadwick finally smiled.

"I am thankful to you, Judy—how much?" he asked.

"$33.27."

"Here, keep the change to cover my rudeness." Chadwick said, handing her two twenties.

Judy smiled her thanks and winked at Eleora. "You have a good guy."

"Thank you! I know, he's pretty great." She

replied, then grabbed the two boxes.

She and Chadwick walked toward the benches to put on their blades, and once they were out of earshot, both began to laugh.

"I love Judy!" Eleora said as she opened her box to see beautiful white rollerblades with silver swirls and silver laces.

"Yeah, she's the best. Also embarrassing, but still the best," Chadwick replied, seeing his sleek black rollerblades with blue shoelaces.

Once they had their rollerblades on, they skated toward the empty rink.

"Wow. Where is everybody?" Eleora commented as they glided around. It wasn't as hard as she thought it would be to skate again. Her instincts kicked in—push off from the center and slightly bend her knees. It was like she'd never stopped.

"I know what you mean; this place seems kind of deserted, eh? But trust me, by 1:10, it will be filled," he told her. Then the music began to play. Eleora recognized the song: Written in the Stars by Tinie Tempah.

"Hey, want to race around the rink?" she suggested.

"Sure."

"Kay, three—two—one—go!" Eleora said quickly and pushed off with all her might, sailing ahead of Chadwick.

"Cheater!" Chadwick called out as he gained on her. He began to pass her as they neared their "finish line."

Oh, hell no. I am not about to lose, Eleora thought, fueled by competitiveness. She did something she hadn't done in years—quickening her pace, she lifted her right leg and crossed it over her left, jumping at the same time. She twirled in the air, catching Chadwick's attention. He slowed as Eleora landed perfectly on her right leg, then sped past him, winning.

"I won," Eleora said smugly, laughing at Chadwick's dazed expression.

"How'd you do that?" Chadwick asked.

"It was something I learned when I was younger," Eleora answered.

"I swear you said you rollerbladed a little. You didn't say you used to rollerblade."

"Oh, I'm worse. I'm a rollerblader," Eleora joked. "I used to be a professional and actually did rollerblading competitions, but I gave it up when I was eleven. Too stressful."

"Wow." He said, still dazed, then Eleora burst out laughing.

"You know I'm joking, right?" she asked, still laughing. Realizing she'd duped him, Chadwick began to laugh too.

"I can't believe I fell for that," he said, shaking his head.

"Neither do I. Why did you anyway?"

"Because you're so good at everything, so it just seemed believable."

"Trust me, I'm not as perfect as everyone thinks. I can't draw to save my life." Chadwick laughed at that, and Eleora smiled. When he laughed, his whole face lit up and his eyes were even more amazing—if that was even possible.

"I'd only be average at dance if I hadn't taken lessons from such a young age. Singing, I was naturally okay at, but lessons helped develop it. Acting is my only true talent—well, acting and writing," Eleora told him. Then, realizing she'd been talking so long that they'd done another lap around the rink, she added, "Sorry for talking so much. Stop me when you need to."

"No, I didn't mind. I like learning new things about you." How did he always manage to say the right thing?

They skated some more, and while they did, the rink began to fill up. The DJ played more great songs by British artists: Live for the Moment by Pixie Lott, Candy by Aggro Santos ft. Kimberly, Beggin' by Madcon, Champion Sound by Fatboy Slim, and more.

After about forty-five minutes of skating, they decided to take a break and get something to eat. Everything was going well. They had a few more races (Chadwick won two and Eleora won one), Eleora taught him a couple of tricks and how to lift her into a spin, and they talked almost the whole time—mostly about their writing.

"Okay, what's the most emotional thing you've written?" Chadwick asked her.

"I wrote this song: Rainy Day. Honestly, it has to be the most depressing song ever, about the sun not coming out because of all the sadness in my heart. I wrote it when my nana was diagnosed with cancer and my family imploded," Eleora said, her voice gaining enthusiasm. "But it made me feel better. Finally, there was something I could control—my words. And that's how everything changed. My dad found my song, and when my parents realized how hurt I was because of everything happening, things got better." Her smile was more confident now.

"I'm glad everything worked out, but I hope you never feel that alone again. And if you ever do, remember, I'll always be here for you. Always," Chadwick told her.

"Pinkie promise?" Eleora asked, holding up her pinky.

Chapter 22

Chadwick had an instant flashback to a few weeks ago when Pastor Gabe had briefly talked about pinky promises.

"How many of you have ever made a pinkie promise?" he asked the youth group. Hands went up all around the room. "Were these made when you guys were little, or are these pinkie promises recent?" he asked.

The youth around the room all said, "Little."

"Exactly, because I'm sure few of you would be caught dead doing a pinkie promise now—it's so 'immature' or 'childish' or 'meaningless,' right? But little kids live for those things. They live for the linking of the pinkies and the keeping of the promise. They all love to make them, and they made them often.

"My daughter, she used to love making those promises. I would say, 'Honey, I love you.' And then she'd say, 'Pinkie promise?' And we'd pinkie promise that I loved her. Then she'd say, 'Well, I pinkie promise that I love you more.' And we'd go back and forth like that."

Some girls started to go "awww," making everyone laugh, and Pastor Gabe smiled.

"Yeah, yeah, it was cute. Honestly, she would bring that out in me. I love her so much." A little bit of pain crossed his face, and we all saw it. We all knew his story—that he'd lost his wife and daughter at the same time and missed them terribly.

He composed himself and continued, "The point is, whenever someone made that pinkie promise, it was because they knew they would keep it no matter what. Whether because they were afraid of their pinkie falling off—which is the suspicion of breaking pinkie promises—or because they really meant it. Pinkie promises, as silly or childish as they may seem, are signs of a child's innocence. Which is what Jesus loved.

"Does everyone know the story? Of when Jesus was hanging out with his disciples and some kids wanted to see him, and the disciples pushed them away? That's when Jesus said, 'Let the children come to me, for they are closer to God than you or I.' That's a paraphrase, but I think you get the point. He was saying that because they are so innocent and don't yet understand what it is to sin, they are closer to God than any of us. We should really try our best to be as obedient, kind, and innocent as children. To start with that, try to pinkie promise a bit more often."

Everyone started to laugh.

"I know it sounds stupid and silly, but hey, it's not going to make life any worse. And at any rate, you can get a laugh out of it."

"Promise." Chadwick affirmed, connecting his pinkie with hers. Then he kissed their intertwined pinkies.

At that moment, Eleora's stomach rumbled. They glanced down at the source of the noise and promptly started laughing.

"Perchance that means it's time to get something to eat," Chadwick joked, playing out a British accent.

"Perhaps it does," Eleora replied with her own British accent.

"I just love your accent!" an older woman said as she skated by them. The two looked at each other and started laughing again.

When they saw an opening in the current of skaters, they broke out of the center and skated out of the rink, still holding hands. They made their way to the snack bar and began to wait in the very long line.

They finally reached the front and were about to order when the cashier exclaimed, "Eleora! Is that you?"

Eleora, who had been looking at the menu on the wall, looked up to see a woman in her thirties with light brown hair and green eyes, and began to recognize her.

"Oh my gosh! Jenny?!" The two did an awkward hug because of the counter between them.

"I haven't seen you since you were around ten years old!" Jenny exclaimed.

"I know! It's been way too long! Sorry, Chadwick, this beautiful woman is one of the two people who taught me how to rollerblade when I was younger. Her name is Jennifer, but she's known as Jenny." She introduced her, and the two shook hands.

"Nice to meet you," he said politely, giving her a smile. Anyone who was special to his Belle was special to him.

"Likewise," she replied. "So Elle, now that you've moved back, will you maybe perform for us one time? Or help out with lessons? You're, like, my best pupil!"

"No problem, just tell me when, and I can see when I'm available!" Eleora replied happily. Chadwick shouldn't have been surprised at her offer, but he was. She had so much on her plate. When would she have time to come here and rollerblade?

"Hey, how long are y'all gonna be? Some of us are hungry!" a guy in his late twenties said rudely with an American accent.

"Oops! Sorry!" Jenny said, flustered. "What would you two like?"

"Did you see anything you like?" Chadwick asked her, taking out his wallet.

"Umm, how about two slices of pizza and a medium Pepsi?"

"Sure, no problem. We'll take four slices of pizza, a small fries, and two medium Pepsis." Chadwick ordered, and they moved down the counter so the American could order.

"So, you weren't kidding about being a rollerblader, eh?" Chadwick teased as they received their food on two trays. Eleora laughed, grabbing hers as Chadwick paid.

"No, I seriously just used to rollerblade. Jenny taught me the basics, and then … my dad taught me how to do tricks. Basically, like figure skating, but no ice. Sometimes I would perform here—to do tricks and stuff—and it all went into my university account," Eleora explained as they walked over to a seat by the window.

He noticed that she tripped over the reference to her father. Once seated, he prayed silently for God's blessing on the food.

"So, I have something to ask you," she said once

he started eating.

"Go ahead."

"Well, my mom would like to invite you to join us for our extended family's Christmas dinner. It's on Saturday, Dec 16th."

He smiled wide at her words. This meant her mom had truly accepted him!

"Sure! Isn't that a bit early to be celebrating though?"

"We do it on Dec 16 to commemorate Simbang Gabi, a series of nine Catholic masses leading up to Christmas. They don't really do that here, but to remember our cultural heritage, we hold it then."

"That's cool! I'll happily join you guys for that," he said easily. He could think of no reason not to go.

Eleora was surprised. "Really? Just like that? No cajoling or bargaining necessary?"

"Really. I want to meet your family, I want to honour your mother's invitation, and I'm definitely not going to pass up an opportunity to eat good food." He started on the fries.

"Wow. I was even going to offer to go to church with you on Christmas to seal the deal. But I'm glad it didn't come to that, I guess?"

Well, damn. Maybe he shouldn't have been so eager. Her coming to church would've been great! He tried to hide his disappointment by eating more pizza.

"You would really like me to come, eh?" she asked gently.

He must not have concealed his disappointment well enough. He took a moment before responding. He wanted to be honest but not pushy.

"I would. But I don't expect it, and I won't try to

force you. I respect you."

His words seemed to land well on her. She smiled in response, even as her eyes looked contemplative. Was she really considering doing this for him?

"Okay, I'll come with you."

He couldn't stop the smile that spread across his face. Chadwick had never expected her to come to church or change her views, but now that this was a possibility, his heart was more excited than he dared admit.

Chapter 23

Eleora tried to calm her nerves as she walked up to Chadwick's front door. She couldn't believe it was already the night of the family Christmas dinner. The last month of dating Chadwick had flown by in a whirl of wonderful memories. In many ways, it felt like they were made for each other; their lives merged so naturally.

Before she could ring the doorbell, the front door opened. And there he was—handsome as ever. His formal black winter coat hung open to reveal a white knit turtleneck that contrasted beautifully with his dark brown skin and paired well with his khakis.

He gave her a wide smile, and her belly flipped. Would she ever get tired of that smile? It didn't seem possible.

"Mom, Dad, I'm heading out now! See you later!" he called, stepping outside and shutting the door behind him.

"Hey, you look beautiful," he said, greeting her with a kiss on the cheek.

She laughed. "You can't even see what I'm wearing under this puffy winter coat!"

He shrugged and grabbed her hand. "You'll always look beautiful to me. Doesn't matter what you're wearing."

She didn't know what to say to that. He consistently caught her off guard with his sincere and affirming words.

"Thank you," she said softly, squeezing his hand.

When they got to the car, Chadwick went to open the back door, but Eleora's mom waved him off. "No, no, Chadwick. Come sit up front with me!"

He shot Eleora a puzzled look but complied. "Good evening, Tita Adalina," he said politely as she pulled out of the driveway.

"Good evening, Chadwick. I'm glad you can join us for the party—it's sure to be a wonderful time. How does your family celebrate Christmas?"

Ah. That was why she wanted him up front. It was an interrogation! The party was in Oakville, a decent drive away—too much time for Chadwick to be cross-examined.

"My family does an Advent calendar starting at the beginning of December, and we go to church on Christmas Eve."

Shoot. Shoot. Shoot. Eleora had managed to hide Chadwick's faith from her mother. She could only imagine what she was thinking now.

"It's nice to have familial Christmas traditions," her mom said smoothly. "Do you go to church often, or only for Christmas?"

Her voice remained calm and friendly, but who knew what was brewing beneath the surface?

"Fairly often. I go with my family every Sunday. Then there's a youth program on Fridays that I attend. I'm often playing piano for part of it."

Chadwick's honesty was one of the things she loved most about him—but at that moment, she almost wished he'd lied.

"Ah. It's nice that you have a place outside of school and home to play the piano. That must be lovely for you."

Eleora released the breath she hadn't realized she was holding. Her mom wasn't going to address the faith issue now—but with the raised eyebrow Eleora caught in the rearview mirror, she knew a conversation was coming later. Joy.

She leaned her head against the cold window and tuned out their conversation, choosing instead to think of the upcoming gathering. She was excited to see her family. With one branch in Ajax, one in Kitchener, and one in Oakville, it wasn't easy to see one another often. They could only count on two times a year when everyone got together: Christmas and Canada Day. But whenever they did, it was a good time. It always made her feel less alone—a reminder she was part of something bigger.

It felt like no time had passed when they turned onto her aunt's street. The house never failed to inspire a bit of awe with its sheer size. With a detached three-car garage, a wraparound porch, and a walkout balcony, it exuded wealth. But it was classy and still felt like a home—not gaudy or flashy.

Her mom pulled into the large driveway and shut

off the car. As she and Chadwick began to get out, Chadwick was already at Eleora's door, opening it for her. She smiled her thanks and reached inside the car to grab some of the food. She handed him one large foil container, then reached for a second. Her mom grabbed the third, and they headed toward the front door.

"Your mom was just giving me the rundown of the family. Do you have any advice for me before we go in?" he whispered.

"Mano po every adult. Address my cousins as Ate or Kuya since they're older than us. Call my aunts and uncles Tito or Tita, and my grandmother Nanay Reyna."

"Isn't Nanay what you call your mom?" he asked, clearly confused.

"Yes, but it's also what you call my grandmother—while I call her Lola. I don't make the rules, I just follow them," she said with a shrug.

He chuckled. "Noted."

They reached the front door. Her mom rang the bell and waved to the security camera. A click signaled the door unlocking, and she stepped inside, kicking off her shoes.

"Who's going to help me with this pagkain?" she called out. Three identical young men approached, each wearing variations of all-white outfits. Their only apparent differences were their glasses.

"We'll help you, Tita Ada," said the one in rimless glasses, smiling as he took her tray and touched his forehead to the back of her hand. The others followed suit, grabbing the trays from Eleora and Chadwick.

"Who's this, Elle?" asked the one with gold frames, gesturing to Chadwick with a raised eyebrow.

"Emmanuel, Felix, and Gian—meet Chadwick, my boyfriend. Chadwick, meet my triplet cousins. They're just a year older than us, each at a different U of T campus. They live here."

"Nice to meet you," Chadwick said, shaking their hands.

"Same," replied Gian, the one with light green frames. The others nodded. Chadwick and Eleora took off their shoes, and she hung up their coats.

The cousins waited for them, and together they walked into the kitchen. Eleora spotted her Tita Blessica at the stove and approached her, touching her Tita's hand to her forehead.

"Kamusta, Tita. This is Chadwick."

"Her jowa," Felix teased.

Tita Blessica raised an eyebrow in surprise, then smiled warmly as Chadwick touched her hand to his forehead.

"It's nice to meet you," he said.

"Ooh. I can already tell you're a keeper. Good catch, pamangkin."

While her cousins set the food on the island, they gave Eleora a big group hug. She laughed and hugged them back.

"Who else is here?" she asked.

"No one. You're the first to arrive," Emmanuel replied. "Ate Cora's still getting ready upstairs."

"Lola is here, though—in the living room," Gian added.

"Then that's where we're going next," Eleora said. Chadwick followed her up a few stairs into a spacious sitting room filled with cozy-looking couches. In the center sat an older woman with black hair pulled into a low bun, dressed in a white and gold top and a white skirt.

"Lola!" Eleora exclaimed, rushing toward her. She touched her forehead to her hand and hugged her.

"My Eleora, you look beautiful." Eleora blushed, relieved that her white sweater dress and leggings were approved of. "And who is this?" Lola asked pointedly.

"Lola, this is Chadwick. My special friend."

He touched his forehead to her hand. "Ikinagagalak ko kayong makilala, Nanay."

Eleora stared at him in shock—his Tagalog was nearly flawless. Her grandmother smiled warmly and patted the seat beside her.

"Ikinagagalak kong makilala ka, Chadwick. Come, sit with me."

He smiled and sat beside her.

"How do you and Eleora know each other?"

"From school. I transferred this fall for piano and acting."

"Oh, a musician! You must play for us tonight," she said, gesturing to the baby grand piano gleaming under the potlights.

"Of course, Nanay."

"Are you hoping for a career in music?"

Chadwick shook his head. "No, Nanay. I hope to work in medicine."

"Medicine! How nice to see a young man with ambition."

Eleora watched the exchange, both shocked and satisfied. She hadn't expected this line of questioning, but Chadwick handled it beautifully.

Then her cousin, Corazon, entered the room and squealed when she saw Eleora.

Eleora squealed right back, racing over to hug her. Despite the few years between them, they were close and always excited to see each other.

Corazon's eyes widened when she spotted Chadwick. She pulled Eleora over to a couch on the far side of the room.

"That's him? Your jowa? He's fine!"

Eleora giggled. "Yes. Yes, he is."

"And it looks like he's already won over Lola. How'd you manage that?"

"I didn't. He did it all himself—learned some Tagalog without even telling me."

"Does he have a brother?" Corazon deadpanned.

They both burst into laughter.

"Okay, but for real—there's gotta be a catch, right? Based on everything you've told me and now seeing him in the flesh, he seems a little too perfect."

"He's not perfect, but…" Eleora paused, debating whether to bring up his faith. She decided against it. "…he's pretty close."

"Hay nako! Look at your face. You love him!" Corazon exclaimed.

Eleora shushed her, glancing at Chadwick. He appeared to be deep in conversation with Lola. She let out a quiet sigh of relief.

"I'm right, aren't I?" Corazon smirked.

"I plead the fifth," Eleora replied, and they collapsed into giggles.

"What about you? Has anyone caught your eye recently?"

Corazon shrugged. "Not at all. I'm actually starting to think that I'm…" She lowered her voice. "…asexual and aromantic. I've been looking into it online, and I resonate with a lot of the blogs I've read. You're the first person I've told."

Eleora nodded, taking it in. "Wow. Thanks for trusting me. That actually makes sense—you never really had crushes growing up. If this feels authentic and true to you, that's what matters."

She noticed tears in Corazon's eyes. "Oh, Zozo. Come here." She opened her arms, and Corazon leaned into her.

"Thank you for accepting me, Rara. I love you."

Before they could say more, a group of voices neared the room.

"Maligayang Pasko! Merry Christmas, everyone!" came Tita Althea's bright voice.

She entered the room with Eleora's other cousins in tow.

Eleora and Corazon stood to greet them, offering mano po and hugs. Bayani looked more manly each time she saw him—towering over most of the room now. Dalisay, Tala, and Marikit looked so alike, you'd think they were triplets, with matching brown eyes and soft wavy hair.

After greetings, they approached Lola, who accepted their respectful gestures, and then she introduced Chadwick like he was her personal guest.

More family members began arriving—Tito Juan with his sons Agapito, Crisanto, and David. Soon, the living room buzzed with conversation as everyone caught up.

The chatter quieted when Tita Blessica cleared her throat.

"Now that everyone is here, the party can begin!" she announced. The room cheered.

"Tito Juan will open with prayer, and then Tita Althea will lead our annual parol contest."

Tito Juan stepped to the front. "Let us pray." Everyone bowed their heads.

"Lord, thank You for bringing us together. Bless our time, draw us closer, and be glorified among us. In the name of the Father, the Son, and the Holy Spirit. Amen."

A chorus of "Amen" echoed throughout the room.

Tita Althea smiled and tucked a strand of hair behind her ear. "Okay, everyone. Downstairs, the tables are set with parol frames. Your task is to decorate them. We've got all the tissue paper and tinsel you'll need. You have 30 minutes. Lola will choose the winner. Let's go!"

Everyone began moving toward the basement. Chadwick kissed Lola's cheek before rejoining Eleora.

"You and Lola seemed to be having a great time. I didn't know you spoke Tagalog," Eleora teased.

"She's remarkable. You're lucky to have her," he said warmly. "We talked about our shared faith."

That made sense—Lola was a devout Catholic.

"Anywho, what's a parol?"

"It's a Christmas lantern shaped like a star. Tita Thea preps them, and we just decorate. I'll show you."

They descended the spiral staircase into the finished basement. Two long tables stood ready with supplies. Everyone took their seats.

Chadwick followed Eleora's lead, decorating his parol in shimmering silver while she created a vibrant rainbow one. The room filled with chatter and laughter as they worked.

Just as they finished, the timer went off.

"Drop whatever's in your hands and back away from the table!" Tita Althea shouted dramatically, causing everyone to laugh.

"This isn't Chopped, Tita!" Crisanto called out.

"You're lucky I'm not judging, or you'd lose points," she retorted.

Lola moved around the room, inspecting each parol. She stopped at a purple, white, and gold one.

"This is the one!"

Marikit jumped up, cheering as everyone groaned playfully.

"Maraming salamat po, Lola!" she said proudly, giving her a hug.

"Now," Tita Blessica said, "take your parol home later. But for now—the food is ready upstairs!"

Chadwick turned to Eleora. "What should I expect food-wise?"

She stepped back to get a good view. "We've got roasted chicken, deep-fried pork, sweet ham, and embutido—it's like Filipino meatloaf. Sides include pancit, lumpia, and steamed rice."

"Sounds amazing! I'm getting a bit of everything."

They loaded their plates and sat with the cousins—boys on one side, girls on the other. Chadwick hit it off with Bayani, who was further along in the med school track and full of advice. Seeing he was in good hands, Eleora focused on her female cousins.

"What are your plans next year, Elle?" Tala asked. She was about to graduate in criminology from York.

"Well… you know my mom wants me to be a nurse, so I've applied to a few nursing programs."

Dalisay tilted her head. "That's fine, but are you sure you can commit to something you're not passionate about? I just started to feel settled in my program."

"Well… promise to keep this between us?" Her cousins nodded.

"I also applied for a Fine Arts degree in writing and theatre. Nanay doesn't know," she whispered.

"Bold! What made you take that step?" Corazon asked.

"Honestly? Chadwick. He encouraged me. He makes me braver."

Her cousins aww'ed in unison, then burst into giggles.

"That's amazing, Elle," said Marikit. "I wish I could be open about my relationship with Miles, but…"

They all nodded. Tita Althea wasn't keen on her dating, so Marikit had kept her three-year relationship under wraps.

"Meanwhile, Dali and I are killing the single life. I'm considering trying online dating," Tala said.

"Okay, go off, sis!" Corazon encouraged.

"There's a guy I like at church, but I'm pretty sure he doesn't know I exist," Dalisay admitted.

"We all know what that's like," Eleora said, giving her a side hug.

Then she noticed her mom waving for attention.

"Hey mag-anak! Dessert is out. We've got bibingka, leche flan, lengua de gato, cassava, and coconut macarons. Plus, Lola made ensaymada for everyone to take home!"

Eleora wasn't sure what to pick. Probably the butter cookies—they always melted in her mouth. She glanced over at Chadwick and smiled as she saw Agapito explaining each dessert to him.

Once everyone had their treats and returned to the living room, Tito Juan stood at the front.

"It's time for caroling! And this year, instead of YouTube, Lola tells me we have a pianist in the house. Chadwick, would you do the honors?"

Chadwick didn't even flinch. He smiled and said, "Sure! As long as I don't have to sing."

Everyone laughed. He sat at the baby grand, tested the keys, then nodded. Tito Juan began "Silent Night," and the room joined in.

If there was one thing the Gonzales family could do, it was sing.

Voices harmonized with ease. The family's perfect pitch shone through. Eleora loved the unity singing brought, even if she didn't believe the lyrics herself. She kept glancing at Chadwick, so at ease and expressive as he played.

When he transitioned into "O Holy Night," Tita Blessica's soprano filled the room. One song led to another, and they ended with Lola singing "Mary, Did You Know." Eleora noticed Chadwick whispering to himself and wiping his eyes.

What was that about? She'd have to ask later.

When he played the final note, the room erupted in applause.

"Thank you, Chadwick," Lola said warmly.

"You're very welcome. You all sounded amazing. Forget the Von Trapps—you're who people should be listening to!"

Laughter rippled around the room.

"Alright, my lovely family—Merry Christmas and Happy New Year!" Lola declared.

People stood and began saying goodbyes. After

more mano pos and tight cousin hugs, Eleora, Chadwick, and her mom made their way to the car.

Once they hit the main road, her mom asked, "How did you enjoy tonight?"

"Oh, it was great! I loved all the traditions—and the desserts were amazing. I'm sorry your husband couldn't make it."

"Yes, it's always a lovely time. A shame he got held up with a big case," her mom replied.

Eleora rolled her eyes. Larry always had an excuse—and Lola didn't like him anyway.

They dropped Chadwick off, then headed home.

After helping her mom put away the leftover food, Eleora went upstairs, changed into pajamas, and called Chadwick.

"Get out of my head—I was just about to call you," he said.

She giggled. "Missed me already?"

"Yes," he replied simply.

Her heart fluttered. "Same," she whispered. "I feel like I didn't even get much time with you tonight. I think Lola saw you more than I did!"

Chadwick laughed.

As they debriefed, Eleora remembered her conversation with Corazon. Was she in love with Chadwick?

He made her feel seen, safe, and special. He accepted her. Helped her see herself more clearly. He was kind, funny, humble—despite his talents and intelligence.

She couldn't imagine life without him. She didn't want a life without him.

Hay nako. I think I'm in love with him.

The thought filled her with both nerves and peace. It felt like the most natural thing in the world to love Chadwick.

For now, she'd keep that to herself—and hope he'd feel the same way soon.

Chapter 24

"Shhh. You're being so loud," Eleora whispered to Chadwick as they walked through the crunchy snow outside their school.

He shrugged. "I can't help the way the snow sounds. Why are we at school again? It's Christmas break!"

This earned him another shush. "It's a surprise," she insisted.

Chadwick wanted to argue. There were so many other things they could be doing for a date tonight. But then, before he could say anything, she turned backwards and smiled at him.

He was dazzled.

When would her smile not have that effect on him? Would he ever get immune to it? Did he even want that immunity?

They approached the front doors of the school, and then Eleora pulled out a key. Chadwick raised an eyebrow in surprise.

"Presidential perks." Her voice was sly as she unlocked the doors to the school.

Chadwick felt eerie being in the hallways when it was so quiet and dark. Maybe this wasn't a good idea.

"Come on. The surprise is still coming."

Chadwick obediently followed Eleora as they walked to the library and then to the back room.

"Didn't you already show me thi—oh."

Chadwick was dumbstruck. The room had been filled with electronic candles and fairy lights.

Eleora giggled at his reaction. "This is only part one of the surprise." She led him to sit on the couch.

And then she slowly unbuttoned and took off her long winter coat to reveal herself clad in red lingerie.

Her smile was confident, but her eyes revealed her nerves. She needed reassurance. She needed to know how in awe he was of her beauty.

"You're..." He searched for the right word and then it came to him. "Wondrous."

The smile then reached her eyes, and he knew he'd said the right thing.

"Now, is this one of those look-but-don't-touch situations or..." He trailed off as she giggled.

"Oh, you can touch." Her voice was sultry now. When had it become like this?

As she walked towards him, he jolted awake.

Chadwick groaned, torn between wanting to continue the dream and being grateful that it ended when it did.

As he glanced down, a wave of shame hit him since he realized he would need to change his underwear after the dream.

Chadwick sighed and opted to take a shower, hoping that he could wash the dream and its impact on him off. He wanted to feel clean. Cleansed. He felt gross, like how he'd feel after watching porn, which he hadn't done in weeks. Maybe even months.

But now he was having these fantasies? About Eleora?

How could his subconscious use her that way? What was wrong with him?

He needed to do better and to be better. That's what she deserved. She was brightness and joy, a sanctuary from his loneliness and self-doubt. She was his everything.

He loved her.

And he didn't want that love to be tainted by his lust.

Chapter 25

Eleora adjusted her dark green knit dress as she exited Chadwick's parents' car. She couldn't believe that she was back at church. She needed no other proof that she was in love with Chadwick; her being there was evidence enough. Her hand itched to hold his, but she kept it to herself. His family still didn't know that they were dating, so she had to treat him as just a friend. It was much harder than she'd thought it would be.

She followed his family into the church building and admired the decor. There were fairy lights and Christmas trees in the lobby. It was a bright space that made her think of a classy rec centre. His family waved to a few people but didn't stop to chat with anyone. Instead, they went through a set of double doors that led into an auditorium. The room was decorated with gold and fairy lights, with a large Christmas tree on the stage beside a wooden cross. Christmas music played in the background, and a large projector screen showed a countdown to the beginning of the service. His family moved to sit near the front on the left side of the room. She sat beside Chadwick and breathed slowly.

Chadwick leaned over to her and bent his head

toward her ear. "It's going to be okay. It'll be a shorter service since multiple ones are happening this morning. I have a feeling that you'll like it, but if at any moment you feel uncomfortable, you can leave and sit in the lobby." His words calmed her. She gave him what she hoped was a brave smile.

The lights dimmed when the countdown hit zero. The room quieted. When they came back on, a young Black woman dressed in green and gold was in the centre of the stage.

"O Christmas tree
O Christmas tree
Your evergreen freshness
Akin to the every season faithfulness
Of Your Maker

O Christmas tree
O Christmas tree
Your lights
On top, beneath, in front, behind
Bring to mind
The One who in the beginning
Spoke brightness into being
Would shine in our hearts through
His coming

O Christmas tree
O Christmas tree
Your star
A sign of the same who shepherded
Strangers
Scholars

Seekers
To their Saviour

O Christmas tree
O Christmas tree
Your wooden frame
Harkens back
To a cradle that held its Creator
To a cross that held its Creator

O Christmas tree
O Christmas tree
You incarnate the good news
And bring Jesus into clear view
For me again and again."

Eleora snapped once she was done reciting the poem. The writing was so well done, as was her performance. What a way to start a church service!

"Amen. Praise God for Eden's poetry that reminds us how everything this season is meant to point us to our Saviour. Feel free to remain seated and reflect upon this song that we're going to be singing over you." This was said by a man with a brown man bun and bright blue eyes. Once he finished speaking, the violinist and cello player began to play. It was a beautiful melody. The song was asking for God to remind them of the deeper meaning behind Christmas even amidst holiday fatigue. But the start of the song was the bridge. The string instruments reached a crescendo as all the singers harmonised, singing:

Glory in the highest

Glory in the lowest
Glory Emmanuel

As this was sung a few times, Eleora blinked back tears. She was familiar with the phrase 'Glory in the highest,' but the idea of glory being in the lowest resonated with her. When the song ended, she clapped enthusiastically along with everyone else.

"Well, we would love for all of you to stand up and join us for this next song!" the leader said, and the room complied. They sang O Come O Come Emmanuel and then We Three Kings. Then a Sri Lankan man came on the stage.

"Merry Christmas Eve, church and visitors. For those who don't know me, I'm Pastor Tavish, but I'm good with being called Tav. I have the privilege of being the teaching pastor here at ACC. We're going to have a good time together this morning! Let me pray for us and then we'll jump in."

To Eleora's surprise, he knelt on the stage and closed his eyes.

"Yahweh, thank You for the first coming of Christ. Thank You for seeking after us even before we ever sought after You. Help me, Lord, to unpack Your word rightly. May everyone who hears this message be drawn closer to You. In Jesus's name, amen."

After praying, Pastor Tav stood up. "Today, we are going to learn about and from the three wise men. Turn or scroll your Bible to Matthew chapter 2. We're going to unpack three Ts in this message. The first one is Travellers. Our text says: Now after Jesus was born in Bethlehem of Judea in the days of Herod the king, behold, magi from the east arrived in Jerusalem, saying,

'Where is He who has been born King of the Jews? For we saw His star in the east and have come to worship Him.'"

"First of all, what does the text mean by Magi? The Greek word used here describes a class of people who were priestly monarch rulers. They were also scholars specialising in astronomy, astrology, and science." So that was why they were called wise men, Eleora thought to herself. "They knew the stars, so when they saw this particular one they deduced that the meaning of it was that a King had been born, one that was worthy of them travelling all that way to worship him.

"Now, some scholars have guessed that the star may have been Haley's Comet or a planetary conjunction, basically two planets touching. In this case, it would've been Saturn and Jupiter. The star could also just be supernatural in origin, and that's why they reacted to it so conclusively — because it was unusual. Regardless of which it is, these magi teach us an important lesson: that the dichotomy we put between faith and science is unnecessary. The two can actually work together. Science is good for learning about what we can observe in the world, but it isn't meant to give us the meaning of what it observes. This is where faith comes in. It takes what we can observe and points us back to the One who made what we've observed possible. In your seeking, you don't have to jettison science and reason."

That was an interesting perspective that he was bringing — that one can be both religious and reasonable. She appreciated him saying this.

"So those are our travellers. Our next T is Trouble. In the next few verses, we see the reaction of King

Herod. He was troubled by the news that these magi brought, and all of Jerusalem with him. Why would that be? Well, Herod was an insecure king. He ruled with an iron fist to overcompensate for his insecurity. The city was troubled because they knew that if he was upset, people were going to die. Now, we might be tempted to lean on an old saying here: 'Power corrupts and absolute power corrupts absolutely.' I want to challenge that idea. The Bible tells us that people come pre-corrupted and that power reveals the corruption that was already there. In every human heart is a little King Herod — an insecure master of our own fate."

How did this man manage to say something so harsh with such gentleness? Eleora felt understood and challenged at the same time. What did insecurity look like in her life? How was she trying to run her life?

"Now, he wanted details about this king because their birth challenged his position. He's advised that he would be born in Bethlehem, as their scriptures have already predicted it. This shows us that in our seeking, we will eventually need to consult the scriptures and learn about God from God directly."

Interesting. She definitely wasn't at a point where she felt comfortable consulting the scriptures. Wait, when did she even accept that she was seeking? Was that why she was really at the service? Was some part of her still curious about her childhood faith? Even after all the pain it had caused her?

"Lastly, we have our last T: Treasure. We read that they follow the same star all the way to Jesus's home. They have finally found the one they were seeking. And what's the result? First, in verse 10 we see joy. Then in verse 11, we see worship. They worship him with three gifts: gold, frankincense, and myrrh. They each have symbolic meaning, which we actually sang about earlier!"

Was he saying that Christmas carols weren't just songs for a season, but that there was intention and depth to be found in the lyrics?

"The gold represents royalty. This is them saying that He is King. Frankincense was used for worship at the Temple. It represents deity or divinity, saying that He is God. Myrrh was a medicine and ointment rubbed on flesh that was used in Jewish burial. It is a sign that God came in flesh to die. And that happened. Jesus did die, taking upon himself the punishment for humanity's sins."

How did the magi know all these things about Jesus to have brought these specific gifts? She wished she could talk to them. It was definitely too on point to be coincidental. But did they really just get all of this from a star?

"And lastly, the third result of their seeking is relationship. Where do I get that? It says that they were warned in a dream about not going back to King Herod. They experienced communication with God that was more intimate than a star. They had entered into a relationship with Him. God loved them and orchestrated events so that they would meet Jesus. How did God do this in your life? How will you respond to Him tonight? You might not have realized you were searching for a king, but He has always been seeking you. If you don't yet believe in Jesus, I would gently challenge you to seek Him honestly. There is joy and intimacy waiting for you once you meet and worship Him."

His words hit her poignantly. Could God actually be real? Was she really seeking Him? Was He really seeking her? Even after she denied Him and turned her back on having any faith? Questions started to swirl in her mind, and she needed answers. Maybe it was time to start intentionally seeking after all.

Pastor Tav came off the stage, and the worship leader was back. They went into another version of We Three Kings, one that had more soul to it. The music was so good that everyone in the room was clapping and dancing. She laughed, amused at Chadwick doing a two-step with his parents to the song.

"We could go all day! But I know that everyone's families have Christmas plans, so we'll wrap up now. Merry Christmas and see you all on New Year's Eve! You are loved!"

Eleora smiled at his parting words; it was a nice sentiment. People started to leave their seats to go and talk to those around them. Some people walked over to their row to chat with Chadwick's parents. She decided to return to her seat. She had a lot to process. Chadwick sat back down too and leaned closer to her.

He wondered how Eleora was doing. She seemed to be engaged during the service, but it was hard to tell. He thought it had been great and that Tav had preached a good message, but had she internalized it?

"How are you doing right now? Do you need some space to process the service alone, or would it be helpful to do so out loud with me?" he asked her gently.

"Honestly, I'm not sure." She paused to think for a moment. "It was a good time! I mean, I enjoyed myself. The music and poetry were really great; and the message definitely has me asking some questions."

"Really?" He was surprised by this admission. He wanted to hope that this could mean she might be closer to accepting the faith, but he also feared disappointment.

"Yeah. For some reason, what he shared resonated with me. Maybe there is a part of me that's seeking? I don't know. With everything with my dad, I just jettisoned Christianity. That it must not be really true or its God must not be real because of everything that happened. I think there's a part of me that wants to be sure though, one way or another, of what's true. I know he mentioned reading the Bible, but I'm not there. It's way too triggering considering my past."

As Eleora would say, hay nako! The service had impacted her more than he'd dared hope. He tried not to show how excited he was about what she said. He didn't want to crowd her processing with his own emotions. "That's a lot that you just shared. Thanks for being so honest with me." He itched to hold her hand but had to school himself.

She nudged him playfully. "Of course I would be honest with you. You're…" She seemed at a loss for words. "…my safe place," she whispered.

Now, he really wanted to hold her hand or give her a hug. "You honour me with that privilege," he whispered back. Wow, he really loved her. How did he ever manage to just be her friend? Recalling that time, he was hit with an idea.

"Wait! I just remembered something. Remember how I told you that C.S. Lewis had written a book about Christianity?"

She nodded and then smiled; it looked like she was catching his drift. "You're thinking that maybe that can be my next step?"

"Yes, exactly! We can read it and discuss it together. How does that sound to you?"

Eleora looked thoughtful, but also excited.

"I love that idea!"

He almost hugged her in his excitement but settled for holding up his hand for a high five. She hit it enthusiastically and gave him a bright smile.

"So, Eleora, how do you feel about more cooking lessons?" Mrs. Nina asked her.

"I would really enjoy that, actually! What are you making?"

"Well, since oxtail is so expensive, I usually only make it for the holidays, so there's that. I was also thinking some jerk chicken and rice and peas."

"Mom, you're making me hungry just talking about all of this good food." His parents chuckled.

"If you're sure that I'm not infringing on family time, then I would be happy to stay, learn, and eat," Eleora said graciously.

"That's settled then. And actually, I think we still have your clothes from the first time you came over. You're welcome to stay in your dress, of course, but those may be more comfortable."

"I will definitely be taking you up on that suggestion."

Fairly soon, they arrived at the house. It had been snowing when they'd left for church, and it was still steadily coming down. After getting dressed in more casual clothes, Eleora and Mrs. Nina met in the kitchen. Chadwick and his dad went outside to shovel the snow.

"Alright, I already have the meat seasoned, and they've been marinating all morning. The oxtail will take about 2 hours, the rice and peas an hour and a half, and the jerk chicken about 45 minutes. Are you ready?"

Eleora rolled up her sleeves and pulled her curly hair into a high bun. "Let's do this."

She was careful to follow Mrs. Nina's directions, and soon the oxtail was on the stove. Then Eleora added the ingredients for the rice and peas under her supervision. Once that was done, Mrs. Nina set an alarm for when to check on it. At that moment, the men came in from shovelling.

"Now, we have some time. Care to join us for one of our family Christmas traditions?"

"Sure! What is it?"

"Jingle Jangle!" Chadwick said enthusiastically as he shook off the snow from his coat and hat. Eleora wished she could greet him with a quick kiss but made sure to hang back.

"It's a Christmas movie musical with a majority Black cast," Mrs. Nina explained.

"Say less. I'm definitely game for that!"

Chadwick got the movie set up on Netflix while his dad brought in some blankets and pillows.

It was easy to get pulled into the movie. The music was wonderful, and the world building was wholesome and whimsical. Every so often, Mrs. Nina would get up and go to the kitchen to check on the food and make sure everything was cooking well. The smell of the food permeated the house. If the movie wasn't so captivating, Eleora probably would've been more aware of how hungry she was. She cried at the movie's ending and inadvertently started to clap when she saw the credits. Chadwick noticed her tears and passed her a box of Kleenex. She smiled her thanks.

"Alright Chadwick, if you could please set the table, that'd be great. The food is ready."

Within a few minutes, everything was ready, and the four of them sat around the table.

"I'll just pray for us real quick, and then we can dig in," Mr. Knight said, extending his hands to his wife and son. They, in turn, each reached out a hand to Eleora. She felt privileged to be included like this. "Yahweh, thank You. Jesus, we are so grateful for your coming and for this time to honour and celebrate it. Lord, bless this food to be a blessing to our bodies. In Jesus's name, amen." With that, it was time to dish out the food.

"So, Eleora. How did you like Jingle Jangle? Do you have a favourite moment from the movie? Mine is the snowball fight. I love seeing Jeronicus beginning to warm up to his granddaughter," Mr. Knight shared and then took a bite of the food.

"Mine would be the importance they place on belief, and how it can lead to life," Mrs. Nina chimed in.

"I always end up coming back to the moment when Jeronicus gives Gustafson the part he needed for his invention and says that he would've taught him everything if he'd been patient. It always highlights to me the importance of our decisions." Chadwick shook his head as he shared his thoughts. "Also, the food is delicious! Well done!"

Eleora savoured the food as she took a moment to think about how vulnerable she wanted to be in her response. She decided to go all out.

"Well, that scene when Jeronicus shows his daughter all the letters he wrote but never sent? That got me all emotional. He was flawed and scared, but he did love her." She started to choke up and cleared her throat, putting down her eating utensils. "See, my father and I were also close like Jeronicus and Jessica, but we don't have a relationship anymore." She was mortified. Was she really about to start weeping in front of Chadwick's parents? "I guess a part of me wishes that what happened in the movie could be true for me too. That my dad still loves me and..." She couldn't say anything more as she was full on crying.

Mrs. Nina scooted her chair closer to Eleora and pulled her into a hug. She leaned into her warmth and allowed herself to cry freely. After a few minutes, the tears slowed, and Eleora began to pull back.

"Sorry about that," she whispered, cheeks flushed.

"You never have to apologize for your feelings, Eleora. Thank you for sharing all of this with us. It was very brave," Mr. Knight said gently, kindness and compassion radiating from his eyes.

"Thank you," she said timidly.

Chadwick smiled at her and then gestured to her plate. "Are you still planning to eat your food, or is it up for grabs?"

Eleora laughed, her smile returning. His grin deepened. "It is most definitely not available to anyone but me," she teased, making everyone chuckle.

With the tension broken, they all dug into the food together. The warmth of the house, the laughter, and the shared meal felt like a balm to Eleora's bruised heart.

Chapter 26

Chadwick was curious about what Eleora had planned for their date. It was Boxing Day, and they were meeting for their post-Christmas gift exchange. She had told him to meet her at the library, and that's where he was—waiting for her to arrive, holding a blue gift bag.

The only thing she'd told him about their time together was to dress warmly. He'd made sure to wear his thickest winter jacket, warm winter boots, and a few layers of track pants.

She came into the building dressed in a light blue snowsuit, thick winter boots, and a tuque, carrying a light green gift bag in her hands. He thought she was the most attractive snow bunny he'd ever seen. It shouldn't be possible for winter wear to be sexy, but on her, it was.

He waved to her as she scanned the room. Eleora gave him a big smile and gestured for him to come over. He obliged and walked over, scooping her into a tight hug when he was close enough. She rested her head on his shoulder and sighed. He pulled her closer and kissed the little bit of forehead exposed beneath her winter hat. Leaning toward her left ear, he whispered,

"It's great to see you, Belle." She shivered despite her warm clothes and pulled back from the hug.

"Are you ready for some winter fun?" Eleora asked mischievously.

"Sure! I'm excited to finally know what you have planned!" he said, his voice excited.

She took his hand and led him outside. While there was a slight chill, the sun was out, adding some warmth to the day. With the bright blue sky, it was a picturesque winter day. "We're walking across the street from the terminal to Chinguacousy Park," Eleora told him.

"Lead the way."

They walked together, sharing how each of their Christmas days had been, since they hadn't had a chance to chat the night before.

"Larry gave me an Amazon gift card for $300," she said with a shrug.

"I've been wondering about him. The times I've been over, he's never home. And he wasn't at your family dinner either."

"He works a lot. That seems to be where he is whenever he's awake. I don't know how my mom manages it."

"It seems like you don't like him?" he probed.

She nodded. "Yeah, I don't. He…" She searched for the words. "…is very charming and likes extravagance and big gestures. But in the little things, I feel like I've never really seen his true character. It was also super awkward because when he met me, he tried to be very dad-like. I didn't want that—it just turned me off. Especially since he never seemed to try to learn about our culture. My mom is the most 'white'…" She mimed quotation marks, "...when he's around." Eleora shrugged again. "It might be stupid, but I think Parent Trap sold me the divorced kid's dream of one's parents reuniting, so Larry also seemed like an obstacle to that."

"It's not stupid. I think it's completely understandable," he assured her.

"Oh, look—we're here," she pointed out as they walked into a large building toward the lockers. She quickly put both their gift bags inside and locked the locker with a lock she'd brought.

"Okay, we're in the chalet. Are we going skiing or snowboarding?" Chadwick asked.

"Well, I'm not sure if you can do either, so I picked something that needs no skill whatsoever: snow tubing!" she said dramatically, awaiting his enthusiastic response. Instead, she got confusion.

"What's that?"

"Are you serious?" she asked, surprised. "You've never been?! It's like a Canadian rite of passage!"

He chuckled at her dramatics. "Well, then I guess I ought to be eternally grateful to you for supplying this opportunity for such an important milestone," he teased, and she giggled.

"I dropped by here a few days ago to get our tickets. We have three hours on the hill. Let's go!"

She playfully dragged him outside to Chinguacousy Hill, toward the far-right side where a stack of what looked like inflatable donuts sat. Eleora grabbed one and gestured for him to do the same.

Once that was done, she led them to the ski lift. It looked like a flat escalator going up the hill.

"Oh shoot, you're not afraid of heights, are you?"

she asked.

"Not really, but I don't like the look of this lift. Does it really hold us? Will we not fall?" he asked nervously.

"Well, all those people on the lift have already made it safely to the top. I think we'll be fine," she said gently. He nodded, and they got on together.

Once they reached the top, she led them to the far right of the hill toward an employee. "Good afternoon!" she said cheerfully. "This is my boyfriend's first-time tubing. Can you give him a good spin for this run?"

"Sure thing, miss!" the employee said kindly. "Now, young man, you're going to want to sit and recline in the hole in the middle of the tube. You can put your hands on these handles, and then I'll send you down."

Chadwick was still unsure what exactly he was about to do, but he followed the directions given.

"Okay, get ready to go down in three, two, one!" the employee counted down. Suddenly, Chadwick was spun around and careening down the hill. He yelled with enjoyment as he built up speed. This was exhilarating! When it ended, he was disappointed—he would have continued downhill much longer if he could.

He got up from the tube and waved to Eleora, who was at the top of the hill. She waved back and soon got into her tube. Within minutes, she was by his side again.

"So... did you like it?" she asked.

"I loved it! C'mon, let's go again." He held out his hand, and she took it eagerly.

"I'm so glad! I enjoyed this a lot as a kid but

hadn't come here yet as an adult. It hasn't lost its thrill even later in life," she shared as they stepped onto the lift again.

Then they spent the next hour going down the hill—individually, together, and even racing one another. They had a blast.

"I love doing this, but I have to say I'm getting pretty hungry," Chadwick admitted.

"No worries. Let's take a break to eat and exchange gifts. We have a pass for three hours, so we can always come back for a few more runs afterwards," Eleora replied.

"Sounds good." They dropped off their tubes and went back inside the chalet.

They got their gift bags from the locker and went to get some food. Once seated beside each other on a couch in the lounge, they exchanged shy looks and gift bags.

"You open yours first," Eleora said nervously.

"All right, I wanted you to open yours last anyway," he said good-naturedly and pulled a long rectangular box out of the gift bag. His curiosity piqued, he opened it to see a stunning black stethoscope with Dr. C Knight engraved on it. He was astonished. This gift made him feel seen and validated in his dream of becoming a doctor.

"Ellie... you... I..." He couldn't find the words to express what he was feeling.

"Crap. You don't like it? Does it feel impersonal? I should've done something el—" Chadwick interrupted with a light kiss on her lips. When he pulled back, he saw a glazed look on her face. He smiled.

"I love it beyond words—that's why I was

struggling to speak earlier. Thank you for such a thoughtful gift."

She gave him a relieved smile. "You're not just saying that to make me feel better? You actually love it?"

"I very much do. Let's test it out." He took it out of the box and put in the earpieces, then placed the diaphragm on her chest, right above her heart.

The thud of her heart brought a smile to his face. He marveled at her gift—and the access to her heart that she was giving him.

"It's perfect." He carefully put the stethoscope back in the box. "Now it's your turn to open your gift." Now it was his turn to be nervous. Maybe it was too much too soon.

Eleora reached into the bag and pulled out a book titled Mere Christianity. "Is this the C.S. Lewis book that we talked about?" She asked him.

"Yep, but that was added after we chatted on Christmas eve. Your OG gift is still in there."

She reached in again and pulled out a small black velvet box. She stared at him aghast. "What did you do?"

"Just open it, Ellie." He encouraged her.

She took a deep breath and opened it to see a sterling silver ring with a small round diamond set in the center.

"It's beautiful." She whispered, shocked.

"Before you freak out, I'm not proposing." He said teasingly and she chuckled. "I'm promising."

"What do you mean by that?"

"Well, back when I first met your mom she asked me what my intentions are towards you. Do you remember that?"

Eleora nodded. "How could I forget? I was mortified."

"Well, you never heard my answer. What I essentially told her was that, for me, the end goal of dating is marriage and that's what I'm pursuing with you." He paused for a moment to gauge her reaction. She looked shocked, but not scared. Maybe, happy? He took her hands in his and made sure to look her in the eye for the next part of what he was going to say. "I love you, Eleora. I know we haven't been together for very long, but that's the only word I know to describe what I feel for you. I want a very long future with you. I'm asking you to accept my intentions towards you and the promise of love that I'm making to you."

She searched his face intently and could only find sincerity in his hazel eyes. Then Eleora gave him the brightest smile he'd ever seen on her face. "I love you too." She said quietly, but loudly enough for his heart to hear her and soar with joy. She loved him back. His feelings were reciprocated. They were truly on the same page and that page was love.

"Yeah?" He said boyishly.

"Yes." She said, her voice louder than before.

"Well, you managed to top your amazing Christmas gift in a matter of minutes. Your love is the best gift you could ever give me."

She blushed at his words and ducked her head to hide it.

Gently, he lifted her head up and pulled her face towards his and kissed her softly, slowly. She smiled with his lips on hers and kissed him back. Before they could get carried away, Chadwick remembered that they were in a public place and pulled back.

"Can you help me put this on?" she asked with glee.

He nodded. "Sure thing."

Chadwick reached for her right hand and slipped it on her ring finger. It was a little loose, but it fit.

"Sorry about the size not being right. I had to guess." He said sheepishly.

"Well, there would've been no subtle way to ask for my ring size." She joked. "No worries, but I don't want it to fall off..." her voice trailed off as she took a moment to think. "Ooh! I think I have an idea!"

Eleora took off her necklace and then slipped the ring off her finger. Then she threaded the ring onto her necklace chain. The ring knocked up against her locket. They looked good together.

"Here, let me help you put this back on." Chadwick offered and she nodded. Eleora turned around so that he faced her back and then lifted her hair off her neck. He placed the necklace lightly on her skin and deftly clasped it.

She let her hair fall back down and turned around to face him once more, smiling. "Thank you. For everything."

He grinned at her and grabbed one of her hands. "You're welcome, for everything."

They stayed like that for a few moments; gazing and smiling and basking in each other's presence and love.

Chapter 27

"I guess it's time to say goodbye now, eh?" Chadwick asked, his face on the screen looking disappointed.

Eleora nodded to him on the video call. "Yep, the titas and Lola will be here soon."

Chadwick sighed dramatically, making Eleora giggle. "You're such a royal, I can't even with you!"

She could understand the sentiment, though. The last few weeks of the New Year had been amazing with him. They studied together after school, unless one of them was working, and they usually hung out all day Saturday. Friday night and Sunday, Chadwick had to be at church, so that's when she spent time with Maryliz and her mom, respectively. It felt weird that she'd only be spending a few hours with him on a Saturday, but it was the only day that worked for planning her debut.

"With this humongous sacrifice that I'm making, this better be such an effective planning time!" She snorted at his dramatics, making him laugh.

"Well, I sure hope so. Debuts are usually super big and expensive, like planning a wedding. I don't need all of that; I'm only turning 18. I'm hoping to keep things small. We'll just see how the family feels about that."

Truthfully, she was a little nervous about how her vision would go over.

"Hey, they love you." His voice oozed reassurance. He must have heard the nerves in her voice. "I'm sure they'll want it to be an event that reflects you."

"Thanks. Here's hoping! I'll see you later, though?"

"Yep, just text me when things are winding down and I'll drive over." He confirmed.

"Sweet. Well, I'm terrible at goodbyes—I never know what to say."

He chuckled. "See you later, Belle. I love you."

She smiled as her heart fluttered at his closing words. She still wasn't used to him telling her that he loved her. "I love you, too. Bye!" She was happy to see his face light up at her response. She loved making him smile like that. He waved at her and then ended the call.

Eleora sighed happily and then got off her bed. She walked downstairs toward the kitchen, where she could hear her mother moving around. When Eleora got there, she saw that her mom was just slicing up some mango.

"I'll put out the plantain chips," Eleora offered. Her mother nodded, humming to herself. She loved seeing members of their extended family.

The living room was arrayed with the prepared snacks when they heard the doorbell ring. Eleora went to get the door and opened it to see her Lola and Tita Blessica. She moved for them to come in, and once their shoes were off, mano po'ed each of them. They gave her hugs afterward and headed toward the living room. She was about to close the door when she saw Tita Althea coming out of her car. She waved and kept the door open for her. When she got to the door, Eleora went through the motions of the mano po and then closed the door.

In the living room, everyone else was chatting happily with each other and snacking on either the mango or the plantain chips.

"Well, now that everyone is here, I think it's time to start!" Her mom said to the room. The women nodded their heads.

"Now, between the four of us, we've planned so many debuts that I think we can get this done fairly easily."

"Now, iha, tell us what you'd like."

Eleora cleared her throat. "I would like a small debut, just family and close friends. Maybe 50 people in total." She paused. The women looked surprised but not aghast. Emboldened by this, she continued. "I already have a venue that I really like. It's called the Alderlea, and it's in downtown Brampton. It's a beautiful house. I've also already found a caterer through them. They don't have any Filipino catering, unfortunately, but there's the option with a roast pig, which I figured would be good for us?" She was babbling.

"Breathe, Eleora. This all sounds very good. You've clearly already put some thought into your debut ahead of the meeting, which saves us a lot of time. Cora didn't know what she wanted! It took forever to plan!" Tita Blessica said, and the other women laughed. Eleora breathed a little easier. This was going better than she anticipated.

"Well, this year your birthday falls on the first Saturday of April. So, let's go with that day for your debut," her mother suggested, and Eleora nodded.

"Great. Can you send me the contact info for the venue and caterer? I'm going to call them now to reserve that date."

Eleora looked up the businesses on Google Maps and then shared the info with her mom over WhatsApp. Her mom left the room to make the calls.

"Are you picky about your photographer or DJ?" Tita Althea asked.

Eleora shook her head. "Okay, well then I can reach out to the ones who did Marikit's debut. They're Filipino, so it's nice to pour into the community."

Eleora wholeheartedly agreed with her. "That sounds great, Tita!"

"Okay, I'll take a page out of your mother's book and call them now. Emailing takes forever!" Tita Althea left the room, leaving Tita Blessica and Lola.

"So, Eleora, I have been using this new thing called Canva. Have you heard of it?"

Eleora nodded, bemused. Canva was a well-known web app.

"Well, I came up with a few invitation templates for you. Come over and let me know if you like any of them. Whatever design you choose can also be used for the program and seating chart."

Eleora took her Tita's phone and looked through the designs. They were actually pretty good! She scrolled until she came across one that she loved. It looked like marble with a mix of pastel purple, sky blue, and gold.

"Ooh, Tita! This one is beautiful!" she exclaimed, showing her the design that she liked.

"Ah, yes, that one is very nice. Now, let's choose your font." They spent the next 15 minutes fine-tuning the design and adding the details.

"Well, that was much easier than I expected!"

"Yes, it is, especially good that you already know what you like. That saves time. Alright, I think we should be good. Let me know when the menu and the seating chart are finalized, and I'll make the designs."

"Kahanga-hanga. So wonderful. Now, we must choose your royal court. We can use that as a jumping-off point for your guest list," Lola advised. "You must decide what you want: 18 roses and 18 candles, or 9 of each."

Eleora thought for a moment. "I want to keep things small, so let's go with 9. Roses are the males and candles are the females, right?" she clarified.

"Yes. You will dance with each of your roses, and your candles will say a word of encouragement to you."

"Well, I—"

"Hold that thought, iha." Her mom walked back into the living room. "We were able to book the place you wanted and the caterer. We just need to finalize the menu and seating with each. That, I can communicate to them over email," her mom informed them.

"Nanay, that's amazing! Thank you!" Eleora got up to hug her mom.

"You're welcome! Also, your aunt was able to get in touch with her people and reserve the date. She went to use the bathroom, so I'm passing the info along. Do you want to meet with them before the event?"

Immediately, Eleora shook her head. "Nope, as long as they show up on time and do what they're good at, I'm fine."

"That's what I thought," her mom responded. "Now, what were you going to say to your Lola?"

"Oh, I can't even remember now," Eleora admitted.

"Well, we've gotten a lot done. Let's see if we can nail down your guest list. Let's start with your court."

"Okay, for the guys, I'll do all my closest cousins, my friend Jason from school, and Chadwick. That's 9, right?"

"Oooh, yes! We need to learn more about this Chadwick," Tita Althea chimed in as she entered the room.

Eleora blushed. "Tita!"

"Your mother tells us that he's courting you. He is thinking of marriage!" Tita Blessica said excitedly.

"He's a nice Christian boy, and he speaks good Tagalog. He will be a good addition to the family," Lola said decisively.

"Maybe we should return to the court and guest list," her mom suggested. Eleora smiled gratefully at her.

"For the girls, I'll take my closest cousins, Tita Blessica, Tita Althea, Lola, and two of my friends from school. I think that makes 9."

"You honour us, niece," Tita Blessica said, her voice grateful.

"Okay, I've been adding your names to a Google Sheet. Including your Tito, Larry, yourself, and me, we are at 22. Who will be the remaining 28?" her mother asked.

"Do we have any remaining family? Because I have no other friends to include," Eleora answered.

"Oo. I shall invite my brother and his children and grandchildren. They are in the States. I think that will cover it. You have more family, but they are all in the

Philippines," Lola answered.

"Okay. Let's try to get all their names and addresses down now," her mother said. Tita Althea and Lola went to sit by her. Lola pulled out a small black leather book and Tita pulled out her phone.

"Between those three, they'll have all the info they need. Let's decide on a program while they do their stuff."

Eleora and her aunt finished the program. Then, she looked through the menu options available to her and picked what she wanted, sharing that with her aunt so she could work on the menu cards.

As they were finishing that up, her mom, Tita Althea, and Lola looked to have wrapped up what they were doing.

"We have a suggested grouping of people for the seating chart, iha. Come take a look."

Eleora obediently went to her mother and looked at her phone. It looked well grouped, divided mostly by gender and age bracket.

"That looks good to me, Nanay."

"Perfect! I will show it to Tita Blessica to make the seating chart."

"Oh! And I chose the menu. Tita Blessica has it."

"Blessi! When the menu and seating chart are done, send them to me, and I can pass them onto the caterer and venue."

"Of course, Ada. Come, look at the design your iha chose. It's beautiful," Tita Blessica responded.

Her mom went over to her, and the two compared phones.

"You have just about everything. We will send the invitations to be printed, and then you can work on mailing them. You will also need to work on a dance with your cousins. Other than those things, and getting a dress, you have no more things to do," Tita Althea told her.

Eleora nodded and added those things to her to-do list on her phone. She glanced at the time and was surprised that a few hours had flown by so quickly.

Her mom and Tita Blessica seemed to be finishing up, so she texted Chadwick to come and pick her up.

"Are we all done for today?" she asked the women.

Everyone nodded. "Oo. It was very productive. We have almost everything done," her mom said. "Would you all like to order in dinner and watch a movie?"

"Oo. There's a new drama on Netflix!" Tita Blessica said excitedly.

"I think I'm going to spend some time with Chadwick, if that's okay?" Eleora said tentatively.

"Of course! You two have fun, but not too much. I do not want to be a Lola anytime soon!" Her mom joked, and her aunts laughed.

"Hay nako! Nanay, of course not!" Eleora exclaimed.

Still laughing, her mom picked up a brochure for an Indian restaurant that she enjoyed. "Here, let us pick out our food."

Eleora listened as they debated which meals to get and then felt her phone buzz. She checked it to see a text from Chadwick saying that he was outside.

She grabbed her purse and made sure that her Mere Christianity book was packed. They were supposed to discuss it together.

"Paalam [Goodbye]! See you later. Love you," she called her goodbye and then left the house. She wanted to run to the car but was conscious of the ice on the ground. Gingerly, she made her way to the car and went in.

Once she was seated, Chadwick leaned over the gearshift to kiss her on the cheek.

"Hey, Belle."

"Hey yourself. Is where we're going a surprise, or can I know ahead of time?" she asked, putting on her seat belt. When he saw that she was buckled in, Chadwick pulled away from the curb.

"Well, I was thinking of a place that's meaningful to our relationship," he said vaguely.

"Are we going all the way to Malton?"

"No, earlier than that. Our first non-date." He hinted, and she smiled excitedly.

"Jollibee!"

Her enthusiasm made him laugh. "I'm guessing you like my idea?"

"Yep! Good decision."

As he drove to the mall, she filled him in on everything they'd gotten done that afternoon for her debut. He listened attentively.

"I'm glad my sacrifice was worth it," he teased, and she rolled her eyes.

Chadwick found a parking spot near the entrance to the restaurant, and they got out. They held hands as they walked over and entered the restaurant. It was fairly empty, which set a nice chill vibe for their time together.

They walked over to the counter, and Eleora ordered for them easily, but this time Chadwick paid for the food. As they waited for it to be ready, he stood behind her, his arms around her waist. She leaned backwards into him and sighed happily. His arms had quickly become her safe place.

When the food was ready, they grabbed a booth and laid it all out on the table. She waited while Chadwick said a quick prayer, and then they began to share their food.

"Okay, so what did you think of the book?" he asked.

"It was not what I expected. It's hard to believe that this is the same person who wrote children's fiction!"

"Yes, it's definitely more intellectual and philosophical," he concurred.

"Right! But it all made sense to me. I'd never thought before that so many different civilizations have had similar moral codes."

"How did you feel about his conclusion that the moral law points to the existence of a Being that gave humans this law?"

"Truthfully? It felt like a bit of a stretch. Humans having a fundamental sense of right and wrong could be an evolutionary development," she pointed out.

"That's fair pushback."

"But there was an argument that was compelling to me. Let me take out my copy; I don't want to butcher the quote." She placed her utensils down and pulled the book out of her purse.

"Okay, so it's on page 13. Yes, he writes: 'These, then, are the two points I wanted to make. First, that human beings, all over the earth, have this curious idea that they ought to behave in a certain way, and cannot really get rid of it. Secondly, that they do not in fact behave in that way. They know the Law of Nature; they break it. These two facts are the foundation of all clear thinking about ourselves and the universe we live in.' I found myself agreeing with these points, especially the second one. While having morality might be explained evolutionarily, our inability to stick to our own morals cannot be so easily explained."

Chadwick nodded. "Yeah, it's like we have the sense to know right and wrong, even if we believe that to be subjective, but we don't or can't follow it perfectly."

"I'm guessing this is where Adam and Eve come in, eh?" she asked.

"Yeah. The Christian explanation for that dilemma is that we were created to be perfectly good, but because of Adam and Eve's disobedience, we are imperfectly trying to be good," he explained.

"That still sounds a little far-fetched to me. But, at least it's an attempt to answer the question," she admitted.

"Yep, it is. Now, what are you thinking for the next section? I think it's like 15 pages or something. When do you think you'll want to discuss it?"

"Well, we have exams for the next week or so and then Valentine's Day. Maybe a month from now?" Eleora suggested.

"Sure." He agreed. She could tell that he was disappointed even though he was trying to hide it.

She felt this sudden need to make him happy by getting to it faster. But she didn't want to "seek" for his sake. She wanted to do it for herself. And moving up the timeline for him would conflate her spiritual journey with her love for him, and she didn't want that. Eleora wanted the two to be distinct.

The last time she'd coupled her spirituality with another person had gone badly, and she wanted it to be different this time.

Chapter 28

Chadwick turned the stove on low heat and then opened the oven to check on the garlic bread. It was coming along nicely. Satisfied that both the pasta and bread were good to go, he took the Caesar salad kit out of the fridge and tossed the salad in an appropriately sized bowl. He found some cling wrap in a kitchen drawer, covered the salad, and then returned it to the fridge. The bread still needed a bit more time, so he decided to set the table. He deliberated whether to put the chairs across from each other or side by side. Deciding on across, he put everything in its place. Then he strung fairy lights around the table and chairs.

Once that was done, he turned off the oven and checked his phone. Eleora's Uber was just around the corner. He slipped on his winter boots and climbed the stairs to the side entrance of the basement apartment.

As he rounded the corner to the driveway, he saw the Uber pull up. A puzzled Eleora emerged from the vehicle. Her confusion was warranted—they weren't at his house, but a random one in Brampton.

"I promise I'll answer your questions, but I didn't grab a jacket, so I'd rather do it inside," he said, rubbing his hands together for warmth.

She nodded and followed him to the side entrance on the right side of the house. Once inside, he led her down the stairs where there was a shoe rack and a coat stand.

When she hung up her winter jacket, he saw that she was wearing a beautiful, form-fitting red sweater dress with black leggings. "You look beautiful, Belle, as always," he complimented, kissing her on the cheek.

"Thank you! You don't look bad yourself," she responded. They matched, with him in a red turtleneck and dark jeans. "Now, where are we?" she asked as she walked through the door into a bright basement apartment. It was an open-concept layout for the kitchen, dining area, and living room—the latter having a large flat-screen TV with what looked like speakers built into the walls and a comfortable-looking sectional.

"This is a VRBO that I rented for our time together. I wanted to do something special for our first Valentine's Day, but I knew I couldn't do that at my place since my parents don't know we're together. This seemed like the next best option," he explained.

"Wow, you just told me it would be dinner and a movie. I wasn't expecting all of this, Chadwick!"

"Well, that's what we are doing. I made us dinner, and then we'll watch a movie that I think you'll really like."

"And that's it? There won't be anything more?" she clarified.

"More?" he asked, confused.

"Well, you booked this place for the night, and I'm assuming there's a bedroom..." Her voice trailed off.

A reddish tint spread across Chadwick's deep brown skin. He had been ignoring the whole bedroom and overnight booking situation. "Oh. Nope, just dinner and a movie," he stammered.

She smiled and placed a hand on his left shoulder. "No worries. Although, for the record, I would've been okay with more."

She would? She would really be comfortable spending the night with him? He gave himself a mental shake. Regardless of her comfort level, he had made a commitment to God that he wanted to keep.

Right?

"But I knew your values, so I wanted to check. It does give a slightly mixed message, though."

He nodded. "In hindsight, I can see that," he admitted. "But truly, I didn't see it as me booking a room as much as it was just a space with a kitchen and a good setup for movie watching. The door to the bedroom is closed, and I'm planning to keep it that way," he said firmly, more for his sake than hers.

"Sounds good. Now, where do you want me?" she asked.

He smiled and led her over to the table set for two. He pulled out her chair and pushed it closer to the table once she was seated. "If you'd just give me a moment, I'll bring the food to the table."

Eleora nodded and gave him a warm smile. He smiled back and quickly brought the salad, garlic bread, and pot of pasta to the table.

"This smells amazing!" she exclaimed.

"Hopefully it tastes that way," he joked. "Mind if I pray for us before we dig in?"

"Sure."

He closed his eyes and bowed his head. "God, thank you for this opportunity to spend time together.

Bless this food that I prepared and our evening. In Your name, amen."

When he opened his eyes, he saw that Eleora had a contemplative look on her face.

"Okay, so what we have here is Caesar salad, garlic bread, and what I like to call glorified mac and cheese. It has chicken, bell peppers, and spinach in it."

"Mmmm. Sounds yummy," she said appreciatively.

They each took turns dishing out their food and then began to eat. Chadwick was relieved that the food tasted good and that Eleora seemed to like it, too.

"So, what movie are we watching?" she asked between bites.

"Belle, to honor Black History Month, my family only watches shows and movies that feature a Black majority cast or share some Black history. This is a movie that my mom found a few years ago and loved. It's based on the true story of a half Black and half White woman who was raised as a gentlewoman in England before the abolition of slavery," he explained.

"That sounds amazing! I love period pieces—Pride and Prejudice, Bridgerton, Downton Abbey... I can't believe I'm just hearing about this movie now!" She said excitedly and enthusiastically took a big forkful of food.

"Whoa, slow down there! I promise we have enough time to watch it," he teased, and she giggled.

They went back and forth exchanging their favorite pieces of Black entertainment until dinner was done.

"For dessert, I just got us some two-bite brownies. Is that alright?"

"For sure! Those things are addictively good," she

said appreciatively.

"Well, I already have the movie set up. I just need to hit play. Feel free to pick a spot on the couch," he directed, handing her the tub of brownies and gesturing to the sectional.

She went to sit on the chaise part of the sectional while he grabbed the remote from the coffee table.

"How close do you want me to sit?" he asked.

She gave him a mischievous grin. "As close as you can. Because of our relationship, I've learned that I'm a cuddler."

He chuckled and motioned for her to move forward on the chaise. She scooted up, and he went behind her so that she was sitting between his legs. Eleora leaned back against his chest and sighed happily as his arms wrapped around her stomach.

"I'm guessing this is close enough?" he teased; she could feel his chest move with his laughter.

"This is perfect! Let's start the movie." She opened the tub of brownies and held it up for him to grab a few as the opening credits rolled.

Chapter 29

She loved it.

Partway through, she started to tear up. When the male romantic interest, Mr. Davinier, proclaimed his love for Belle, she squealed excitedly. When the ending credits started, she began to clap.

"That was better than I could've anticipated! There's just so much about it to love. Now, Knight, you know I love you, but Mr. Davinier would a hundred percent be my hall pass. He's just the perfect example of an ally. He treasures her Blackness without fetishizing it. He owns up to his mistakes and advocates for equality and true systemic change. If a woman of color marries a white guy, Mr. Davinier is the standard," she said enthusiastically.

He nodded. "I don't even feel a ways because he's as great as you said. I never thought of the purpose of the law as giving society boundaries and holding a teaching function until him," he said, reaching for a brownie.

"And the intersectionality! Like, the way they showed the complexity of race, gender, and class. Like Belle—less privileged with race and gender but rich. While Mr. Davinier is a white male, but poor. I just love how they gave us a multilayered view of people."

"Right. I also think this movie shows us the problem of color blindness. Mr. Ashford is a nice enough guy, but he sees her race as something to ignore or overlook. That's so problematic. Recognizing and honoring diversity is important! Like, if God had wanted us all to be the same, He would've made us that way—but He didn't!"

"It's the passion for me!" Eleora teased, and he laughed softly. "On a serious note, what does your faith say about race, if it addresses it at all?"

He was pleasantly surprised at her curiosity. "Well, it doesn't really talk about race. It more so focuses on ethnicity."

He felt Eleora nod. "That makes sense since race was literally a construct made by white people to subjugate others years after the Bible was put together."

He was impressed. "Okay, Ms. Academic. Go off!"

She giggled. "Was there more you were going to say?" she asked.

"Yeah, just that the Bible doesn't ascribe more worth to one ethnicity over another. Like, even when the Jews were the chosen people, there were foreigners still a part of their community. And beyond that, it says that in the future, heaven will be filled with people from every ethnicity and culture. There will be both unity and diversity," he explained.

"I love the way you put that: unity and diversity. I feel like I rarely see both of those things together. We're either super divided or people just take on color-blindness. What you described is so different but really beautiful," she commented.

He smiled at her openness to—and affirmation

of—a part of his faith. She was really getting closer to believing in God.

"Was there any way you related or resonated with Belle, seeing as you're both biracial?" he asked her.

"Hmm. Good question." A few moments passed before she spoke again. "Well, I think I relate to her feeling as if she doesn't fit in anywhere. My extended family on my mom's side has never made comments about my being darker or treated me differently, but I did struggle with the fact that I looked so different from them. With my mom, it's hard. She's always been the standard of beauty for me with lighter skin and straight hair. I used to wish we looked more alike so that I could be as beautiful as she is. That scene in the movie where Belle is struggling to comb her hair and the Black maid helps her? That was so real. One of the biggest losses from everything with my father was not having his mother in my life anymore. She's the one who knew how to do my hair. I've had to learn from trial and error and YouTube instead. Anyways, I've been talking for too long, haven't I? I'll shut up now."

He shook his head. "Aht aht. Oh no you don't. Your voice matters to me. I want to know these things about you, okay? I'm just glad you've trusted me enough to share all that you did. Really," Chadwick tried to put as much feeling into his words as possible.

"Thanks," she said quietly.

He was about to give her more reassurance when she surprised him by turning around to face him. Before he could fully register her change in position, she kissed him. His arms went around her, his hands on her waistline as he kissed her back. She leaned forward into him and put her arms around his neck, escalating the kiss. When he started to feel himself moving downward on the chaise to a horizontal position, he reluctantly broke the kiss and gently pushed her away.

"Well, that was unexpected," he said as he tried to catch his breath.

"I just didn't know how to put what I was feeling into words, so I kissed you instead," she explained breathily. "But I guess I totally disregarded our rules, eh? Sorry about that."

"I can't honestly say that I'm upset about it, though I probably should be," he admitted.

"Well, I'm glad that the pleasure I get from us kissing is mutual," she commented cheekily.

"Oh, it is. I pushed you away before you could feel just how attracted I am to you," he said dryly.

She looked surprised and then glanced down very quickly. "Oh."

"Yes. And on that note, I should bring you back home."

"But you still have so much cleaning up to do!" she protested.

"I can do it after I drop you off."

"Nope. Your mom rubbed off on me. You cooked, so I should clean—or at least help with the cleaning," Eleora said firmly.

He held up his hands in surrender. "Fair enough. I really just have to put the remaining food in the compost and then rinse the dishes and run them in the dishwasher. It shouldn't take too long."

She got off the couch and walked toward the kitchen. "Alright then, let's get to it."

He followed her to the kitchen, and they made quick work of cleaning up. Before long, they were done. While she went to the bathroom, he did a final cleanliness check and then started to put on his winter wear. She joined him fairly quickly, and they left soon after. They drove in peaceful silence.

With a quick kiss on the cheek, Eleora jumped out of the car and walked quickly to the front door. When she got inside, she was happy to be warm again.

What an amazing Valentine's date. He had sure made her first memorable, even if they couldn't be together on the actual day. She had been stuck on what to do for him until an idea hit her when she was rinsing the dishes. A poem had started to form in her mind. She had gone to the bathroom to grab a few moments to write down her ideas. Now that she was home, she could get it all down.

***

It was now Valentine's Day. For the past couple of days, she had been going back and forth on how to deliver the poem to him. But she'd finally landed on what she was going to do. It was harder than she expected to hide this from him. She hadn't realized how instinctive it had become to tell him everything.

Finally, it was lunchtime. Her hands shook with nerves as she packed up her books and walked to her locker. After dumping her books, she headed to the cafeteria. She just hoped Maryliz had been able to come through with getting the help of the A/V club.

When she entered the room, she saw Maryliz beside a speaker and holding a cordless mic. Eleora rushed to her and gave her a big hug. "You're the best!"

"Yes, I am. Are you ready?"

Eleora nodded. "As I'll ever be."

She only had to wait a few moments for Chadwick

to enter the room with Jason, who had been under strict orders to delay Chadwick's arrival until Maryliz texted him that they were all set. Taking a deep breath, she walked on top of her friend's table. The room slowly started to quiet down at her ascent. Phones were held up to record whatever was about to happen.

Then Chadwick noticed her and stopped in his tracks. Feeling emboldened by the love she felt at seeing him, she turned on the mic.

"Happy Valentine's Day, my Lions!" she started, and people began to cheer. "I hope y'all don't mind me monopolizing your time for the next few minutes. Chadwick, this is for you." She took a deep breath and then recited the poem she'd written and memorized:

He calls me Belle
And my heart smiles

Belle
The bookworm in an old fairytale
Who fell in love with a soul hidden within a Beast
Her sacrifice a key into the love story
That was better than anything she'd read

Belle
Dido Elisabeth struggling to know her place in this world
Where black and female are equally of no merit
No matter the wealth, it's your skin you inherit
And must learn to cherish
For few people will

Does he have any clue what this

Nickname does to the core of me?
What a treasure it is
How precious it is to receive
And my soul longs to respond

I will be your Belle
If you will be my Beast
Becoming my best friend
Who sweeps me away into a dance
That I trust you to lead well
A library of chance
A more-than-montage romance

And I will be your Belle
If you would be willing to break social convention and
barriers to be with me
If you would let your zeal and convictions drive you to
action
If you would see and treasure my biraciality

Yes, I will be your Belle if you'll be my Beast
My tale as old as time
I will be your Belle if you'll be my Mr. Davinier
Championing the causes of today

I am His Belle
And He is all of the above to me
And more
I wonder what our future has in store
I just hope it will include
You as my escort for my debut.

The room was silent for a moment, then applause

erupted. She barely noticed the cheers; all she cared about was what Chadwick thought. He looked dazed but happy. She stepped off the table and walked over to him.

"So?"

"Yes. Of course I'll come to your debut with you!" he said, picking her up and spinning her around. She laughed with glee. When he put her down, he pulled her into a tight hug. "Thank you for that poem. I loved it. I love you," he whispered into her ear.

"I love you too. Happy Valentine's Day," she whispered back. And then they kissed to the hoots and hollers of the cafeteria.

Chapter 30

"Chadwick! We're leaving in five minutes!"

He groaned at his mom's loud voice. He was so tired after staying up with Eleora the night before. A part of him wanted to stay in bed and skip church that Sunday morning.

Yet, he felt a strong sense that he needed to be at the service. Chadwick hadn't felt God's presence in a while, probably because he was barely praying or reading his Bible, so this impression he was getting from the Lord felt like a friend he hadn't seen in a while reaching out to him.

Someone he missed.

Quickly, he got out of bed, brushed his teeth while throwing on clothes, and rushed downstairs.

His dad raised an eyebrow at his bedraggled appearance but then gave him a warm smile. "I'm glad you're coming this morning, son."

"Thanks, Dad."

His father surprised him by giving him a quick but firm side hug before walking to the car. Chadwick blinked back tears at his father's unexpected embrace as he followed him to the vehicle.

The ride over to the church was quiet, almost as if his parents could tell he needed the silence—that this morning was going to be significant in some way.

As soon as they arrived at the church building, they parked in their usual spot and went straight to the right side of the sanctuary, where they often sat.

While his parents mingled with other church members, Chadwick stayed in his seat. Deep in his soul, he felt antsy—like something was coming.

But he wasn't sure it was something he would like.

Soon, Pastor Ben's familiar face came on stage and began leading them in a lively song about being God's family.

"All His children,
Clean hands, Pure hearts,
Good grace, Good God,
His Name is Jesus."

As they sang this part of the bridge a few times, Chadwick began to wonder what it meant to have clean hands and a pure heart.

To his surprise, after only one song, Pastor Tav came on stage.

"Hey everyone. We're going to dive into the message today and then respond in song. Please join me in bowing your heads as I pray." Per usual, Tav knelt on the stage. But this time, he was silent. Then, Chadwick heard him crying. Concerned that his pastor might genuinely not be okay, he wanted to bring him a tissue.

"Lord," Tav started in a choked voice, "we need You to speak. Let Your Word do what only it can do—change hearts by Your power. Let there be repentance and personal revival. May the wanderers return to the flock. May I not get in the way. Amen." Tav got up and faced them. "I know it may seem odd to see your pastor cry, but Jesus wept, amen?"

"Amen!" a few people called out in response.

"Thank you." Tav gave the room his customary warm smile. "Now, today's word is a hard one. But it's necessary. It was needed for me personally, and it is my prayer that it is a blessing to you. Please turn your Bibles to James chapter 4. We've been going through this book slowly, but today we're knocking out a whole chapter! I want you to see at least three things in the text today: our sin, God's invitation, and our response."

He took a swig of water. "Let's dive in. The first five verses describe the sinful attitudes and behaviors of the believers James was writing to. They are following the ways of the world—lusting, envying, and doing things motivated by self-interest. They do what they want no matter the cost, be it quarrelling, fighting, or even murder! James calls this adultery, as if these Christians are cheating on their covenant with God. One commentary writer put it this way: 'Are you following the wisdom of the world while claiming to be a Christian believer? If so, you're cheating on God with this world system of serving yourself first and at all costs.'"

Chadwick felt exposed. He was struggling with lust. And even what he prayed—when he did pray— was for Eleora's salvation. But that was from a place of self-interest, wasn't it? Because he wanted to stop avoiding the guilt he felt at dating her. He wanted to be with her, no matter what. Even if it meant compromising his integrity and values.

"Anyone else feeling convicted in the room?" Tav

said lightly, causing nervous chuckles to erupt. "Now, we go to God's invitation. Let's read verses six through twelve. Let's start with verses eleven and twelve. There are two implications of this: we don't slander others in our judgment because we are not the Judge. We also cannot judge ourselves to be right when we are wrong; only God gets to determine what's right and wrong. God is the one with the right to judge us. But verse six tells us that He gives greater grace! Even when He opposes you in your sin, He doesn't necessarily reject you. He is willing to offer grace—we must only repent. Verses seven through ten describe six aspects of repentance: we resist temptation, we go to God, we surrender our hearts, we change our actions, we weep over our sin and what it has done to our relationship with God, and we humble ourselves before God."

That was what the clean hands and pure hearts meant. Repentance. Tears came to Chadwick's eyes. God was in opposition to him and his choice to date Eleora, but he was not rejected or kicked out of God's family. God just wanted him to return, to repent.

"We serve a good God who can be both just and gracious because the penalty for our sin was paid for already in Jesus' death on the cross. Praise God! Now, it's time for our response. Let's look at the last five verses of the chapter."

Chadwick read them on his phone and was a bit confused.

"It seems a bit out of left field, eh? To be talking about boasting and making plans? The point James is making is that of humility. One commentary put it this way: 'In true humility, Christians understand that their lives are fragile and short. Unless God allows it, they can accomplish nothing.' We must respond to God's invitation to repent with humility and dependence upon Him. This humble dependence on God leads to obedience and righteousness, which we see in verse seventeen. I'll read it for us: 'Therefore, to one who knows to do the right thing and does not do it, to him it is sin.'"

Chadwick felt a chill go up his spine. He'd continued to tell himself that he technically wasn't sinning because he hadn't married a nonbeliever. But this verse threw that out. He knew the right thing to do and wasn't doing it, so he was in sin.

While these thoughts hit him, Pastor Tav left the stage and Pastor Ben took his place with the band.

"We're going to respond in song to this message as an opportunity for prayerful reflection. You can stand, sit, or even kneel. The point of this time is to connect with God and get right with Him."

Chadwick opted to sit as a simple song asking God to give them clean hands and pure hearts was sung. He struggled to sing the words. He knew what he should do, but really didn't want to do it.

The next song was about God leading them to the cross to behold Jesus's sacrifice and respond with surrender. His tears returned. He couldn't think of the cross without being moved by the sacrificial love of God. Jesus literally died the worst death for him. All He asked was that Chadwick would live for Him instead of for himself.

Lord, I love You. I want to live for You. But I don't want to give up Eleora. I love her, too.

"As we sing this last song, I want to invite you to be real with God. Repentance isn't something we muscle ourselves through with willpower and theological truth. Repentance is a work that the Spirit does in and with us. So, ask Him for help to do what He's called you to do." After saying these words, Pastor Ben led them in a song expressing their need for God.

Chadwick bowed his head. God, I know what You want me to do. You told me from the very beginning to just be Eleora's friend. But I didn't listen. Now, I love her and I don't know how to go back. I don't want to go back. I need Your help. Help me repent. Amen.

As the band wound down, Pastor Tav came back on stage. "It was a hard message today, but needed. I want to invite you to speak to your small group leaders or pastors or parents about what came up for you from today's services. We repent as individuals but are held accountable in community. Have a great week, family. You are loved!"

He heard Tav's words about speaking to someone but felt hit with so much shame. Opening up about Eleora and asking for prayer would expose all the lying and hiding he'd been doing for the last few months. He couldn't bear the thought of Pastor Gabe's or his parents' disappointment in him.

But he also knew that he couldn't get right with God by himself either.

What was he to do?

Chapter 31

Eleora sat on her bed, rereading the email on her phone screen.

Dear Eleora,

Congratulations on your academic achievement! On behalf of the University of Victoria, I am pleased to offer you conditional admission beginning in September 2025...

She got in.

She'd applied on a whim and was accepted!

She nearly dropped her phone in shock.

Eleora didn't know how to process this. She knew she should feel joy, but all she felt was despair. Even though she got in, she couldn't actually go.

She'd already received offers for the nursing programs she'd applied to. And her mom didn't even know she'd sent an application to UVic. She began to regret applying. It was worse to have to reject the program of her dreams than to have never applied at all.

Eleora wiped the tears beginning to form in her eyes. Why had she even applied? That was stupid. She was stupid. How could she indulge her fantasy like that? Why did she have to dream of a future where she studied what she wanted? Having now tasted the opportunity of a life that would really bring her joy, anything else would be a stark disappointment. Now, a future that could have been satisfactory would feel burdensome.

Hopeless.

Not even worth living.

But what was the alternative? Follow her dream but lose the only parent she had?

That wasn't a future she wanted either.

She should've never put herself in this position. She was so stupid for doing so.

"Stupid. Stupid. Stupid," Eleora whispered aloud. And suddenly, a thought came to mind that had always been lurking but was normally kept at bay:

No wonder her dad hadn't wanted her in his life.

That one thought opened a torrent in her mind.

He knew what everyone else had yet to realize: that she was worthless.

Worthless. Worthless. Worthless.

And stupid. Stupid. Stupid.

Only a burden to the people around her.

Eventually, they'd all realize this about her and reject her too.

Her mother.

Maryliz.

Chadwick.

She'd be all alone.

Eleora started to sob as her mind ran that thought on a loop.

Alone. Alone. Alone.

No one would love her.

No one. No one. No one.

With blurry vision, she swiped to call Maryliz.

"Belle?"

Looks like she'd called Chadwick by mistake.

His voice just made her cry more. One day, he wouldn't call her Belle anymore. He'd call her burden. She'd have to be without him. Eleora couldn't even imagine that.

"Belle, are you okay? It sounds like you're crying. Say something, please."

"Just break up with me already. Rip off the bandaid. Stop pretending to love me." She said hysterically between sobs.

For a moment, there was silence. Maybe he'd hung up to not be in her life anymore.

"I'm coming over," he said firmly. She heard movement in the background: drawers opening and closing, rustling clothes, the clink of keys, doors opening and closing, and then the sound of an engine starting.

"I'm driving now and have you on speaker. I'll be by soon."

She barely registered his words, curling into a ball on her bed and crying her eyes out.

It felt like no time had passed when she heard a knocking. Eleora looked around to find its source and saw Chadwick at her window. She walked over in a trance-like state to open it. As soon as she undid the latch, he pushed open the window and let himself in.

He dropped his backpack, took off his shoes, and pulled her into a hug. She collapsed in his arms, her legs barely holding her up, her head against his chest. He adjusted to bear her weight. "I've got you, okay, Belle? I've got you. I'm not going anywhere."

She vehemently shook her head. "No! You're

going to leave me!" she exclaimed, still sobbing.

He tenderly lifted her head to look into her blurry gray eyes. She was struck again by how beautiful his hazel eyes were. "I have no idea where this is coming from, Belle. But I'm not going to leave you. I love you. I want to be with you."

Eleora started to shake him again, but he stopped her with a light hand. With his other hand, he touched the ring he'd given her resting just above her collarbone. Then, he took one of her hands and brought it to the ring. "Do you feel that? That's the ring I gave you. That's the promise I made to you. I'm not going anywhere, Belle."

The touch of the cool metal against her fingertips lifted the haze she was in. She looked at him with a more focused gaze. "You're not going to leave me?" It was more a question than a statement.

He nodded emphatically. "That's right."

"You don't think that I'm worthless and stupid? I'm not a burden to you?"

"You are none of those things, Eleora. I have never thought of you that way. Ever."

She clung to him tightly at those words, desperate for them to be true.

He deftly lifted her, scooping her legs under one arm, and carried her to her bed. He tried to put her down, but she wouldn't let go, afraid he really might leave her.

"I'll come right beside you, okay? I'm not going anywhere." He repeated.

Eleora nodded and reluctantly let go. Within seconds he was sitting beside her, his back against the headboard. Chadwick wrapped an arm around her, and she leaned into him. Her ear was against his heartbeat. The thump-thump of his heart began to drown out the thoughts until she had a semblance of mental quiet. Exhausted and finally at peace, she fell asleep.

Chapter 32

Chadwick was flabbergasted. He had no clue what had just happened, what was going on with his girlfriend—the hysterics, the self-hateful things she'd said.

He was worried.

With his free arm, he took his phone out of his sweatpants pocket. It was only 7:20 a.m., but he felt like a whole day had gone by. He swiped to call Maryliz.

"Chadwick?"

"Hey Liz. So, I'm with Eleora right now. She's... had a rough morning and I don't think she'll be making it to school today. Think you can cover for her?"

"Of course." She answered immediately.

He released the breath he hadn't realized he'd been holding. "Thanks."

"No problem. It's the Friday going into March Break anyway, so there won't be much to miss. But what exactly is happening?"

"I'm genuinely not sure. She called me sobbing and saying that I was going to break up with her. It was high-key confusing and worrying, so I drove over. It took some time for her to believe me, and then she fell asleep."

"Hmm. You know what happened with her dad, right?" Maryliz said cautiously.

"Yep." He answered.

"Well, I low-key think Elle has a whole fear-of-abandonment thing because of that. I recently learned about something called the Enneagram, have you heard of it?"

He shook his head and then remembered that she couldn't see him. "No, I haven't."

"Well, it's not important to go through it all right now, but it's like a personality thing. I was looking into it and came across one of the personalities—they call them types—that felt like it fit Eleora to a tee. I legit felt like I was reading about my best friend. Basically, they try to be perfect to be loved and struggle with a deep fear that the people they love will reject or abandon them."

"That's both interesting and heartbreaking," he commented.

"I know, right? And I love Elle, but she does so much. Student president, all the different clubs, working, and three specializations. It's a lot. She would run herself ragged doing all these things. I've always wondered why. But now it's hitting me that she may do it all because she's worried about not being loved if she doesn't. That's a pretty compelling motivation." She paused. "Truthfully, I'd been on the lookout for burnout until she started dating you. Then she started to actually rest and have fun, so I was less worried. I don't know what triggered all this, but something must have made this fear come right to the surface."

"That makes sense." He agreed. Then something

else came to mind. "She also talked about being a burden. Isn't that idea connected to depression? I'm trying to remember things from the intro to psych class I took last year."

"I think so. Let me Google that real quick." He heard a tapping sound.

"Yikes. It is. And it's a thought that can be associated with suicidal thoughts."

He gasped. "Suicide?"

"Yeah." Her voice was solemn. "Okay. Let's not rush right to the worst-case scenario here. But maybe you should stay with her." He practically heard the words: Just in case.

"I was already planning to."

"Great. I'll come over after school. Also, according to Dr. Google, be on the lookout for these things: appetite changes, sleepiness, irritability, and lack of interest in things she normally likes."

"Got it. Thank Liz."

"No problem, Chad. Take care of our girl."

"I will." He promised, and they got off the phone.

Still feeling worried, he decided to pray. "Lord, I don't know what's happening right now with Eleora. But You know, and You've got everything in Your hands. Help me to be the support and encouragement she needs. May I be a vessel of Your love to her. I can't do this without You. Amen."

Gingerly, he moved the arm that was around Eleora and positioned her more comfortably on the bed. Then, he went to get his backpack. He brought it back to his spot on her bed, reached into his bag, grabbed a book he was reading, and settled into a comfortable position.

About an hour passed before Eleora woke up. He felt her stare and looked up from his book.

"Hey Belle," he said carefully. "Where are you at right now?"

"I don't know."

"That's okay. Do you want to rewind for me and tell me what happened?"

She sat up. "Well, first this happened." She handed him her phone.

He saw the email from UVic. "This is great news! Congratulations."

Eleora shook her head. "No, not congratulations. I can't even go."

"Well, I know your mom is a barrier, but it's not impossible."

She started to look angry. "You just don't understand. Can we just drop it?" It wasn't a question.

He held up his hands to indicate surrender. "Consider it dropped. Do you want to get something to eat from the kitchen?"

"No, I'm not hungry. I just want to lie here."

"Are you sure? We could go for a jog together. It's not too cold outside; it's a pretty nice March day," he suggested.

"No. Staying in bed sounds better to me."

"Okay, then staying here is what we'll do. Want me to grab a book for you from your library?"

"That would be great, actually." Finally, he got to see her smile.

He smiled back. "Sweet. What would you like?"

And just like that, they spent a few hours reading. When they had both finished their books, Chadwick ordered some Jamaican food for lunch. She didn't eat much, but at least she ate something.

Then, they went back to reading more books until Maryliz texted that she was outside. Eleora showed no signs of moving from bed, so he went to get her.

"How is she?" Maryliz asked as she walked in.

"Irritable, not eating, and refusing to leave her bed. The only good thing is that she's still interested in books."

"Okay. Could be better, but also could be worse," she summarized.

"Exactly." He agreed.

They walked upstairs together. "Hey Elle!" Maryliz said in a lighthearted tone.

Eleora's face brightened slightly. "Hey Maryliz."

"Mind if I kick out your boyfriend for some girl time? It is Friday after all."

"Oh, that's right. I'd forgotten what day of the week it was," Eleora responded numbly. "Sure."

"Okay then. I love you, Belle." He leaned down to give her a kiss on the cheek and grabbed his backpack. "I'll see you tomorrow?"

She nodded.

"Text me if you need anything." Now both nodded.

With that, he left the room.

Later that night, Maryliz called him. "Hey Chad, I figured you'd want an update on Elle?"

"You figured right," he responded. "What's happened since I left?"

"Pretty much what seemed to be happening when you left. She would only read books. She didn't want to talk about anything. I had to force her to eat something and then she fell asleep. I'm worried about her. Especially since her mom and Larry decided to go on a cruise for the next week, so she'll be alone at home."

He didn't know her parents were going to be away. This wasn't good.

"Shoot."

"Yep, my thoughts exactly. I figure we can maybe alternate days of being with her over the course of the week? If she's primarily worried about being abandoned, hopefully us being with her every day will be a tangible reminder that her fear is unfounded."

"Okay, I like that idea. We may not know exactly what she needs, but at least we can offer her our presence. Hopefully, that'll prove enough to bring her back to herself."

"Yeah, hopefully." Maryliz didn't sound hopeful. He could understand why; he was worried about Eleora as well.

He went to bed that night praying for her and woke up with her on his mind. He quickly got ready and started to drive to Eleora's house. Chadwick stopped at Tim Hortons on the way and picked up Timbits and bagels for breakfast. When he arrived, he called her.

"Knight?"

She said tentatively.

"Yeah, Belle. It's me. I'm outside, but my hands will be too full to climb up your ladder this time."

"Don't worry about that. The door has been unlocked since Maryliz left last night." He was concerned she didn't realize how unsafe that was but decided not to say anything right then.

"Okay. Do you want to meet me downstairs to have breakfast?"

"No. I want to stay in bed." Well, he'd tried.

"All right, then breakfast in bed it will be," he said,

trying to infuse cheer into his voice. "See you soon."

She hung up without another word.

"Lord, please help me today with Eleora. Help me to love her well. Help her to open up. I can't do this by myself. Amen." He uttered the prayer as he left the car and walked to the front door.

As she'd said, it was unlocked. He took off his shoes and brought everything upstairs. She was still in bed, wearing the same clothes as yesterday.

"Hey Belle," he said and gave her a kiss on the cheek. At least that made her smile.

He settled beside her and spread out the food on the bed. He was about to prod her to eat when she suddenly said, "I wrote a poem."

"Yeah? What about?"

"About how I've been feeling." Her voice was nervous, but he would take nervous over numb.

"Will you share it with me?" he asked.

She nodded, pulled out her phone, and started to read:

Empty breaths
That's all (I feel) I am
Smiles and cries
Displaced by intermittent sighs
Bereft of zeal
Void of drive
Blah incarnate
Meh personified
Aimlessly
Drifting
Waiting for
Something to wait for

Besides my death.

"You never fail to amaze me with your writing, Belle."

She cracked a smile at that. "Thanks."

"I appreciate you giving me a window into what you're feeling. But I have to ask—you referenced death. Do you have a suicide plan?" He asked carefully. From what he'd read online, you have to confront suicidality head-on.

Eleora shook her head, and he inwardly sighed in relief. "Okay, I have another question if that's okay?"

She nodded.

"Your poem sounds like it's describing numbness. Is that right?"

She nodded again.

"So, my question is: what led to this numbness?"

A moment passed without her responding. He was about to redirect the conversation when she said, "It's the only way to turn off the despair and silence the thoughts."

"So, it serves a purpose. Like it's... protecting you?"

"Yes." She sounded relieved that he understood.

"All right. Would you be able to tell me what the thoughts are? Maybe I can join the team fighting against them?"

She shook her head. "I'm afraid if I let myself go back to the thoughts to share them with you, I'll drown in them."

"That's heavy. Okay, understood. From what I remember from yesterday, there seemed to be a thought of me leaving you and a thought of being a burden. Is that right?"

She nodded.

"Well then, let me speak to those thoughts. I love you. I want to be with you. You're not a burden—you're a blessing in my life. Maryliz and I, and many others, want you here."

He saw tears form in her eyes as a result of his words.

"I needed to hear that. Thank you."

"You're welcome. Maybe we can make this a routine? You can continue to write poetry to describe how you feel, and then we can talk about it together?" Would she go for this idea? Was it something that would actually be helpful? He had no idea what he was doing, but he wanted to sustain momentum.

"Okay, we can try that. Now, could we maybe start eating? I'm starving." He smiled at that. She was actually initiating eating something! Maybe there was reason to hope after all.

Chapter 33

Maryliz's words from earlier that day reverberated through Eleora's mind. "You might need to talk to someone about how you're feeling besides Chad and me. Or, maybe you could at least journal about how you're feeling? I don't know. I just want you to feel better, Eleora." She'd held out a silver-gray journal to her that had an attached pen.

Eleora sighed. She wasn't ready to consider therapy, but she could journal. It would help with her writing poetry to share with Knight anyway. She was also curious about using something beyond her phone's Notes app for writing.

She grabbed the journal and stared at the blank page. How should she start this?

Dear   Journal,

There. She could do it like a letter.

I'm so thankful for Maryliz being with me today. Her friendship is such a gift to me. She gently, but firmly, made me take a shower. I didn't realize that doing little personal hygiene tasks was so important for my mood. It felt good to care about myself. We even left the house to go for a walk! The fresh air felt nice, refreshing. It was a good reminder that the world is bigger than what's happening in my head.

My head still feels really bad in here. Both the shower and the walk helped me break out of my numbness. But now it's like an onslaught in my mind of all these hateful and dark thoughts. I feel like the angry voice is yelling at me, trying to drown out the love I feel from Maryliz and Knight.

Hmmm. A poem is brewing in my head.

Eleora paused, took a deep breath, and then let the words flow out of her through her pen onto the page.

> *There's a tension between*
> *What I know and what I believe*
> *They love you*
> *They despise you*
> *You're wanted*
> *You're tolerated*
> *You're a blessing*
> *You're a burden*
>
> *A battle being fought*
> *An identity tug-of-war*
> *A tennis match of thoughts*
> *One side a whisper, the other a roar*
> *This conflict is exhausting*
> *I just want to rest*
> *Respite from all the pulling*
> *Maybe I can find that in death?*

Tears fell onto the page as she reread her poem. She hated that death seemed so appealing to her. She was scaring herself a bit.

But numbness wasn't really an option either. At

least now she could also feel the good, even if it seemed lesser in weight than the hard.

It felt frightening to feel because her emotions were a mess—a chaos that threatened to consume her until there was nothing left.

Chapter 34

It was Monday, and Chadwick was back at Eleora's house. He'd been praying for her all Sunday and shared what was going on with his parents so they could be praying too. He texted her that he was outside, and within a minute, she opened the door for him. She had a little more color in her face and smiled when she saw him.

Chadwick smiled back and leaned down to kiss her quickly on the lips. Her smile grew wider.

"I hadn't realized how much I'd missed that," she admitted in a teasing tone.

"That makes two of us," he joked as he entered the house and closed the door behind him.

"I have another poem for you, that is if you still want to go forward with that plan?"

He was glad she remembered. "I would. Do you want to go to the living room or your room?"

"Down here is fine." They walked to the living room together and sat down beside each other on the couch.

Then she proceeded to read him her poem.

He snapped appreciatively when she finished. "Somehow, you managed to top your previous poem."

She smiled at his response. "Thanks, Knight." He warmed at the use of her nickname for him. She sounded a bit more like herself.

"I have to ask, you mentioned death again. Are you having suicidal thoughts?"

"Vaguely? In the poem, I mention this tug of war. It just feels like my mind is constantly yelling at me now that I'm not numbing out anymore. I don't know how to get it to stop other than dying. But I don't have a plan or anything," Eleora explained.

"Thank you for sharing all of that. It gives me more of an idea of where you're at and how I can love you," he told her earnestly.

"You're honestly too loving, Chadwick. This is why I feel like I'm a burden," she said abruptly.

"I don't follow." He was genuinely confused. How did she get that from what he'd said?

She sighed heavily and looked down at her hands. "It's just that I feel like I'm on the receiving end of so many wonderful things by being your girlfriend. And that makes me think, 'What do you get from me? What good do I bring to your life?' I can't think of anything, and so I feel like a burden."

"Belle, I'm going to need you to look at me for what I'm about to say," he said firmly.

She looked up, partly in surprise at his tone.

"Eleora Gonzales, you bring so many amazing things to my life. One that immediately comes to mind is how you've helped to alleviate my loneliness."

"What do you mean? You're so sociable. Everyone loves you!"

"I have a lot of acquaintances but few friends. Like at my church's youth group. I usually leave spiritually full but emotionally empty. No one really takes the initiative to know me, so I often feel disconnected and unseen."

Concern filled her gray eyes, and she reached over to take his hand. "That's awful, Knight."

"Yeah. It's made worse by the reality that most guys primarily bond by doing stuff together. But that's not me. I bond by talking and going deep with a person. That makes it hard to have guy friends. At school, it's easier to ignore the loneliness because my purpose is to learn and get good grades. But for so long, it would be unavoidable outside of school. And—only one other person knows this—I used to watch porn just to escape the deep loneliness I felt." Now he was looking down. He didn't want to see the revulsion in her eyes.

"Chadwick, look at me."

He took a deep breath and acquiesced. All he saw on her face was love.

"What you just shared with me doesn't change the fact that I love you. I need you to know that."

Her sincere tone nearly had him crying and gave him courage to keep sharing. "But then, Eleora, I met you. And we became friends. And I wasn't as lonely anymore. The quality time that we spent together gave me room to share my heart. You weren't just capable of making me laugh, you also managed to engage me in deep conversations. And then the stethoscope you got me? It was the most known I've ever felt."

Now she was starting to cry. He gently wiped away her tears as he spoke. "Belle, I used to think that I could only expect intimacy with God. That it just wasn't a thing for my human relationships. You've nullified that thought process. You've brought closeness and connection into my life on a scale beyond any other relationships that I've had. You bring so much to my life. Being with you is one of the greatest blessings I've ever received."

"Chadwick, I…" she seemed at a loss for words. "I love you."

He smiled at her statement. "I'll never get tired of hearing that. I love you too. So, now that we've discussed a bunch of heavy stuff, what do you want to do today?" he asked her.

"Are you down for bingeing a series with me? It would help me not to constantly hear the thoughts."

"Say less," he responded, and that's what they did.

Chapter 35

Dear Journal,

I don't know what I'd do without Maryliz and Chadwick. It was wild to hear how lonely he's felt and how I help him not to feel that way, just by being me. The thoughts got a bit quieter after that revelation. Then, watching Heartland was just what I needed to rest and tap out without being numb. I could cuddle and consume media with Chadwick forever.

I think it made me more ready today to talk to Maryliz about what sparked this whole mess. My father. His rejection of me has really screwed with my self-perception. I hate that I'm so afraid of everyone I love leaving me because of him. Maryliz tried to reassure me that she and Knight aren't going anywhere, and there are people beyond them who love me deeply. I know what she's saying is true, but it's hard to believe it. The opposite thoughts are stubbornly persistent. It's hard, no, exhausting, to keep fighting them. Like swimming upstream and beginning to drown in the process. But I will. I have to hold onto the words that have been spoken to me outside of my mind. I have to trust that they're true. Like a lifeline.

Ohh. I think I have an idea for my next poem to

share with Knight!

Heaviness hangs onto me through hateful thoughts:
They don't really love me.

They're self-deceived into thinking it's love.
Or
They don't really know me.
Or
They will stop eventually.

My death will leave everyone better off.

My breath no longer a burden.
And
My life no longer a leech.
And
My funeral replete with relief.

I am not good, beautiful or worthy.

Horrible describes my nature best.
Plus
My features are an offense to eyesight.
Thus
I only deserve languishing and loneliness.

I know these self-slanderous statements aren't truth.
But repetition begets belief.
Opposing this onslaught akin to swimming upstream.

And it's exhausting, easier to concede.

"I love you"
"I'm not going anywhere"
"You bring so much to my life"

Are linguistic lifelines
Stopping a suicidal submerge
Commissioning me to challenge these
cognitive combatants with compassion, a
courageous act when criticism is my
conditioned cadence.

Eleora read over the poem and felt pride. The writing was good, but the message even better. Suicide felt like less of an option today than it did yesterday, or the day before.

She was getting a bit better, although she knew that she still had a long way to go.

Chapter 36

Chadwick was pleasantly surprised to be greeted with a hug and kiss when Eleora saw him at her front door.

"Well, hello to you too." He said warmly. "How are you doing today?"

"Wanna hear a poem to answer your question?"

"Bet." He said, following her into the living room. He went to sit on the couch but she motioned for him to turn to sit on it lengthwise. He complied and stretched out. She sat between his legs and leaned back against him, sighing happily, then read her latest poem.

He whistled in appreciation. "Belle, literally you're writing is just getting better and better."

"Well at least that's one thing that poor mental health is good for." She said dryly.

He chuckled. "I noticed that your poem has ended on a hopeful note. Is that how you're feeling?"

"Yes? I'm cautious to use that word but I think that's where I'm at. I still feel these thoughts coming at me, but they feel less strong. Like, I have some breathing room. I don't feel this need to distract myself to drown them out. It's like I've been able to turn the volume down. I don't know if anything I'm saying is making sense."

"You're making sense, Belle. What do you think has helped turn the volume down?"

"Honestly you and Liz. You guys just spending time with me has provided evidence that those thoughts aren't true. And then being able to talk about where these thoughts come from has helped. I'm guessing Liz told you what we'd talk about yesterday?"

Chadwick nodded. "Yes, that it connects to your dad."

"Right. I'm trying to work on reframing what happened so that I don't blame myself. It's difficult though because I've been feeling this way for a long time, I was just good at hiding it away."

"That does sound hard. May I ask, what brought it up?"

"Well, you know I got accepted to UVic?" He nodded. "Well, I thought about what might happen if I tell my mom and choose to go there. But then, this fear hit me that I may lose my relationship with her. And that would be awful because then I would have no parental relationships. And then my dad came up."

"I'm following the thought process. Do you really think your mom would be that upset?"

"I don't know. I've never gone against her. I've always done what she wanted, so I have no idea how she'd react if I didn't."

"That's fair." It sounded similar to what Liz had thought was going on with her, doing things that other people wanted to be loved. Keeping that in mind, he asked, "Do you feel like this is only something you do with your mom? Or does this apply to other people as well?"

"That's a good question. Hmmm. I guess I might do this with more than just my mom actually. I don't want people to ever be mad at me, because …" she was starting to tear up.

"… because they might leave?" Chadwick finished for her. He felt her head nod against his chest. "Okay, you're going to need to turn around so you can see my face."

Eleora turned around so that they were face to face. "Eleora, you can't live your life in fear and you can't live your life for other people. Even if others aren't happy with you, it doesn't mean that they've stopped loving you. And even if they do stop showing you love, that's more their problem than yours."

She sighed. "I know what you're saying is true. But it's hard to believe. And it's even more difficult still to live out."

"Yeah, it is." He agreed. And then something came to mind. "Wait, Belle. You reading CS Lewis and being on your spiritual journey, have you been doing that to make me happy or have you been doing it for you?"

"That's for me." She said automatically.

"You're sure?" He clarified.

"Yes. I knew that I didn't have to convert for you to like me. So, I know I'm seeking for myself. Not you."

"Phew."

He remembered something Liz had brought up that was helpful for people-pleasers. It was relating to boundaries. "Hey, have you ever thought of setting boundaries?"

"I'm not sure I even know what that means." She admitted.

"Truth be told, neither do I. Let's google it?"

"Sure." She agreed and went back to her original position.

He typed out their question and then scrolled through the results. "Aha. I think I found something. 'A boundary is a limit or edge that defines you as separate from others'. It tells you what you're responsible for and what others are responsible for. For instance, every person is responsible for their own thoughts, feelings, and behaviors. Let's use happiness as an example. No one is responsible for your happiness but you. It's yours. Likewise, you're not responsible for other people's happiness. That's theirs to take care of."

"I feel called out! I definitely feel like I'm responsible for making people feel a certain way or do certain things. It's radical to be told that that's not true." She sounded stupefied. "So, this means I'm not responsible for my mom being happy with my decision. That's her choice to make. Like with UVic?"

"I think so. How does it feel to say that?"

"Weird. It's a lot."

"Well, then. Do you want to table it for now?"

"Yeah." She said thoughtfully. "I think I'll take more time to ponder it tonight. Maryliz gave me a few suggestions at the beginning of the week. One was to maybe see a therapist. I'm still on the fence with that. The other was for me to journal out my thoughts every night. So that's what I've been doing. It's where the poems have been coming from. I definitely feel like I have a lot to journal about tonight. Now, I have a surprise!"

"Oh?" He asked, not expecting this.

"I made us breakfast. It's a Filipino dish called

suman. Basically, rice cooked in coconut milk that was steamed in plantain leaves. Normally, people serve it with coconut syrup but I'm Canadian, so I eat it with maple syrup. Does this all sound too weird or are you game for trying it?" She sounded so excited, so much like her normal self, that he would've even eaten cockroaches.

"I'm game."

"Sweet, you can join me in the kitchen and we can eat at the breakfast bar." He followed her there and they enjoyed the meal together. He actually liked the suman.

"Okay, so you mentioned before that you don't feel a need to distract yourself anymore. Does that mean we're not watching anything today?" He asked in between bites.

"Yep. I feel like we may have some schoolwork to do."

"I'm glad that I brought my school stuff just in case!"

Eleora led him to their dining room where they cracked open their books and started to work. They did that for the whole day, taking breaks to eat snacks. When it started to get late, Chadwick started to clean up his stuff. "I've gotta get going but I'll see you tomorrow."

"Tomorrow?"

"Yeah, so that Friday can be for you and Liz. Unless you're getting sick of me." He teased. He was pleased to hear her giggle.

"Not a chance." She said and leaned over to where he was sitting to kiss him.

"Since you're seeming better, do you want to meet at the library tomorrow? I don't know if I can handle being in a house alone with you if you keep kissing me like that."

"Can't handle the heat that I'm bringing Knight?" She teases, batting her eyelashes at him.

"That's exactly right." He said with no guile.

She laughed.

"And this is how you respond to my pain?" He said dramatically, making her laugh harder.

"Okay, okay. You win. The library it is." She conceded.

They got up from the table and she walked him to the front door.

"I love you, Belle." He told her and kissed her on the forehead.

"I know. I love you too." She responded back.

He waved at her before walking the path to his car.

Chapter 37

Eleora closed the door and leaned against it. Gosh, she loved him. And wow, it had felt good to laugh like that again. To feel like herself again.

She went upstairs to do some journaling. After grabbing her journal from her nightstand and a pen from her desk, she settled into bed. Opening her journal to a fresh page, she began to write:

Hey Journal,

Today was a good day. I was able to go through a day without having to use media to distract myself. I was able to lower the volume on the thoughts. I was able to belly laugh today, something I haven't done in almost a week.

I'm so thankful for Knight and Maryliz. I don't know where I'd be without them this week. My thoughts were going to some scary places, way more suicidal than I'd let on to Maryliz and Chadwick. I just didn't want them to worry, I felt like being with my not-fun self was a burden enough. Why add to it? And yet, they haven't let up on caring for me. They've been here every day. Loving me when I didn't want to get out of bed or talk or go out. They are proof that my worst fear of people leaving me because I'm not enough isn't true.

I repeat, I'm so thankful for them.

Every day, I feel like I've been able to make more sense of my inner world. And today had a huge revelation in store for me. I didn't realise how much I lived for others approval of me, of receiving people's love. But I do. Oh boy, do I ever! I have really crappy boundaries. Where I'm taking responsibility for things that aren't mine and making others responsible for what's mine to take care of. This really needs to change, but I confess: I don't know where to start. Hmm. I think it's time for a poetic break. I'll be back journal, I have a poem to write.

Eleora put down her pen and picked up her phone, swiping to open the notes app. She'd realised that she preferred writing poems on her phone. The words flowed out of her and she had fun playing with a different kind of rhyming scheme. She read it over and smiled. It was good.

My back hurts
From all my bending over
To meet others' expectations

I'm habitually hunched over
My people pleasing posture
A popular position

I contort myself to be loved
Finding safety in being approved of
Despair at any condemnation

I just want to breathe
Without waiting for another's happiness

To give me permission

I want to be at peace
in others' anger or disappointment
Free from the responsibility of others' emotions

It's time to do the work
Of forming boundaries
For they will be freedom's foundation

Proud of her poem, she went back to her journal and resumed writing.

Now where was I? Right, how do I start this process? Maybe it can start with me not doing things for other people's happiness? Like, if I actually don't want to do something, I can give myself permission to say no. That sounds so much more difficult than it probably should be. Maybe, I can start with listing out things that I want.

I want to go to the University of Victoria for a Fine Arts degree in writing and theatre.

There I said it! Err, wrote it. It would honestly be such a dream come true. If the only reason I wouldn't do it is because I want to make my mom, then (it seems) like that's not a good enough reason. It's not my job to make my mom happy. Maybe if I repeat it, I'll start to believe it more.

It's not my job to make my mom happy.
It's not my job to make my mom happy.
It's not my job to make my mom happy.

But if she's unhappy with me, will she still love me? I hate feeling like her love is so conditional but didn't my dad prove that love isn't unconditional? That people can choose to stop loving you for any reason?

Yikes. So, maybe I'm not ready yet to take hold of my UVic dream. But I can pay more attention to what I want and need and arrange my life in such a way that those get met.

Hmmm. What else do I want (or need)?

I want to know what I believe in a spiritual sense. Whether I should confidently embrace atheism or whether Christianity is worth thinking about. Not judging it based on my dad's behaviour but based on it itself. What could I do to meet this need? Well, I haven't read that book in a while. We were supposed to discuss the second section ages ago but I hadn't read it yet. Maybe that's what I can do now.

Okay journal, thanks for this processing time. Until tomorrow!

Eleora Gonzales

Satisfied, she closed her journal and put it on her nightstand. Then, she got up from her bed and went to her purse where the book was. She returned to her bed and opened it up to the second section of the book.

When Eleora got to the second page, she read something that made her stop in her tracks.

'And, of course, that raises a very big question. If a good God made the world why has it gone wrong?'

Yes! Exactly, C.S. That's what I'm saying! Eleora thought to herself. She continued reading and then had to reread it again slowly.

'My argument against God was that the universe seemed so cruel and unjust. But how had I got this idea of just and unjust? A man does not call a line crooked unless he has some idea of a straight line. What was I comparing this universe with when I called it unjust? If the whole show was bad and senseless from A to Z, so to speak, why did I, who was supposed to be part of the show, find myself in such violent reaction against it?'

'Oh my gosh. He's right.' She thought to herself. She couldn't find a flaw in his reasoning. To believe that God couldn't exist because of evil, she'd have to question where her idea of evil and good came from and why she even wants the world to be good in the first place. And atheism could not answer those questions.

"Well, crap. I don't think I can honestly say that I'm an atheist anymore." She said aloud and then went back to reading.

Eleora found herself agreeing with his take on dualism not being quite right. She underlined a line that stood out to her: "Goodness is, so to speak, itself: badness is only spoiled goodness." She kept reading and understood what he was saying about free will. It's like what people often say about consent: if someone cannot really say no then they cannot really say yes either. So, it is with free will. If humans couldn't choose not to love, then they can't really choose love either. Free will has caused its problems for sure, but there's no better alternative.

Eleora continued to read and was stopped again once C.S. started to talk about Jesus. This was another section paragraph that she had to underline and reread.

'I am trying here to prevent anyone saying the really foolish thing that people often say about Him: "I'm ready to accept Jesus as a great moral teacher, but I don't accept His claim to be God." That is the one thing we must not say. A man who was merely a man and said the sort of things Jesus said would not be a great moral teacher. He would either be a lunatic—on a level with the man who says he is a poached egg—or else he would be the Devil of Hell. You must make your choice.'

"Oh boy, C.S. You're really bringing the guns out." Eleora muttered to herself and kept reading, a chill going down her spine as she read his last few sentences about Jesus.

'But let us not come with any patronising nonsense about His being a great human teacher. He has not left that open to us. He did not intend to.'

Shoot. He was right. Either Jesus's claim to be God is true or he's a horrible person or had some sort of mental illness. But the stories she remembers from her childhood about Jesus conflict with either of those conclusions.

Eleora couldn't read anymore. She had too many questions. Intellectually assenting to there being a God was one thing. But, was she ready to believe that Jesus is God? Wouldn't that make her a Christian? Didn't Islam have something else to say about Jesus? How did they square the circle of what Jesus said about himself? Unless, the Quran had Jesus saying different stuff. If that's the case, then which one is more trustworthy? The Bible or the Quran?

She did a quick Google search and was inundated with a bunch of information; things like textual criticism and dating of copies and the number of manuscripts. Beyond the jargon, most held up the Bible as more historically reliable and holding up to its claim better than the Quran.

Eleora put down her phone and stared up at her ceiling. She remembered Pastor Tavish's words, that eventually in one's seeking they'll wind up reading the Bible. It hit her that she was at that point now. This realization stirred surprising emotions. She felt humbled. She felt nervous. But the dominant feeling that she was experiencing was excitement. Maybe even yearning. Something was happening in her. Eleora didn't quite know what it was, but she liked it.

A lot.

Feeling invigorated, she grabbed her phone and called Chadwick.

Chapter 38

Chadwick was surprised to see a call from Eleora. "Miss me already, Belle?"

"I just have something really important to share with you."

"Okay. Go ahead." He said in a bemused voice.

"I'm no longer an atheist. And I think I might believe Jesus is God? And I want to read the Bible to be sure."

Did he hear her correctly? Was he dreaming? "You're going to have to rewind a bit for me. First of all, what brought this on?"

"I was reading the C. S. Lewis book, and he just said something that floored me. I couldn't intellectually be an atheist anymore." She explained.

"Wow, okay. So now we are in deism territory. Now what were you saying about Jesus?"

"Just that I think he might actually be God? I don't know what I believe anymore, but I know that I want to read the Bible to find out."

"Well then. I 100 percent support this step." More like a Google plex percent.

"Good, because I need help. I haven't touched a Bible since I was in elementary school. And I know that there are going to be things that I won't understand. I don't even know where to start with all of this." She admitted.

"Well, you're not in it alone, okay? First, you're going to want to download a Bible app on your phone. The company should be Youversion."

"Alright, that's done."

"Cool, now you want to learn more about Jesus. The good news is that there are four accounts of his life to read in the Bible. It's just a matter of choosing which one to start with." He informed her.

"Which one do you think I should start with?" She asked, starting to feel a little overwhelmed.

"It depends on what you want. Luke is best if you want a detailed account of Jesus' life. Mark is the opposite, it just gives you the essentials. John explores the why behind the things Jesus did and Matthew shows how Jesus fulfilled a bunch of prophecies." He explained.

"I can't decide between Luke and John." She told Chadwick.

"Okay. Let's flip a coin. Heads Luke, tails John." He grabbed a quarter from his night table and flipped it. "And we have heads, so you'll be reading Luke! Are you good with that?"

"Yep. I'll start reading it tomorrow, probably during our study time, since I got a lot of work done today."

"Sounds like a plan, and I can be there to answer - or at least attempt to answer - any questions that you have as you read."

"Thanks. Okay, good night, Knight." She giggled at the homonym.

"Good night, Belle, I'll see you in the morning. Love you."

"Love you too."

With that, she ended the call. Chadwick stared at the phone in his hands. He loved the sound of her voice, especially when it was full of such joy and hope. She'd sounded so much like the opposite for the past week.

She was clearly feeling better psychologically, for which he was thankful, but where she was spiritually was blowing his mind!

She could very well become a Christian soon.

The spectre that had been haunting him for the past few weeks, made especially worse by Eleora's poor mental health, was that he needed to end things with her because of their differing beliefs.

How good it was that he hadn't!

She was scared of abandonment and would've taken a breakup so hard.

Like her dad all over again.

No, he was not her dad. He would stay. She would always know that she was loved by him. And, soon, he may not have to break up with her anyways.

Chapter 39

If someone had told Eleora that she would be going to church by her own volition because she was considering following Jesus, she would've laughed in their face. But, here she was.

This was her second time visiting Chadwick's church. She adjusted her black pencil skirt and pulled at the puffy sleeves of her champagne blouse. Then she played with the pearl earrings that she'd borrowed from her mom. She couldn't help but fidget, she was so nervous.

"Welcome everyone to our Sunday service! Please stand and join me in song."

Eleora stood up and started to clap to the beat. It was a high energy and catchy song. She glanced at the corner of the projector screen and saw that it was titled: My Testimony. Then they transitioned to a slower song. The lyrics struck her. The idea of God knowing her as a child moved her for some reason. She took note of the title of this song: Hidden. The next song was about praising God even when life was hard. She noticed people around her openly crying as they sang. Others were kneeling or bent over in their seats. This song was really hitting people hard.

As it ended, people began to sit and a Black woman came on the stage. Eleora recognized her as the one who'd performed the Christmas poem. She felt excited for what she was about to hear. With no preamble or introduction, she started to perform.

"I don't like what You're doing right now.
I'm angry – angry with You.
I'm disappointed.

Your wisdom and goodness are on trial for perjury because it feels like You've fooled me and now Your omnipotence and sovereignty no longer bring comfort to me.

Faith in You is exhausting when the yoke You invited me to co-carry has become far too heavy.
I'm tired."

Yes, you are allowed to pray prayers like this.
I used to think it was blasphemous to speak to Yahweh in this way.

The only confident approach we can make to the throne is reverence, gratitude, praise.
There was no room for my frustrations, grumblings and complaints.

My soul is only allowed to smile and pray the pain away.
Right?
Isn't that what worship is supposed to look like?

Except, worship is the meeting of Spirit and truth

directed towards the only One who can bear the weight of it.

Sometimes, worship looks more like weeping than smiles.
Sometimes, complaints are the most authentic parts of ourselves we can bring.
Sometimes, the Spirit groans and grieves and following Him means doing likewise.

In lament, faith and blasphemy seem differentiated by a thin and blurry line.
Grace beckons us to visceral honesty. Love meets us there in comfort.
Hope reminds us it won't last forever.
Faith is our response to the invitation.

Like our forerunner, blind Bartimaeus – faith is in the question of asking, not knowing what the response will be, but knowing Who we're asking and expecting a response.

Lament is far more audacious and authentic than our tidy Christian traditions would have us believe – and grace is far more lavish and extravagant to welcome it at all.

So, I will lament.
I will bravely and honestly bring You my questions, that aren't for intellectual gain or curiosity but are birthed from the labour pains of life thus far.

I will remember. I will exhaust myself of all that

currently tangles up my present until all I can do is see
Your past faithfulness towards me.

It is there.
I will see it when I've casted all that I can currently see
onto You.

I will petition. I will not just have enough faith to give
but to ask to receive. I will believe that You are not just
able to meet my needs – but that You care to do so at
all.

I will trust that You too are grieving the brokenness of
this world and my life – and I will join You in it.
I will enter what is so radically intimate.
I will lament."

Eleora snapped as hard and fast as she could. The
writing! The vulnerability! She wished she could sit
with the poet and unpack the meaning of it all. As the
poet walked off the stage, Pastor Tav walked onto it.

He knelt down and prayed aloud. "Yahweh. Be
with me today as I share this message. Speak Lord! Let
me not get in the way. And may everyone within the
sound of my voice be impacted. Speak to your people.
Would no one be able to leave here the same. Amen."
Eleora heard the amens of the congregation around her.

"I'm about to get really, real with you, church. Can
you handle it?" Someone called out "Yes Pastor!"

"Okay. Because of trials I've been through, I've
asked God the question: why did you write my story
this way? I can't be the only one in this room who has
felt like this, who has asked the burning question of

why."

Eleora felt exposed.

"Praise God that He answers us when we pray. And He answered with His sovereignty, His love and His glory - and that's what I want to share with you.

If you're taking notes, the first point is this: God is sovereign. A sovereign is one who has supreme power and authority. This is true of God. There is absolutely nothing that happens in the universe that is outside of God's authority. Don't mishear me this morning. I'm not saying that God causes everything, for then we brush up against the evil and brokenness of this world. No, what I'm saying is that He has the final say on what happens."

This made sense, it was similar to what she'd read in Mere Christianity.

"Scroll or flip your way to Isaiah 46:9-11." She took out her phone and went to the passage. "It reads: 'Remember the former things, those of long ago; I am God, and there is no other; I am God, and there is none like me. I make known the end from the beginning, from ancient times, what is still to come. I say, My purpose will stand, and I will do all that I please. From the east I summon a bird of prey; from a far-off land, a man to fulfill my purpose. What I have said, that I will bring about; what I have planned, that I will do.' Now follow me to Colossians 1:17-18." She scrolled to Colossians and went to those verses. "It reads: 'He existed before anything else, and he holds all creation together. Christ is also the head of the church, which is his body. He is the beginning, supreme over all who rise from the dead. So, he is first in everything.'

"Hallelujah! You see, God's answer began with a

reminder of who He is. He took my eyes off of myself and reminded me that History is really just His Story - not mine. Everything is done by Him, through Him, for Him and nothing is outside of His authority- authorship. It's not about me; about us because we are not God, He is. He is the infinite one, not us."

That doesn't feel like an answer though, Eleora thought, but just a direction to shift perspective. She listened to see where he was going with this.

"This first point might make it seem like God is impersonal. That because it's not about us, he must not care about us. That is so far from the truth! God is not just infinite, He is intimate. That's our second point today: God is intimate and intentional. He intentionally wrote us into His Story. Psalm 139:16 says: 'Your eyes saw my unformed body; all the days ordained for me were written in your book before one of them came to be.' Family, He cares. What is this book that the psalmist refers to? I believe it's the book of life."

This was curious to Eleora. What was he talking about?

"You thought that I was just being metaphorical when I was referring to our lives as stories and God as the author, eh? I wasn't. The book of Revelation tells us two things about the book of life. For the sake of time, I won't read the passages but I'll mention them for you to read on your own. They are Revelation 17:8, 20:11-15 and 22:22-27. First off, we learn that everyone will be judged by what book holds their story. Those in the book of life are saved and destined for God's holy city. Those not in the book of life are destined for the lake of fire. Secondly, it tells us that our names are written in the book from the creation of the world!"

She shivered at the mention of hell. Eleora respected him for bringing it up but was thankful that he wasn't focusing on it.

"This is actually parallel to Ephesians 1:4-6 which says: 'For he chose us in him before the creation of the world to be holy and blameless in his sight. In love he predestined us for adoption to sonship through Jesus Christ, in accordance with his pleasure and will— to the praise of his glorious grace, which he has freely given us in the One he loves.' There's three things here that I want to point out. First off, we see the sovereignty of God in Him choosing and predestining us. Second, we see the love of God making us a part of His family. Thirdly, we see the reason for it all - and that's His glory.

Eleora really liked the way Pastor Tav clearly articulated what was happening in the Bible in a way that she was able to understand.

That's our last point today. After he reminds of who He is and of who we are to Him, the answer for the things that happen to us are that somehow they contribute to the glory of God. Romans 11:36 says: 'For everything comes from him and exists by his power and is intended for his glory. All glory to him forever! Amen.'"

Ah. That was the real answer. His glory. What did glory mean?

"Family, He is involved in the macro of all of human history and the micro of the intricacies of our hearts. He is sovereign and soul mate. He is holy and home. When we begin to actually grasp this, our why's become worship. We stop asking the question of why He did what and begin to praise Him for writing us in at all, not wasting any detail and using every single aspect for His glory.

"I want to close with Revelation 12:11. It reads: 'They triumphed over him by the blood of the Lamb and by the word of their testimony; they did not love their lives so much as to shrink from death.' The 'they' are believers and the 'him' is the devil. 'By the blood of the Lamb' is a reference to Christ's sacrifice on the cross."

Eleora appreciated the explanation, she was a little lost when he first read it.

"Satan was utterly defeated as sin would no longer be the master of humanity. But why mention 'by the word of their testimony'? Because it is the sovereignty of God and the intimacy of God playing out to the glory of God in reconciling someone the enemy thought he had claimed to Himself!

"So, here's our application from today's message. If you're struggling with things God has allowed to happen in your life, hear me. Remember who He is, remember who you are, and trust that somehow glory will come from it. Don't pull away from God, but draw near to Him. Engage in the practice of lament that our sister shared about poetically. This too is worship. This too is faith. Remember He loves you. He wants you to be intimate with him about what you're feeling. And just because He's allowed something doesn't mean He isn't grieved by it too. Remember, Jesus knew that Lazarus' death was going to end in God getting glory through His resurrection but He still wept."

Interesting. So, he was saying that you could actually approach God with whatever you're feeling.

"The second application is for those in the room

who may not believe in Jesus yet. I caution you, hell is a real place that is waiting for those who are not in the book of life. Take your spiritual journey seriously, and don't delay in trusting in Jesus."

These words struck a chord in her. She was taking it seriously, but was she delaying unnecessarily? What was she waiting for to believe? What was missing for her?

"My third application point is for believers. If you are a believer in Jesus, you have a testimony. Share it. You get to participate in God's triumph over the enemy when you do this. And I'm going to model this for you guys right now by sharing my story with you."

Oh wow! Eleora wondered how vulnerable he would get with hundreds of people in the room.

"I came to Canada when I was 17 near the end of high school. My father was abusive to me, my siblings and my mom. We nominally practiced Hinduism. By the end of high school, people tend to already have their friends so I was lonely and bullied because of my accented English. Then someone befriended me who happened to be a Christian, Brian. When I would study at his place after-school, I was always surprised at how loving his dad was to them. One day, I asked why his dad was so loving and he said it was because he was a Christian. I didn't understand how religion could make someone so loving." His voice cracked at this. He cleared his throat and continued to speak.

"I had been surrounded by religious people, but they weren't loving like that. It made me curious about why Christianity was different. I started going to Brian's youth group and it was starting to make sense. I was shaken by the idea that a god could love me so much. After a few months during one of the services, I gave my life to Christ. But life didn't get better. My dad was angry with me for changing religions and took it out on my mom. Eventually, I was able to get my mom to leave but I, as the oldest, had to take care of the family. I barely graduated high school because I had to work for us to have our needs met. Eventually, my mom and siblings came to faith and my mom was able to go back to school to get a new job. Once that happened, the pressure was off of me and I felt God calling me to ministry. And here we are, years later. I have the privilege of being one of your pastors."

She hadn't anticipated his story to be so heavy. He was brave for sharing it in such detail with them all.

"I love my story because it is how He purposed for me to know Him. It is our love story, with not a detail missed. From my family and all the generational curses to my personality - it was all for His glory of shaming the devil as yet another was brought back into relationship with Him.

I have no clue what your story is. It could be riddled with abuse of every and any kind or, on the flip side it could seem average and basic. But hear this, it is your part in His Story. It is beautiful. It is victorious. It was written with intention by the infinite and intimate God. We can rest and rejoice in this when things are going well - and we can weep and worship in this when everything hits the fan. Let's worship God together now."

Eleora hadn't even realised that the band was on the stage again. Everyone in the room stood up as they sang a song about glory being given to Christ. Fitting, when she considered how the sermon had ended. When the song was done, Pastor Tav came back onstage. "The service is officially over. If you'd like to chat with me, I'll be sitting right here. You are loved!"

She couldn't explain it, but she felt the need to go talk to the pastor. She wasn't sure what about, but it just felt so important for her to go to him. She leaned over to Chadwick. "Hey, I'm going to go and talk to him. Is that alright or do you guys need to leave right away?"

"That's no problem, Belle. We normally catch up with people while we're here. Go for it." He encouraged her with a warm smile. She smiled back. Noticing that his parents were distracted, he took her left hand in his and gave it a comforting squeeze. In response, she quickly kissed him on the cheek and then headed toward the stage.

Chapter 40

Chadwick watched Eleora walk away with hope in his heart. She was so close to believing in Jesus. He wanted to know how the service had landed on her and what she was talking to Pastor Tav about, but he hadn't wanted to crowd her. They'd have time later to process anyways. He sat down in his seat when he heard a voice call out his name. He looked around to find the source and smiled when he saw who it was.

"Hey Pastor Gabe!" Chadwick said warmly as he walked over to him. As he drew closer, he saw that his mentor looked unhappy. "Is something wrong?" He asked.

"Well, you tell me. From where I was standing, it seems like you and Eleora are more than just friends."

Crap. There was no point in lying.

"Yes, we are." He admitted.

"How long?"

"About 5 months."

"And you neglected to tell me this in all the times we met together. This deceit is unlike you, Chadwick. Is this why you also haven't been as committed to meeting up?"

Chadwick started to feel defensive and just

shrugged. "I didn't feel like I needed to, since I had my problem handled."

"The biggest danger is if you think pornography is the problem. It's actually your makeshift solution to the problem." Pastor Gabe said firmly.

"Well, my problem was loneliness and being with her has solved it."

Pastor Gabe raised an eyebrow. "So, you're using her instead of porn?"

"No, I love her!" Chadwick was thankful that the room was so full of lively conversation, so no one had heard him.

"Chadwick." Pastor Gabe sounded more disappointed than angry. Somehow that was worse. Chadwick couldn't meet his gaze anymore and instead looked at the floor.

"It's not that simple as that day in your office. I love her." His voice was quieter this time, but no less rich with emotion. "I'm in too deep now. I know I was not supposed to date her, that doing so is a sin and that I'm basing my actions on a technicality. All I was supposed to do was be her friend and lead her to Jesus. But—"

"Well, colour me surprised." He heard a familiar voice say. He looked up to see Eleora behind Gabe.

"Belle, I can explain."

"Explain what? That since the day we started dating you've been lying to me?" Her voice was cold, but he heard an undercurrent of hurt.

"I can explain it. Really." He repeated.

"Save it, Chadwick."

"But Belle, if you would just give me a—"

"You should probably quit while you're ahead. She

doesn't want to hear it." Pastor Gabe said sympathetically.

Chadwick saw Eleora freeze. Her face was paling like she'd seen a ghost. He could find disbelief and hope in her expression. What was going on?

"D ... Da ... Daddy?" She stammered.

Daddy? Her father was here? Where? He was about to look around when he saw the look on Pastor Gabe's face.

No, he couldn't be.

Could he?

Chadwick watched in alarm as Pastor Gabe turned around to face Eleora and said, "Hello Ra-ra."

Chapter 41

Eleora didn't know how to compute this. She had never really thought through what she would do if she saw her father again. A part of her wanted to run into his arms when she heard his nickname for her. Another part of her wanted to kick him in the nuts for all the ways that he'd hurt her. She didn't understand the look on his face, sad and yearning. Why would he be feeling those things? He's the one that had given her up. Did he regret his decision all those years ago?

She shook her head as if that would prove to change what she was seeing before her, but nothing changed. It was really her father standing in front of her. He looked good in a light blue button-down shirt and khakis. He was bald now with a thick beard and was wearing pretty cool looking glasses. The gray eyes that she'd inherited from him began to fill with tears.

"Ra-ra, I ... you ..." Now he was stammering. Then he cleared his throat and tried again. "You've grown into such a beautiful young woman."

The world became blurry as her eyes filled with tears. She didn't know how to handle this situation. She needed to leave. "I can't do this. I have to go."

She grabbed her purse and then speed-walked from

Chadwick and her father. As she made her way to the lobby, she pulled out her phone and booked an uber home. She tried calling Maryliz, but then hung up before it started ringing. Eleora had never really told Liz the full story of what had gone down with her dad and she didn't have the energy to go into all of it right now.

Her uber came quickly and the ride was exactly what she needed; quiet and uneventful. She was able to hold herself together until she walked into the house and then the tears started.

How could he do this to her? She wasn't even sure which he she was hurt by the most. Her father for rejecting her, Chadwick for lying to her or God for ... allowing all this to happen?

Through blurry vision, she walked up the stairs to her room. She needed to get into some comfortable clothes. Eleora was about to enter her room when she remembered that the earrings she was wearing were her mom's. She decided to go to her room first to put them into her jewellery case on her dresser. But her blurry vision was making her clumsy, so much so in fact that she knocked over a bunch of envelopes that were on her mother's dresser. Eleora shook her head in dismay as she squatted to pick them up and organise them.

As she did so, she realised that one of the envelopes had her name on it. She wiped away her tears so that she could see it more clearly. Maybe she had imagined it?

Nope, there it was: Eleora James. And the sender was Marielle James; her nana.

She hastily checked to see what was in the envelope, but it was empty. What was going on? What had her nana sent her? Why had her mom taken and opened her mail? She sat on the floor, stumped; unsure of what her next steps should be.

Eleora heard the front door slam and footsteps coming up the stairs. They were light and focused, her mother's steps.

"Iha, what are you doing here?" her mother asked, her voice confused but warm.

"Nanay, how could you do this?" She blurted out.

"Do what?" her mother said hesitantly.

Eleora wasn't even sure that she had an answer to the question because she was so confused herself. Finally, she said. "Withhold this information from me."

Her mother's face blanched. "How did you find out?"

"With all due respect nanay, I would rather that you not answer my question with a question. I deserve answers." Eleora said firmly, but with a tremor in her voice.

There was silence for a moment and then her mom started to cry. "I just didn't want to lose you too."

What? What was she talking about? Lose her? "I don't understand. Why don't you start from the beginning?"

"Well, okay." Her mother sat down next to her on the floor. "So, I had already lost your father to the church. And you guys were so close, I didn't want to lose you as well. That's why I wanted us to have a new life. I looked for jobs far away from where my heart had been broken and betrayed, and the furthest I could find was British Columbia."

Eleora was so confused. What did this have to do with a letter from her grandmother? She was about to interrupt, but something made her stay quiet. Clearly, there was more going on than she'd realised.

"I told you that your father knew we were leaving that day, but I lied to you. He didn't. The reason it had taken him so long to contact you was because it had probably taken him that long to track us down." That week of no contact, it wasn't because he hadn't cared. It was because he hadn't known!

"And before he could contact you, I wanted to be sure that you would choose to live with me. But, you guys were so close - bonded by your shared faith. I figured I didn't have a chance in hell. Unless ..." she took a deep breath. "Unless something severed your relationship with him. The only thing I could think of was if you thought that he didn't love you anymore. That's when I signed into his email and wrote that email to you."

It felt like someone had just drenched her in ice cold water. That email that had torn her apart. That she'd thought was proof of something being wrong with her that made her unlovable and easily rejected. It wasn't real? Her dad had never typed out those words and sent them to her?

"Once you read it, all that needed to be done was nail down the custody agreement. You were at an age where your voice mattered the most to a court. If you said that you wanted to live with only one of your parents and not the other, they would go with that. And that's what happened on that phone call."

It sounded like her mom was done sharing, but Eleora was still confused about what receiving mail from her nana had to do with all of this.

"And nana? What happened with her?"

Her mother nodded. "Right, I forgot to mention that I passed on our contact information to her when I had begun to feel guilty about what I did. Every so often she sends you a letter and a check. But when the first letter arrived, it hit me that everything could unravel if you two stayed in touch. So, I've deposited the cheque into your RESP and hidden away the letters."

Eleora needed a moment to think about all the things her mother had shared with her. The shock she had been feeling was giving way to something else: anger.

"How could you do this to me?" she said, beginning to shudder with rage.

"I told you. I didn't want to lose my relationship with you. I love you. You're the most important person in my life, iha a-"

"Don't call me that." Eleora interrupted her curtly.

"I know you're upset now, but I did the right thing. We're together and we're good, thriving without your father." Her mother said confidently, putting an arm around Eleora.

She shrugged her off and stood up. "Are you kidding me right now? I am not good. I have not been thriving. For the last 8 years, I've thought that there was something wrong with me, some flaw that made me someone who my father would abandon and reject. I gave up a faith that I loved because I thought God must be cruel and awful or not real for this to happen to me. And all this time, the problem wasn't with me, my dad or God. It was you!"

Her mother stood up. "Eleora Gonzales, you better watch that tone. I am still your mother and you must respect me."

Eleora laughed bitterly. "Respect is the furthest thing I feel toward you. You're still my mother? What type of mother is that? The type to see hurting her daughter as a means to an end of making herself happy? Yeah, that's not the mother that I want."

"What are you saying? I did this for you! For us!" Her mother exclaimed.

"No. You did this for you." Eleora said quietly. Here came fresh tears. The anger was giving way to deep sadness.

For the first time in this interaction, her mother's face looked remorseful. She went to touch Eleora, but she stepped away before her mother could touch her. Her mother flinched at the rejection.

For the second time that day, Eleora needed to exit a situation. "I need to go." She grabbed her phone from her mother's dresser and left the room. She ordered another uber that was about 10 minutes away.

This gave her enough time to pull out a duffel bag from her closet and stuff it with a bunch of clothes. Eleora could feel her mother staring at her from her room's doorway, but she blocked it out. She tried to pay attention to what she was packing - and failed. As long as there was underwear, bottoms and tops, she'd be fine. When she was done, Eleora went to leave her room but her mother was in the way.

"Iha, please. Don't do this. I love you." Eleora looked in her mother's eyes and could see that she was being sincere.

"That may be true, nanay. But you love yourself more." She said sadly and pushed her way past her mother. She hurried down the stairs and slid into her sneakers.

Her uber arrived just as she stepped out of the house. Thankfully, the driver didn't comment on her tear-strained face or the over-stuffed duffel in her arms. He simply and quietly drove her to her destination.

The last time she'd been to Malton, she had been with Chadwick and hadn't paid attention to where they were going. She was just enjoying being with him. She felt another stab to her heart just thinking about that day. This time, though, she took notice of the turns they made and streets they were driving on. She was pleasantly surprised to see that it had only taken about 15 minutes to get there.

They had been so close to each other, this whole time.

With a quick thank you to the driver, she slung her duffel bag over her shoulder and left the car. Eleora took a deep breath and walked up the stairs to her grandmother's porch.

Her hands shook with nerves. What if she didn't want to see her? What if she wasn't even home? What if - her thought process was interrupted as the front door opened before she'd even knocked.

Behind the still-locked screen door was her nana.

She had a few more wrinkles on her face and her hair was in sister locs, their colour a mixture of white and gray, matching her gray eyes.

There was a beat of silence as her Nana gave her a full perusal, her face displaying surprise. Then, suddenly the screen door swung open and Eleora was pulled into a tight hug.

"My beautiful granddaughter. You've come back to me." She heard her nana whisper.

It was disconcerting to be taller than her, but soon the shock wore off and she let herself put her full weight on her grandmother, tucking her head into her nana's shoulder.

They stayed like that for a while and when they pulled apart, both of their faces were wet.

"Well, come on in sweetie. It's still a little chilly out there, eh?" She said kindly, her voice carrying her faint Jamaican accent. Eleora nodded, her heart warming at the familiar nickname and walked into the house that had barely changed in all these years. She placed her duffel bag down and took off her shoes.

"I have a feeling that we have a lot to talk about. How about I put on some tea for us?" Her nana suggested.

Eleora smiled. "Peppermint?"

Her nana smiled back. "With a dash of cinnamon."

Eleora nodded and went to follow her down the stairs to the kitchen but her nana stopped her. "No, sweetie. You go relax on the couch. Just rest. I'll be back in a few minutes."

"Okay nana." She deferred and stepped into the sitting room to her right.

Its familiarity was comforting. The bronze linen couch, the cream doilies. The only real difference she could find was a flat screen TV that was playing a church service. It looked familiar and then she realized that it was a livestream of the service she had just left earlier today. I guess it made sense that her nana and her father would go to the same church. Just thinking about her father brought everything back to her.

Eleora sat on the couch and sunk deep into the cushions. It helped her relax as she contemplated the last two hours. So many things had gone topsy-turvy and she didn't know how to handle it.

Her nana walked into the room holding two mugs of tea. She handed Eleora hers and then sat down beside her.

"Okay, sweetie. Tell me everything."

"Oh nana. I don't know where to start. Everything is a mess."

"Let's start with what brought you here. What made you want to come and visit me?"

"Well, you're the only one I feel like I can trust nana. My mom, she lied to me. She severed my relationship with daddy and hid all of your letters! I didn't even know you'd been writing to me. I swear nana, I would've responded. I would've visited. I didn't know that you still loved me. I thought you felt the way daddy did. Or how my mom convinced me that he did. And normally, I would take all of this to Chadwick but he lied to me too! This just seemed like the safest place for me."

Eleora paused her rambling and took a few gulps of the delicious tea.

"I must confess that I only caught parts of that. How about we go a bit slower, eh?"

Eleora nodded and they began to slowly untangle and process all that Eleora had learned and what had brought her there. By the end of it, her head was in her nana's lap and she was asleep.

Eleora's hunger pangs woke her up. She was startled to not be in her bedroom and then remembered everything that had happened. That's right. She was at her nana's house. She reached blindly for her phone and saw that it was almost 5 pm. And she had a few missed phone calls from Chadwick. There were also some texts that she swiped away from the lock screen. She couldn't deal with that right now. She had to focus on food. Breakfast had been ages ago. No wonder she was so hungry! She sat up and stretched out her arms, rolling her neck from side to side and shimmying her shoulders.

Once she had gotten rid of some of the soreness she had been feeling, she smelled Jamaican curry. Oh man, one thing she had definitely been missing these last several years was her nana's cooking!

She began to head downstairs to the kitchen, and as she did she heard her nana talking.

"...so that by two unchangeable things in which it is impossible for God to lie, we who have taken refuge would have strong encouragement to hold firmly to the hope set before us. This hope we have as an anchor of the soul, a hope both sure and reliable and ... shoot. I forget. Let me try that again. 'So that by two unchangeable things in which it is impossible for God to lie, we who have taken refuge would have strong encouragement to hold firmly to the hope set before us. This hope we have as an anchor of the soul, a hope both sure and reliable and ... one which enters within the veil, where Jesus has entered as a forerunner for us, having become a high priest forever according to the order of Melchizedek."

Eleora stopped in her tracks. The words that her grandmother recited had pierced her soul. '...it is impossible for God to lie' and hope being an anchor for her soul. She had been lied to by the people she'd trusted most, but according to the verse that her grandmother had recited, God wouldn't - actually couldn't - lie to her. Which made Him trustworthy. Which meant that she could have a hope for her future that was sure and reliable.

She sat down on the middle step and began to sob.

All these years, she had thought that everything to do with God had been a lie. She had thought that Christianity wasn't trustworthy. She had thought God to be cruel or non-existent. But this whole time, He was the trustworthy one. The reliable one. Very real and able to give her hope.

Eleora barely heard the footsteps coming towards her, but she felt her grandmother's arm around her, pulling her in.

"Oh sweetie. Talk to your nana. What are you feeling?"

"I don't even know, nana. This whole time, all these years, I had been blaming God for everything that happened. And now, I find that it wasn't His fault. I've been wrong all these years. I've treated God terribly. How could he ever forgive me? How could he ever want me back?"

"Eleora, there is nothing you can do to make God stop loving you. 'For I am convinced that neither death, nor life, nor angels, nor principalities, nor things present, nor things to come, nor powers, nor height, nor depth, nor any other created thing will be able to separate us from the love of God that is in Christ Jesus our Lord.' Did you hear that? Nothing can separate you from His love, sweetie. Is that what you want? Do you want to receive His love?"

Eleora thought for a moment. All her intellectual reasons for not believing in God had already been dealt with. And now, the personal hang ups that she'd had with Him had been resolved. What was stopping her from believing again?

"Yes, nana." She said finally. "That's what I want."

"That's wonderful, sweetie. Now, do you want to pray on your own or would you like me to help you with that part?"

It wasn't even a question. "Your help please. I haven't done this in a while."

Her grandmother invited Eleora to repeat after her and she did, feeling every word. "Yahweh, I'm sorry for not believing you. I'm sorry for blaming You for things that weren't Your fault. I believe that You exist. I believe that Jesus, you really did live, die and resurrect. I believe that you are trustworthy and that you love me. Forgive me for all my sins and make me new. Let me join Your family and be filled with You, Holy Spirit. I ask these things in Jesus's name. Amen."

Eleora felt different.

Something in her felt lighter, like her soul was floating in a sea of calm and peace. She felt this overwhelming sense of being loved. The pain she had been feeling for the last few hours wasn't gone, but she felt a keen comfort. Like she was receiving the warmest and tightest hug.

"How do you feel?" her nana asked her.

"Different. A good different. It's hard to put into words." She answered.

"That's completely alright. Now, dinner will be ready soon but I know that there's someone who desperately wants to talk to you."

Eleora stiffened. She wasn't ready to talk to either of her parents. Or Chadwick. Who could her nana be talking about? "Who?" she asked, pulling away from her grandmother to see her face.

"Your lola. She and I have been in touch throughout the years. She's sent me pictures of you growing up and updates on how you've been doing. I was just chatting with her on the phone while you were napping. She didn't know about anything your mother had done and really wants to talk to you. I also know that she'd be thrilled to hear about the decision you just made. What do you say, shall I make the call?"

Eleora was touched that these two women had stayed in contact and was relieved to hear that her mother's deception may not extend to her whole family. "Yes, nana. Go ahead."

"Well, my cell phone is on the kitchen counter. Let's go." She said happily. They got up from the steps and walked to the kitchen.

When they got there, her nana put a spoon in the pot on the stove and then brought it over to Eleora. "Can you taste this for me? I need a fresh perspective."

Eleora opened her mouth and was hit with the spicy curry flavour. "This tastes great! Are you making goat or chicken?"

"Chicken. I'm glad you like it, it's what we're having for dinner tonight." Her nana told her while tapping on her cell phone.

Eleora put the spoon in the sink and then waited for the phone to be passed to her. "Ate! Eleora would like to talk to you." Her nana's voice was filled with warmth. The two really were close to each other. "Okay, here you go!"

Eleora took the phone that was being held out to her and then tentatively said, "Hello?"

"Apong babae [granddaughter], how are you?" Tears sprung to her eyes at the term of endearment.

"I'm a mixed bag, lola. In many ways, I don't know how to move forward. But, something good did just happen."

"Oh? And what is that?"

"I just became a Christian." She smiled as she said those words. It still felt surreal for her.

There was a moment of silence during which she wondered if the phone call had cut off, and then her lola shrieked. Eleora nearly dropped the phone in shock. She had never heard her lola be this loud before. "That is the most wonderful news you could ever give me. I've been praying for you, apong babae, for years."

"Thank you lola. And thanks for staying in touch with nana too!"

"Of course! We became like sisters when your parents got married. On the topic of your parents, I don't even know what to say. I was shocked when Marielle told me what had happened. I did not know that my iha could be capable of such deception." Her voice took on a disappointed and angry tone. "I tried speaking with her, but she refuses to admit that what she did was wrong. We are currently not speaking."

"Oh lola. I'm sorry."

"It is what it is. I've talked to your aunts and they didn't know about all this either. They are figuring out for themselves how they're going to interact with your mother."

Eleora breathed a sigh of relief. It was hard to know what she would do if everyone else had been involved.

"I want to let you know, though, that your debut is

still on - if you still want it. Your mother doesn't have to be involved in the rest of the planning."

Eleora hadn't even thought about her debut. It was happening soon, in just a few weeks! Maybe it would be better to cancel and just take the loss of the deposits. She didn't want to deal with any family drama and it would be hard to go without Chadwick in attendance. But, it was an important milestone. She would only turn 18 once. And she had really been looking forward to it.

"Yes, I still want it, Lola. I'm not sure yet what to do about nanay, but I know I want my debut to happen." She said confidently.

"That's my girl! Okay, we can talk about more of those details later. Your aunts and I will take care of everything. We love you, Eleora."

"Thank you, lola. I love you all too."

"And I'm so glad to hear about you giving your life back to the Lord! Do you mind if I pass this news on?"

"Oh! Sure, I'm okay with that."

"Lovely. Well, I have to get going for dinner. Would you like to come over? We always have room."

"Thanks for the invite, Lola, but I'm dying to have nana's food again. It's been a very long time."

"Too long." Her Lola agreed. "But that all changes now. Okay, have a good time. I'll talk to you later! Mahal kita."

"Bye lola, I love you too!"

She heard the click of the phone call being hung up and then gave the phone back to her nana who placed it on the counter.

"Now, Eleora, I have something else to talk to you about." She said seriously.

"That sounds slightly ominous. Is something wrong?"

"Well, normally I have dinner with your father on Sundays since we're both alone. Given everything that's happened, I could tell him not to come and we can just have dinner with the two of us. But I didn't want to make that decision for you."

Eleora appreciated her grandmother's thoughtfulness and took a moment to think about it. She had spent so many years angry with her dad, anger that he didn't even deserve. But she'd missed him too. She was nervous as to how to go about talking with him, but she wanted to hear about his life and share about her own. She'd have to see him eventually; and it would probably be easier with her nana than the two of them alone.

"I'm okay with having dinner with the two of you." She finally said.

Her nana took Eleora's hands in her own and squeezed them affectionately. "I'm very proud of you, sweetie. He will probably be here in the next half an hour or so. Now, while that's a very classy outfit that you're wearing, you might want to put on something more comfortable, hmm?"

Eleora glanced down at her black pencil skirt and her now crinkled blouse. "Yes, that sounds like a wonderful idea nana."

"I thought so. I put your duffel bag upstairs in your old room."

"Oh nana! You didn't have to do that! I know that it was heavy."

"Don't let this white hair fool you, sweetie, I'm still strong enough to do some things!" Her voice was teasing so Eleora knew that she wasn't really offended.

"Okay, okay! You're fit, eh? Running a marathon soon?" Eleora teased back.

Her grandmother threw her head back and laughed. "Oh, I don't run. Not even when I was young and spry did I do that. No, my exercise of choice is Zumba. I get to shake what the good Lord gave me!"

Eleora burst into giggles. "Nana! Not you shaking it for the Lord!"

"As Pastor Tav said today, everything is for his glory!" Her nana added and they both laughed.

"I'm going to head upstairs to get changed, nana. Please shout for me if you need help with anything."

"Go, go!" Nana shooed her off.

Eleora went to her old room and found it filled with pictures of her over the last several years. Most of them were from school picture days. This must've been Lola's doing.

She rummaged through her duffel bag, looking for something to wear. What did one wear when reconnecting with their father? She wanted to look good, but not like she had tried to look good. But it was her dad, he probably wasn't expecting her to be dressed up. She settled on a pair of black skinny jeans and a gray sleeveless turtleneck. Eleora added some leave-in conditioner to her hair and brushed out her curls, then put half her hair up and let the rest hang loose. She knew that she looked good, but she was still nervous.

A part of her itched to text Chadwick. They hadn't ever gone this long without speaking. She wanted to tell him everything. Eleora nearly texted him, but then she remembered his lie and put her phone in one of her pants pockets.

As she descended the last stair, the door opened and in walked her father. She froze. Even though she was expecting him, her body still didn't know how to react. For years, it had been in a state of fight and flight when it came to him. Now, she didn't know what to do.

He tentatively smiled at her and put down a satchel that had been on his shoulder. Then, he took a step towards and opened up his arms. "Eleora, would it be okay if I hugged you?"

She nodded her head and stepped into his arms. He held her tightly. Her head landed right over his heart and she could hear it beating fast. He was nervous too.

"Ra-ra, my beautiful ra-ra." He kept repeating over and over again. At the nickname, she started to cry and she could feel his body begin to shake with sobs.

Eleora wasn't sure how long they stayed like that. But eventually her tears stopped and his body was no longer shaking. They pulled back from the hug and looked into each other's identical gray eyes.

"Papa, I missed you." She said quietly.

"Same here. I want to hear everything about your life. Absolutely everything!" He said eagerly and she laughed.

"I would like that as well, but dinner is ready. Maybe we can do the catching up while we eat?" She heard Nana's voice and turned to see her watching them.

"Sounds great." Eleora agreed.

They all went to the dining room table. Her grandmother sat at the head, her dad was at her right and Eleora was at her left. "Let's pray." Her nana said, holding out her hands to each of them. Eleora took their hands in hers and closed her eyes. "Yahweh, thank you for this time together. You are good and good to us. Thank you for Eleora re-dedicating her life to you! Bless her walk of faith. Bless the food and our time talking together. In Jesus's name, amen."

"Is it true? You've given your life to Christ?" Her dad asked with a raised eyebrow.

"Yes, just about an hour or so ago." Eleora answered shyly.

"That is the best possible news I could receive. I want to know everything else happening in your life as well."

And so over curry chicken, rice and salad, a lengthy conversation ensued. She updated them on her hobbies and activities at school. She told them about how she'd been doing spiritually leading up to that day. She told them about Maryliz and how thankful she was for that friendship. She even shared about getting into her dream program at UVic. They asked her great questions about each topic and along the way they got into a rhythm of playful banter as well. And then, she landed on Chadwick.

"I guess the only thing I haven't told you guys about yet is that I've been dating someone for the last 5 months." She said, her voice sad.

Her dad nodded but her grandmother looked confused. "What's wrong? Why do you look like that? Is the guy a loser? Did he hurt you?"

"He did hurt me. You probably actually know him, nana. It's Chadwick Knight." She could see her grandmother thinking, mentally running through a database of people she knew and then she smiled.

"Why, he's a lovely young man! Very handsome and passionate about the Lord … oh." She started off happy and then understanding dawned. "He was dating you while you both were in different places spiritually, wasn't he?" She said glumly.

"Yes. The day that he asked me to be his girlfriend, I asked him whether there was anything in Christianity that said we shouldn't date. And he said no. He lied to me."

"He made a mistake, Ra-ra. He shouldn't have lied to you. But I do believe that he cares for you a lot. Have you thought about talking to him? Giving him a chance to explain?" Her dad suggested.

She began to shake her head, but stopped when she heard the sound of her ring and locket knocking into each other. Her hand went to the ring and she remembered the day that he gave it to her. The promise of love that he'd made to her. She knew that he loved her. Or, at least she thought she knew. She didn't know what was true and what wasn't anymore. All she knew for certain was that she loved him. And maybe that was enough, at least to have a conversation.

"Okay, I'll do that. Now enough about me. I want to hear about you two!"

They smiled at her deflection but obliged her. The next hour passed by quickly as she was told about how her grandmother was spending her retirement and was still in remission. As for her father, he'd gone to seminary and had become a pastor for the youth and young adults at Agape. It was amazing to see that even amidst all the hardship that they went through, they had both held onto their faith in Jesus.

"Your faith amazes me. It kinda makes me awful though about how I just turned away from God when everything happened." She admitted.

"Eleora, you were 11 years old. Your entire world had been turned upside down and you'd been lied to. How you responded is completely understandable. You did what you needed to survive. There's no shame to be felt for that." Her dad said, his voice filled with compassion.

She wiped away a few tears. "Thank you. I'm still shocked that God would take me back even with how faithless I was."

"He loves you. Like Tav said today, every detail of your life was already known by him. He grieved with you and now he celebrates with you, that you've re-joined the family of faith. I honestly think that he was pursuing you through Chadwick. Do you think you would've ever stepped foot in church again or read Mere Christianity if not for falling for him?"

Eleora took in her dad's words. They were like cool water on a scorching hot day. "No, I wouldn't have. So, all this time, God had still wanted me?"

"Yes. One thousand percent, yes." Her nana said firmly. "Jesus himself said that He is a shepherd, willing to leave the 99 sheep to go back for the one that goes astray. He has always been trying to get you back to where you belong. I have no doubt about that."

"Thanks nana. And you too, papa!" They all smiled at each other.

"Now, Ra-ra. I think there's a phone call that you need to make, right?" Her dad prodded.

She sighed. He was right. There was no more deflecting. She needed to talk to Chadwick.

Chapter 42

"Chad! Dinner is ready. Come downstairs!" He heard his mom call out.

He took a deep breath and then yelled, "Thanks, Mom, but I'm not hungry! I'll eat later!"

"Okay!" She replied.

He breathed a sigh of relief, glad that he didn't have to share why he wasn't hungry. He didn't know where he and Eleora stood, and it was driving him nuts. He'd called and texted her a few times with no response. He was worried for her. While he was concerned about the conflict, he was more concerned by her seeing her dad again. That was a lot. How was she handling it?

It was still bizarre to him that his youth pastor, his mentor, was her father. When the shock had worn off, he had just been angry. How could he claim Christ and work in ministry and have done that to his daughter? But then Pastor Gabe had given him his side of the story. It sounded different than what Eleora described. He didn't mention an email or taking so long to get in touch, just that he hadn't known where his daughter was and when he finally got in contact with her, she said she didn't want to live with him.

Some key thing was missing here, but Chadwick couldn't figure out what.

He picked up his phone to try Eleora again when he saw that he had an incoming video call from her. He quickly answered the phone.

"Belle. I'm so glad you called." He said, his relief palpable in his tone. Just seeing her, even through the screen, brought him a sense of calm. Something about her seemed different but he couldn't put his finger on what it was.

"Well, I was convinced to give you a chance to explain. So, explain."

"Yeah, so." Why hadn't he planned what he was going to say? "That day at the park, when I lied to you? I didn't have some already established plan to deceive you. I just knew that I couldn't be happy being your friend anymore. I just ..." He tried to find the right words. "... didn't want to lose you." He saw her flinch at his words.

"I'm so tired of hearing those words. At being manipulated and lied to instead of being trusted to make informed decisions." She said, her voice hard. But he heard the hurt too.

"Wait, that sounds like more than what's going on between us. Did something else happen?"

"It's a long story. Basically, my mom is the one who wrote the email to manipulate me into staying with her in BC. I left home to come to my grandmother's where she, my dad and I have been catching up."

"Whoa. That's a lot, Belle." She nodded. "But, you seem to be handling it all really well." He commented, and he wasn't just trying to flatter her. She seemed to almost glow even amidst all that she'd just described.

"Thanks. That's probably due to another thing that happened today. A good thing." He saw her eyes brighten.

"It's the suspenseful buildup for me." He joked and was rewarded with her laugh.

"I became a Christian today. Again, I guess. My nana put it a different way. I rededicated my life to Jesus."

He let out a happy whoop, making her giggle. "Belle, that's amazing. It's an answer to prayer. For real."

"Thanks." She said shyly.

"So, a lot has happened, eh? I'm just wondering about where we're at. How do you feel about me, about us?" He asked her nervously.

"I love you." Her words would've brought him relief if they weren't said in such a sad tone. It sounded like there was a 'but' coming. "But, I can't trust you Chadwick." His heart sank. What was she saying?

"What does that mean for us?"

"I don't know. I don't want to break up with you, but I don't know how to be with you either."

"Belle, please. Don't do this. Don't break up with me." He didn't care that he was basically begging. He couldn't imagine his life without her in it. Especially since she was now a believer too. There was so much more that they could share now.

He saw that she'd begun to cry, two tear tracks on her face. He wished he could be with her and wipe away those tears.

"Chadwick, a lot of my life is in flux right now. I just made a huge decision to have faith again. I need to figure out what it looks to have a faith that isn't entangled with another person. I need the space to explore who I am now. And honestly, I think you need some space from me. Somehow, I became the most important person in your life. You were willing to put me above God. Which actually made me God. I can't be your God, Chadwick."

There was a sharp pain in his chest, like his heart was literally breaking. He wished that he could argue with her, but she wasn't wrong. He had done that. He began to cry too. For how his relationship with God had deteriorated and for his relationship with her ending.

"You're right." He admitted, his voice cracking on the words.

"I know that this is the right thing to do. I feel it deep down, but it hurts. It really hurts, Chadwick." There were more than two tear tracks now. Her face was shining with tears.

"I echo that. It might be best if we end this call. The longer we hold on, the more it'll hurt."

She nodded. "You're probably right. But I don't want to say goodbye."

"It's not goodbye. We'll see each other tomorrow at school."

"Yeah, but I think we'll need to stay away from each other. To be near but unable to be together..."

"... would just hurt more." He finished for her. "Well, Belle, I love you. Somehow even more now than I did before. I'll see you around."

"Goodbye Chadwick." With a little wave, she hung up the phone.

He stared at the now black screen through blurry eyes.

It was real. They had broken up. He curled into the fetal position and just let out all of his emotions. He was devastated and angry.

"How could You do this to me? How could You take her away? After she finally comes to faith! I love her! Doesn't that matter to you?!" He sobbed in between his words.

He was so lost in his grief that he didn't hear the footsteps approaching his room, nor his bedroom door opening. When he felt a hand on his back, he nearly jumped in fear. Then he saw his parents, sitting on his bed, looking at him with so much compassion. His mom was actually crying too.

"Mom? Dad?" He stammered out.

He tried to find the words of what to say, but his dad simply looked him in the eye and said, "We know."

"What?" He asked, confused. Were they saying what he thought they were saying?

"We know that you two were more than friends." His dad elaborated.

"How?"

"You don't think we know you well enough to notice you being in love? We know the signs. We were your age and in love once." His mother said gently. "And based on your state right now, I'm guessing you guys aren't together anymore?" She asked, somehow her tone was even more gentle than before.

All he could do was nod. He couldn't say the words. Not yet.

"Oh Chaddy. I never wanted you to experience this kind of pain. I'm so sorry, son." She opened up her arms and he fell right into them, closing his eyes.

"She said that I'd made her my God and she was

right. How do I come back from this? What do I do? It all hurts." The words rushed out of him.

"Son, I need to share something with you. I was wondering why this passage kept coming to me today. And now I know, it's for you." He opened his eyes at his dad's words.

"What passage?" He asked.

"Let me find it for us." His dad swiped and tapped his phone. "Here it is, Genesis 22:1-14."

As his dad read the story of Abraham being commanded to sacrifice Isaac, it felt like he was hearing the story for the first time. When he was finished reading, there was a moment of silence as the three of them took in the powerful story.

"Praise God." His mom said, breaking the silence.

"Indeed, Nina. We must praise him because He always gives us what we need." His father said.

"My relationship with Eleora is Isaac?" Chadwick asked, tentatively. His parents nodded.

"I believe so, son. It's easy to wonder why God would ask Abraham to do such a horrible thing. But I think it's because this son that he had given him could've - or maybe had already - become an idol in his life. God was testing who he loved more. His willingness to obey God showed that Isaac was not his God. I'm sure Abraham wrestled with it. Especially on the final part of the hike. Now Chadwick, I can't promise that your story will have the same ending. Maybe you won't get a relationship with Eleora back. While it's possible, it's not the point. You don't act like you're going to make the sacrifice so that God will say He's just kidding. You actually need to set in your heart to love Him first, whether He provides or not. So, I've gotta ask you. Where's your heart? Do you still love God?"

Chadwick pondered his father's words. He was still heartbroken and angry, but the confusion he'd been feeling was gone. He felt a keen sense of clarity. And in the midst of everything he was feeling, there was still love. Not for Eleora, but for God. There was a conviction for how he'd wandered away, but also a gratitude that God was giving Him an opportunity to come back.

He finally nodded his head. "I do, I still love God."

His parents gave him large smiles. "That's my boy." His mom said warmly. "This might be a good time to pray." She suggested. Both him and his dad nodded in agreement. "Great. I'll start us off. Yahweh. We praise you. You are the only God we could ever need or want. Forgive us for when we turn to idols, but thank you that you love us enough to point out our idolatry and root it out of us. We welcome your intervention, even when it hurts. Oh God, be with Chadwick. Draw him back to you. Let him remember his first love is you. Give him grace to receive and remain in and reciprocate your love for him. In Jesus's name, amen."

After whispering amen in unison with his dad, Chadwick began to pray. "Oh God, I'm so sorry. I'm so sorry for neglecting my relationship with you. I'm sorry for replacing you with Eleora. You are worthy of my love and attention. Forgive me, Lord. Help me to focus once more on my relationship with you. Give me a joy for your word and a steadfastness in prayer. Even now, Lord, my heart is longing for you to say no. Like how you did with Abraham. That you would give me back

Eleora. But Lord, I'm not entitled to a relationship with her. May my heart be genuinely and sincerely for you. Amen."

His parents echoed his amen and then they all opened their eyes.

"Well, son, how are you feeling?" His dad checked in.

"Better. My heart still aches, but I feel ... renewed? I think that's the word."

"That's good to hear. Now, do you want to come downstairs and get something to eat?" His mom asked.

"You know what? That's a good idea, mom. You guys didn't already eat?"

They shook their heads. "Nope. And I'm famished." His dad admitted, getting up from the bed. "I love this whole bonding situation, but can we walk and talk?"

Chadwick and his mom laughed and followed suit. Together they headed downstairs to enjoy dinner together.

Chapter 43

"How is it possible to feel so awful and amazing at the same time?" Eleora asked her nana and father over brunch. She'd opted to miss school for the day to recover from all that had happened on Sunday.

"What do you mean, sweetie?"

Eleora smiled at her nana's term of endearment. "Well, the pain at breaking up with Chadwick is so intense, but so is the joy at being in a relationship with God again. It's confusing."

They nodded their heads in understanding.

"Well, it's been argued that there are three parts to human nature: body, soul, and spirit."

Eleora looked at her father with curiosity. Where was he going with this?

"Body is self-explanatory. The soul is where we get our mind, will and emotions. Our Spirit is the part of us that is connected to God. It sounds like your soul is hurting because of your heartbreak, but your spirit is rejoicing in its revival. Does that make sense?"

"It does actually. It helps put words to the tension I've been feeling within me. Thanks, daddy."

"I vastly underestimated how much I missed that title being used in my life." He blinked a few times and

Eleora realised that he was beginning to tear up.

His tears had a domino effect on her own eyes, making her vision blurry. She put down her fork and reached for one of his hands. "Trust me, I missed saying it."

He squeezed her hand gently and offered her a smile.

"You two are going to make me cry, too! And I have just mastered my makeup routine, so we need to nip this in the bud and get back to eating."

Eleora and her dad laughed at Nana's teasing words. Lunch passed in a pleasant blur of good food and heartwarming conversation that lasted for a couple of hours. When Eleora took out her phone to check the time, she was surprised to see that the school day had already ended. She was even more surprised to see 30 unread texts and 10 missed calls - all from Maryliz. Eleora hastily swiped across her name to call her back.

"Eleora, I don't know whether to be angry or grateful! How are you? Where are you? Do you realise that the last time I saw or heard from you, you were in a mental health crisis? I contacted Chad, he said that you guys had broken up. I go to your house; your mom doesn't know where you are. I thought that you had ... that you had ... killed ..." Maryliz couldn't get the words out because she was sobbing.

Understanding dawned on Eleora as she realised what Maryliz had been going through. "Oh Liz, I'm alive and well. I'm heartbroken, but also really good. I will happily fill you in. I'll drop the address of where I'm staying, and you can come over whenever, okay?" Eleora kept her voice gentle and quickly typed out her nana's address.

Maryliz's sobs eased into sniffles. "Okay. I look forward to hearing the tea, but I'm even gladder that you're safe. I just looked up the address you sent. It should take me about 20 minutes to get there."

"Perfect, I'll see you soon."

Eleora hung up the phone and then poked her head into the kitchen where her nana and dad were still talking. "Hey, is it okay that I've invited a friend over? With everything that's happened, I haven't been super communicative, and I felt that it would be best to go over it all in person."

"That's no problem at all. If anything, she can stay for dinner! I look forward to meeting one of your friends."

Eleora smiled at her nana's hospitable heart.

"Thanks, Nana!"

Eleora took a quick shower and changed into some comfy clothes that weren't pyjamas. As she was brushing out her hair, she heard the doorbell and went downstairs. She barely had the door open before she was tackled in a huge hug.

Laughing, she hugged Maryliz back. "It's good to see you too, Liz! Come on in, there are a couple of people that I'd like you to meet."

"It's the suspense for me." Liz joked as she followed Eleora into the house and kicked off her shoes. But then, she stopped in her tracks. "Eleora, who are these people who have the same eye colour as you?"

Eleora smiled. "This is my nana and my dad. Nana, daddy, this is Maryliz. She is my best friend."

"It's great to meet you, Maryliz. I'm Gabe."

Maryliz shook his hand with wide eyes.

"And you may call me nana. Any friend of my

sweetie might as well be another grandchild to me." Nana pulled Liz into a tight hug.

Eleora knew this was meaningful to her, since she had just lost her grandmother a couple of years ago.

"It's great to meet you guys. Ellie, you have a lot to catch me up on."

Her family laughed. "Feel free to head upstairs to catch up. Dinner will be ready in a couple of hours."

Eleora nodded at her nana's words and led an awestruck Maryliz to her room.

When they settled beside each other on her bed, Maryliz looked like she would burst. "Spill. Now."

And so Eleora did. Liz gasped at the interaction with her father, squinted her eyes in confusion at Chadwick's lie, gasped again at her mother's deception and teared up at the reunion with her nana, crying when she heard about the breakup between her and Chadwick, and turned thoughtful when Eleora spoke of her rekindled faith.

"Well, no wonder you couldn't answer my calls. You were going through it! I'm thankful that the truth came out and that you've reconnected with this side of your family, but I'm sad and angry about Tita Ada. I know Chadwick lied, and that sucks, but I'm confused as to why that warranted a breakup. Especially since you're a Christian now too, right? So, didn't it all kind of work out?"

Eleora considered Maryliz's words. "I don't know how to trust him anymore. I feel very manipulated, like I wasn't given a chance to really choose our relationship because he withheld information from me."

"Ooh. Kinda like a consent thing?"

Eleora nodded. "Yeah, and it's also an integrity

thing. His faith is supposed to be so important to him, but he disregarded part of it for me. Like, how can I trust that he won't disregard other things he says are important to him?"

Maryliz nodded. "I'm following you. I'm just sad. I know he loves you so much. And you guys are so good together."

"I love him, too. I just need to trust him again. I don't want things to be secretive. I want to know that he gets that what he did was wrong and wouldn't do it again."

"That's fair. Okay, do we need ice cream and sad romance movies?"

Eleora laughed and leaned her head against Maryliz's shoulder. "Thanks, but I'm actually alright. My heart may be broken, but my spirit isn't. I feel more alive than I've felt in ages."

"What do you mean?"

"I just feel so loved by God. Even after I rejected Him and was angry with Him, He would still welcome me back into a relationship with Him. It's amazing to me, that kind of forgiveness."

"That's beautiful, Ellie. I'm happy that you've found your truth."

Eleora furrowed her brow. "Well, Jesus said He was Truth. So, it's not just my truth, but truth in general. Does that make sense?"

"Hmm. Kinda? I'm just glad that you've found something that works for you and makes you happy. Atheism never seemed to do that in your life."

Eleora laughed. "That's true. It made me bitter and pretty intolerant to other people's views. I don't even think we've ever talked about your spirituality because of that. What do you believe in, Liz?"

Maryliz didn't answer right away, but Eleora didn't rush her. It was a big question.

"I think I'm agnostic since I don't know if there's a God or if we can even know if there is one for sure. I believe in people, I guess? The goodness of humanity and that everything happens for a reason. Maybe more fate than God. I don't know. As I talk it out, I'm not sure if I'm really okay with my answer. I might need to explore this more."

"That's fair, Liz. Well, if you ever want to explore Christianity with me, I would love that. If you don't, you're still my bestie."

"I think I might want that. Where do I start?"

"I just started reading the book of Luke in the Bible. You could join me if you want. Oh! You can ask my dad and Nana at dinner! They would explain it better than me."

Maryliz nodded. "I'm down for that."

Eleora smiled. It would be so wonderful if Liz also became a Christian one day and that this could be something they share.

Chapter 44

Chadwick was living in paradox. Every day, he felt joy and peace at his revived intimacy with God. There was consistency in reading the Bible again and it felt like a treasure trove of wisdom, encouragement, comfort and revelation. Yet, he also felt an intense sadness at not being in Eleora's life anymore. The past two weeks had been torture, seeing her in nearly every class, but not being able to talk and laugh with her. He had to constantly dodge questions about what had happened to them. It was just salt in the wound to see Jason with Maryliz heading into dance practice with Eleora for her debut.

He was thankful to be heading into the weekend. While he would still miss her, at least it was sure to be an Eleora-free zone.

Or so he thought.

Chadwick walked into his church for youth group on Friday night and was shocked to see Eleora there, speaking with Cass.

He immediately went to the bathroom and splashed his face with water from the sink.

"Lord, help me. I love you. I love you more than I love her. Help me get through tonight. Give me strength. I need you, Lord. Come through for me. Please."

He felt an inflow of peace. God was with him and everything would be okay.

He decided to sit with some guys from the worship band. His plan went perfectly and the evening was everything that he needed. The songs done were all about surrendering to God and His timing. He took note of one that he hadn't heard before, Seasons by Hillsong. It brought tears to his eyes.

When the band was finished, Pastor Gabe came to the front of the sanctuary. He looked happier than Chadwick had ever seen him.

"Good evening guys. Well, normally we save poetry for Sunday morning but tonight, we're going to have someone share a poem. Eleora, come up here!"

He watched Eleora get up from where she was sitting beside Cass and join her dad at the front. "This is my daughter and she wrote a poem about giving her life to God! She will actually be baptized on Sunday!" The room erupted in cheers, Chadwick among the loudest of them. This was fantastic news. And she was going to be sharing her poetry with a group of people? That was huge for her! He was so proud.

Pastor Gabe handed her the mic.

"Well, hi everyone. My name is Eleora and this is my first time sharing my poetry like this. I hope ya'll like it." She took out her phone and took a deep breath.

"My soul is overwhelmed by Your love for me
It sings with words that cannot be understood
It praises in a way that cannot be contained
It cries one word

Again and again and again
Hallelujah

Chadwick was in awe at her courage and the raw theology she was demonstrating in her poem. At one point, she put down her phone, closed her eyes and started to recite the poem from memory.

"My soul belongs to The Lord, my God
It is marked with Christ's signature:
It is finished written
in His blood

Darkness said grave
God said grace
Darkness says hate
My soul says mate

Yahweh,
Your love is unbelievable
It blows me away
You gave your life for my soul
You are my Soulmate.

Thank you."

Chadwick couldn't snap fast enough. And he wasn't the only one. The room was full of applause. Cass was even giving her a standing ovation. People around the room whistled and cheered.

The truth in her poem was hitting him. God really was the true soulmate. He had brought incredible healing and transformative power into his life. He was worthy of all the praise he could ever give and more! It didn't matter if he and Eleora got back together or if he was single for the rest of his life.

He had God, and that was more than enough.

After this thought, he felt something shift in him. Like a final puzzle piece had clicked into place.

'Now, it is time.'

There was God's voice. Time? Time for what? He lifted his head to see Eleora, who had been looking at the floor after saying thank you, slowly lifting her head. His heart skipped a beat. He'd forgotten how amazing her smile was.

'Time to pursue her. The right way this time.'

The right way. This time, with total honesty and in community, not hiding anything from his parents or his mentor.

Ideas began to percolate in his mind.

'Later'. He told himself. He would pay attention to what the Lord would teach him through Pastor Gabe's sermon first. It was powerful, how God is one of reconciliation and relationship from the story of the prodigal son.

He felt like the prodigal son that had just come back home to God. Warmly welcomed and restored back with favour.

As soon as he got home, he spent some time mapping out a plan. He had hid truth from Eleora, and their relationship from his loved ones. The opposite of that would be to publicly declare his care for her and acknowledge his wrongdoing.

But how?

He thought of Eleora and what he knew meant so much to her: words.

Maybe he could write her a poem?

Chadwick nodded to himself. Yes, that felt right.

And he spent the next couple of hours refining his plan, praying that it would work.

Chapter 45

Eleora took a deep breath to calm her nerves. It was almost time for her to make her grand entrance to her debut. Her aunts and grandmothers had been so helpful with pulling together the remaining details for her and running interference with her mom.

She felt a pang in her heart at the thought of her mom. She hadn't seen her since that Sunday a few weeks ago when she'd left the house. Eleora had been mentally prepared to only have one parent at her debut, but she had been wrong about which one.

It still felt surreal to have her dad back in her life. Sometimes, it felt like no time had passed. They had such an easy rhythm with one another. But then, she'd mention something from her pre-teen years, and it became apparent the different things that he'd missed. While she was enjoying reconnecting with him, she was grieving too. And trying not to be bitter. Eleora knew that she needed to forgive her mother, but she just wasn't there yet. It was hard though to not have her mom in her life anymore.

Eleora shook her head, trying to dislodge those thoughts. She tried to focus on something else, something that made her feel good; like the dress she was wearing. Maryliz had outdone herself. Her ballgown had a silver-gray shimmery bodice and an ombre skirt, going from gray to blue to purple, with a transparent shimmering overlay. The sweetheart neckline emphasized her curves without making her feel exposed, and the off-the-shoulder cap sleeves added an air of modesty. With her face fully done up with makeup and her curly hair pinned up with a sparkling silver clip, she was a sight to see.

This was the most beautiful that Eleora had ever felt.

One of the staff gave her the cue that it was time to make her entrance. As she descended the stairs, she heard the strains of the score for Wakanda from Black Panther begin to play. Here came another heart pang. For both Chadwicks. She missed him so much. While her rededicated faith had brought unspeakable joy to her life, there was still sorrow over not being with Chadwick anymore. She missed their conversations and how safe she always felt with him.

She saw phones out as she walked into the room and remembered to smile. This was a big day, a good day. She was 18. This party was to celebrate her. She ought to be in the moment and enjoy it.

"Isn't she a vision of beauty and grace? Let's hear it for our girl, excuse me - young woman, Eleora Gonzales James!" Her Lola's words felt like stepping into a patch of sunlight, all warmth and light.

The applause that ensued almost brought tears to her eyes. She was loved. Eleora smiled and sat at the head table with her 9 candles.

"And now, it's time to eat. I'm going to let Eleora's other grandmother, Marielle, pray for our night and the food." She handed off the mic to her nana.

Eleora closed her eyes. "Yahweh, thank you for this day to celebrate Eleora's life. Bless this time with sweet fellowship and deep joy. Bless this food and the hands that prepared it. In Jesus's name, amen."

Eleora whispered amen along with the rest of the group and then opened her eyes. Her nana put the mic on its stand and then returned to her seat next to her Lola.

Waiters seemed to appear like magic to serve the food as music began to play in the background. Eleora took in the event happening around her with a bittersweetness. On one hand, it was lovely to see the event come together so well. So many people she loved were in the same place at the same time. On the other hand, she remembered planning this with her mom. She'd also envisioned being there with Chadwick; two people she loved were absent and it was hard to ignore that.

Once dinner was done, it was time for the candles and roses parts of the evening. Her lola went to the mic once more, holding a tea light in her hand. "Now, it is time for Eleora's nine candles to share some words with her - and all of you! I have the privilege of being her first candle. There's so much I could say." Her Lola turned to face Eleora sitting in the center of the head table. "I've seen you grow from a tiny baby into a young woman. You have been beautiful since the day you were born. And you have grown to be intelligent, capable and kind as well. I have never known you to be less than honourable to your elders or to bring less than your best to everything you do. We may be the ones holding the candles, but you are the one who lights up every room that you enter. I love you, my dear girl. Happy Birthday." Eleora blinked back tears as people in the room clapped.

She got up to hug her Lola tightly. "Maraming salamat po." She whispered into her ear.

"You're welcome. I meant every word." She said back.

And so it went. Her Titas were next, sharing moments when they felt proud of her and grateful for her. Then it was time for her female cousins; they each shared a cherished memory with her. By the time they got to Maryliz, she was openly crying and wiping away tears.

"So, for those who don't know me. I'm Maryliz, Eleora's best friend from school. I met Eleora in grade 9. I was intrigued by this girl who I didn't remember seeing in middle school; this girl who happened to be the first to have a triple specialisation. When we first interacted, I came in with confidence, bordering on arrogance. It's cringey to think about. And then, somehow she fully disarmed me by asking me what tends to make me smile. I'd never been directly asked a question like that, one that would go beyond the superficial things of life. When I answered with reading, her eyes lit up and that sealed our friendship. After school, we would regularly go to the library together and show each other our finds. When we finished our books, we would discuss them in detail with one another. Eleora thought deeper about things than most people I knew, she made me better. The last 4 years of friendship have been amazing. They haven't been without arguments. We've had some doozies." Eleora chucked, she was telling the truth there. "But we've always come back from them stronger. Our friendship has even started to involve faith and spirituality which has only made our bond deeper and stronger. Eleora, I am so thankful for you. I'm thankful for your kindness, depth, sense of humour, and good advice. I don't know what my life would be like without your friendship, except that it wouldn't be as bright as it is now. I love you, best friend."

"Oh Liz!" Eleora exclaimed and dabbed at the tears making their way down her face. They hugged tightly and then both sat down. This last slot was supposed to be for her mom, but instead her nana would be sharing.

"Hello everyone! I have the honour of being Eleora's other grandmother. And I mean honour in every sense of the word. I never knew that someone who bore my genes could be so creatively gifted. I don't know if you've heard her poetry, but if you haven't - you're missing out! She is so talented. It's also been a blessing to witness Eleora's spiritual growth. When she commits to something, she goes all in. It's been beautiful to see her embrace faith, walk in the Spirit, understand and draw insights from the Bible that even I haven't seen or noticed before. You amaze me, Eleora. I believe that your future will only be brighter from here. As you finish high school and go onwards to your post-secondary education, I know that God will bless you with everything and everyone you need. I declare goodness to be in store for you! I truly believe that God has a wonderful plan for your life, and I'm just honoured to be able to see it and play a tiny part."

While everyone's words had moved her heart, this

final message from her nana had stirred something in her soul. A deep peace for the future, that it truly all would work together for good; even the hard and messy parts that she was experiencing right now.

She got up to hug her grandmother and then went to the mic. "I'm so thankful for the words from these beautiful women. My speech is coming later though, so I'll spare you for now." People all over the room chuckled. "Now, it is time for my roses' dance."

Eleora walked over to the middle of the dance floor and waited for the music to start. With her back to the head table, she was unaware of what each of those women were doing. As she saw people point and take out their phones, she turned around to see that each of the women were holding a letter lit up. Together it spelled, Mahal kita, I love you in Tagalog. While this was unexpected, she found it to be a sweet surprise. Then she heard the song from Beauty and the Beast begin to play, which was not the right song.

Chapter 46

Chadwick heard the music playing and knew it was his cue.

His heart hammered in his chest, so much so that he struggled to breathe. Is this what anxiety felt like?

"Breathe, son, you can do all things through Christ who gives you strength."

Pastor Gabe's words released the tension in his chest, helping him to breathe. It brought him back to the conversation they'd had after he'd made his plan.

Chadwick knocked on Pastor Gabe's slightly open office door.

"Come in."

With a deep breath, Chadwick pushed open the door and stepped inside, immediately looking to the ground.

"Chadwick."

It was the compassion in Pastor Gabe's voice that made him look up with a question in his eyes.

"Come, sit down. I was hoping you would reach out at some point."

Chadwick did as instructed, still confused. "You want to see me? After everything?"

Pastor Gabe smiled. "Yes. I was disappointed, but

that doesn't hinder the immense care I have for you. You have always been like a son to me, Chadwick. Your hiding doesn't change that. I am protective over Eleora and how hurt she is right now, but I know that's only because she cares for you so much. And she cares for you so much because she's seen what I have, you're a wonderful person. You made a mistake, but there's mercy and grace for our wandering."

Chadwick swiped away a few tears. "I needed to hear that. I came to beg your forgiveness and blessing to pursue Eleora the right way this time."

"Well, begging is unnecessary. What do you have in mind?"

"But what if she rejects me?"

"Then you'll make it through, because Christ will be your strength."

Chadwick nodded. "You're right. I want her back in my life so much, but I don't need her. I need Jesus. And I'll always have Him."

"Amen, now go!" With a gentle shove, Pastor Gabe sent him into the ballroom.

As Chadwick walked into the ballroom, his stage presence as an actor kicked in and he was filled with confidence, flicking on the handheld mic with ease. He stopped just a few feet away from her in the middle of the dance floor. "Eleora, happy 18th birthday. You look …" He paused to find the right word. "Wondrous. I love you and wanted to share a poem with you and your loved ones about how I feel about you. If you're okay with that. If you're not, just shake your head and I'll go, and you can pretend that this never happened." He took a deep breath. What would she choose?

And, ever so tentatively, she nodded her head.

This is what hope felt like.
"Thank you. Here goes it.

In all the times before
When I imagined of mon amour
I never dreamed I would be floored
With grand poetic gestures
Having my heart treated as a treasure
A prized possession,
Shown such careful attention and deep affection

By this Beautiful Belle
With the clever wit of Dave Chappelle
a never-ending list of stories to tell
Every conversation causing my joy to swell

Around her, my multiple personalities
Find the ability
To run wild and free
Allowing to be who I am within
I guess this is what it's like to be Aladdin
Having the eye of someone with the class of Jasmine

Then it went bad
Bad, not like that Michael Jackson song
Something cool that makes you want to sing along
No, more bad, like seeing her in world of hurt
And knowing that the cause of her pain is you
Because you were too cowardly to tell the truth
So the words never fell off your lips
For your fears had the firmest grip

Now your rom-com is a horror story

Where no words of sorry
Feel like they'll ever be enough
All you feel is shame,
Wondering will things be same
Will she ever forgive you?
Will there be an us or just her without you?

This is the place where our Saviour draws near
Where He's made it clear
In our brokenness, He stands victorious
In Him, our worst moments become glorious

In Him, we are loved as we are
But never left as we are
Cause this love is far bigger than our mistakes
Like thinking you need a girl more than the One who
commands the daybreak

I should have pursued Christ
In whom satisfaction is of infinite supply
But now, I can love you beyond my means
Cause I've been loved beyond my wildest dreams

Will you give me another chance?
Just to talk while we do your first dance."

Chapter 47

When the song started playing, Eleora knew something was up.

She wasn't expecting to see Chadwick.

He walked in, wearing a navy slim fit suit with a white, gray and purple bowtie. He was outfitted in a way that was completely complementary to her.

She was frozen, unsure of whether this was real or if she was just having a really elaborate dream. But, even in her greatest dreams, she had never imagined that Chadwick could look so handsome.

Then, he'd called her wondrous. Bringing her back to the night she'd realised he'd seen her. A time before the lie.

It was that one word that got him the chance to share his poem.

She was stunned.

He must've worked so hard on that. He admitted his wrongdoing and had shared the gospel, not just to himself but to everyone in the room. And now, he just wanted to talk. Could she do that? Should she?

Without thinking, she glanced around the room for her dad. He smiled at her and gave her a thumbs up. That was what she needed. If her father and his mentor thought hearing him out would be wise, she could do it.

After all, it was only one dance.

With a deep breath, she closed the gap between them and took his offered hand.

He put his other hand at the small of her back and she instinctively put her other hand on his shoulder. Then, they began to dance.

"Eleora, I'm sorry. I hid something important from you, and I wrongly put you above God in my life. He's been teaching me about Him being enough, and losing you has shown me that my faith in Him can last even when it hurts. I feel that now I can be the godly boyfriend that I'm supposed to be. I love you and I want us to be together again. I have so much vision for what we could be like, with both of us being believers in Jesus … and it's, well, glorious. I know you might not feel ready to be my girlfriend again, but would you be open to going one date at a time?"

She took in everything he said and everything he'd done. He'd had to put in a lot of work to pull this off. And then there was the dance. He was leading her as if he was in the dance specialisation, not her! He must've spent so much time practicing and preparing for this. Her heart warmed. He had gone to such lengths to show her how he felt.

She had no doubt of his sincerity.

And that sting of manipulation was being eased with every opportunity he was giving her to opt out. With taking things slowly.

They'd had something special, now they could have something sacred.

She could see what he was talking about, how their shared faith would only make what they had before so much better. She loved hearing him mention where he and God were now at; his faith in God that used to be a thing to ignore before was now the most attractive thing about him. The thought of them being able to pray and study the Bible together made her almost squeal in glee.

Was she willing to take that step?

As he twirled her out and in, she heard her locket knock against her promise ring. The ring she hadn't been able to remove from her necklace. The promise that she still wanted to be kept, even when she was hurt by its maker.

As she looked him in the eyes, she saw something that made her breath hitch. Not just determination and focus, but surrender. He would truly let her go if that's what she wanted - if that's what God wanted.

'God, what do You want?'

In answer, a verse came to mind: 'Your word is a lamp to my feet and a light to my path.'

Eleora smiled as she remembered her nana explaining to her that sometimes, that light on the path only gives us enough sight for one or two steps forward. How it requires moment-by-moment surrender to and dependence upon God.

This could be God's answer. To just trust Him enough to take a step forward with Chadwick. To not have the whole future figured out. They had fallen so hard and so fast, now they could go slow.

Eleora smiled at Chadwick. "Thanks for giving me time to think and, honestly, pray just now. I am open to taking things one date at a time."

The smile that lit up his face warmed her up, from her toes to her heart. He twirled her out once more and brought her in close such that their faces were only centimeters apart.

She saw the heat in his gaze, the fire in his hazel eyes. He wanted to kiss her.

She wanted him to do so.

He leaned and she held her breath, ready for the kiss. Instead, he bent his head to her ear, his exhales on her skin making her shiver in anticipation. "Slow and steady, Belle."

Eleora nodded, relief and respect welling up in her. This was a Chadwick she could trust. One willing to lay his desires aside to honour God's pace.

As the song ended, she barely registered the cheers around the room because she realised that she was at peace. Agreeing to being with Chadwick felt like something inside of her had clicked into place. Like two puzzle pieces that helped make a beautiful picture of all that God was doing.

Epilogue

Eleora people watched from her booth at Stir It Up, the only place to get Caribbean food in Victoria. The trees were in full autumn glory. If not for the overcast sky, it would've been a picturesque October day. She smiled when she saw Chadwick walk up the path towards the restaurant's entrance. He was wearing his UBC sweater, the one she'd been hoping to borrow (indefinitely). The maroon colour complemented his brown skin.

She waved to alert him to her presence and stood up to give him a hug when he got to where she was. Eleora wrapped her arms around his neck. At the small of her back, his thumbs moved back and forth, caressing the little bit of skin exposed from her sweater lifting up. She sighed happily.

After a few moments like that, they partially pulled apart, their noses almost touching as they stared into each other's eyes. Each time they reconnected on the weekend, she felt like she had to commit every detail to memory. It helped her get through them being apart on the weekdays. They might be in the same province, but they were still a few hours away from each other.

"Wow, it's great being with you again. One hug

from you makes the bus and ferry trip worth it." His words made her smile grow even larger.

"If I haven't said it before, thanks for making the journey to see me every weekend. I appreciate it." She told him.

"You're welcome. It's also a great time to get readings done and work on my labs."

He gave her a quick kiss on the nose and then broke the hug. "So, what are we having tonight?" He asked, perusing the screens with the menu items.

"Well, I was going to go classic and just get a jerk chicken." She shrugged. "You?"

"I'm in a curry goat kind of mood. Have you already ordered?"

Eleora shook her head. "No, but I can cover it. You're the one dishing out money for a weekly trip on a student budget."

"A budget that has some breathing room since I work part-time." He pointed out. That was true. He'd gotten a job calling alumni for donations. It was only a few hours on weekday evenings. It cut into their video call time, but facilitated their in-person time together.

"Okay, okay." She conceded.

They ordered their food and sat back down in the booth to wait for it to be ready.

"How are you feeling about this weekend?" She asked him.

"It'll be weird not being home for Thanksgiving. I don't think I've ever spent one without my parents before. I'm thankful …"

"Very punny, Knight." She cut in, her voice teasing.

"Thank you, Belle." He said with a wink. "But

seriously, I'm grateful that Sam and Claire invited us to join their Thanksgiving meal."

"Same." She agreed.

"Here's your order!" The cashier called out to them, gesturing to their packaged food.

Chadwick went to the counter and thanked her for the food. "Shall we eat here?" He asked Eleora when he got back to their booth. She checked the time on her phone. It was just hitting five o'clock.

"Well, sure. I guess we have time. It shouldn't take long to drop your duffel off at the dorm and get to Community Group for 7:30."

"Sweet. Wait, do you think we should get something for Jeff? I wish there was some way to thank him for letting me sleep in his room every weekend."

Eleora thought for a moment. Is there something that he would like? She realised that she didn't know him all that well. Just that he was the only other Christian on her floor in her residence and was local to Victoria, so he spent the weekends at home. While she was thinking, Chadwick checked the packages to see whose food it was and passed her the container with the jerk chicken. "Hmm. He'll be gone by the time you get there, so I don't think getting him food is the best bet. We'll think of some way to thank him. It's because of him that we even have a church out here."

"And I'm so thankful to be attending Central Baptist. I miss Pastor Tav's preaching, but I love the way they really help people get connected in the church."

"Right? I'm really looking forward to Community Group tonight. I've been loving the book of Acts and our discussions on it." She picked up her fork to begin to eat and then realised that she'd forgotten to pray.

"This food smells amazing. Let me pray for us real quick and then we can dig in." She nodded, then bowed her head and closed her eyes. They held hands across the table. "Yahweh, thank you for getting us through another week and for helping me to get here safely. Thank you also for this food and the hands who prepared it. Bless it to our bodies and bless this weekend. May we have fruitful discussions about Acts tonight, fun times together this weekend and a gratitude-rich Thanksgiving meal with Sam and Claire. In Jesus's name, amen."

"Amen." Eleora echoed him and picked up her fork again. She took a spoonful of rice and chicken and nearly groaned at how good it tasted. "If this food is any indication, we have a great weekend in store for us."

Chadwick reached across the table to hold and squeeze one of her hands. "Yeah, we definitely do."

They smiled at each other and then dug into their food.

"Hey, guess what memory came up on Instagram today?" Eleora said after a few moments of silence as they ate.

"No idea, what?"

"This was the weekend that we first hung out at the library and then watched the Magician's Nephew."

"Wow, that feels like ages ago. I'm shook that it's only been a year since then." He commented.

"Right? Like, did you think that we would end up here? There I was telling you about my dream school, and now I'm actually in that program! God is so kind!"

"He really is. I wonder what life will look like a

year from now. What would be your dream situation?" He asked her.

"Hmmm. My mom and I would hopefully be less awkward with each other. I'm glad that we're talking again, therapy has definitely helped with that, but it feels like we're starting our relationship from scratch. I would love for it to feel normal to have her in my life. What about you?"

"Honestly, if it looks similar to life right now, I'd be very content. Maybe, I could go on an overseas mission's trip and see what my parents loved about that type of ministry?"

"Yes! I love that for you!" She said enthusiastically.

He laughed. "Slow down there, Belle. It's still very much in the idea stage."

"But, it doesn't have to stay there." She pointed out.

"True. Why do I feel like you just became an accountability partner for this?" He teased.

"Because I have." She said matter-of-factly. "But, I'm not going to be pushy so I'll change the subject for now. Where do you think we'll be in a year?" She asked, tentatively.

"Hopefully, still together and closer to Jesus and one another." He answered immediately.

She breathed a sigh of relief. "I was hoping you'd say that. I feel the same way. I love you, Chadwick."

"And I love you, Eleora. I'm not worried about our future. I'm confident that God has the best for us already planned out." His words washed over her like a calm wave.

She knew he meant what he'd said. And she knew

he was right. She wasn't able to predict everything that had happened in the last year, but so much good had happened. So much transformation. She could trust God with the next year and everything that it held. Right now, she just needed to enjoy the present.

And staring across the table at Chadwick, it was easy to do so.

Dear Reader,

This story has a special place in my heart. It's the first contemporary novel I ever started. It's the story I struggled to finish. It went through two significant rewrites. This story, more than any of the others, feels like a true birth after much labour.

I hope it's brought life to you.

These are not easy topics: interfaith dating, pornography addiction, and a minor depressive episode. Thank you for sticking with me through them.

My hope is that you have been able to see the light-bearing and life-giving power of the good news of Jesus in all these dark and trapping spaces. As I say with every book, if you are triggered - please talk to someone.

I volunteer as tribute if you can think of no one else.

I love you, God loves you most.

"The grace of the Lord Jesus Christ and the love of God and the fellowship of the Holy Spirit be with you all" (2 Cor 13:14).

Sana'

To my Filipina sisters who gave me permission to represent their rich and beautiful culture. Katelynn, Sophia, and Khadione - thank you.

To the team at Winged Publications, and Cynthia specifically for what is probably my favourite cover of the series, thank you.

To Gordon and Saidah, who saw the earliest drafts of this story over a decade ago. Thank you for nurturing my author dreams and encouraging me. Young Sana' needed you. This story would not be here without you.

To my husband who offered such wise insight into Chadwick's healing journey. Who has loved me through all my depressive episodes. Who heard all of these poems first. I love you. Thank you for loving me like how Christ loves us.

To the one who entrusted me with this story. "Amen! Blessing and glory and wisdom and thanksgiving and honor and power and might be to our God forever and ever! Amen" (Rev 7:12).